WINE INTO WATER

WINE INTO WATER

Flynn's Crossing Romantic Suspense Series
Book 6

Yvonne Kohano

IK
E

Nanokas Press
A Division of Kochanowski Enterprises

WINE INTO WATER
FLYNN'S CROSSING ROMANTIC SUSPENSE SERIES BOOK 6

Nanokas Press/KE Press books may be ordered through booksellers or by contacting:

Kochanowski Enterprises/Nanokas Press
PO Box 1274
Clackamas, OR 97015-9594
www.yvonnekohano.com
yvonne@yvonnekohano.com

Blooms on the Bones is a work of fiction. People, places, events, and situations are the product of the author's imagination. Any resemblance to actual persons, living or dead, or historical events, is purely coincidental.

This book contains an excerpt from the forthcoming book *Love's Touch of Justice* by Yvonne Kohano. This excerpt may not reflect the final content of the forthcoming edition.

Any people depicted in stock imagery provided by Thinkstock are models, and such images are being used for illustrative purposes only.

Certain stock imagery ©Thinkstock
Cover design: John Kochanowski

ISBN: 978-1-940738-36-9 (sc)
ISBN: 978-1-940738-98-7 (e)

Original Publication: 10/23/2013
Nanokas Press re-release date: 6/20/2015

Also by Yvonne Kohano

FLYNN'S CROSSING ROMANTIC SUSPENSE SERIES
Pictures of Redemption, Book 1
(Serena & Dane)

Flashes of Fire, Book 2
(DK & Vince)

Naked Intolerances, Book 3
(Gabby & Rick)

Tastes and Consequences, Book 4
(Mac & Roxy)

Blooms on the Bones, Book 5
(Tess & Powers)

Wine Into Water, Book 6
(Marguerite & Deke)

Love and the Christmas Tree Nymph, A Flynn's Crossing Seasonal Novella

Love's Touch of Justice, Book 7
(Jake & Marlee)

This Proposal Between Us, A Flynn's Crossing Seasonal Novella

Measure Twice, Love Once, Book 8
(Geno and Agnes)

And more to come!
Learn about upcoming releases at
www.YvonneKohano.com.

Subscribe to Yvonne Kohano's enewsletter to be among the first to learn about new releases and special offers. Visit www.yvonnekohano.com for more information.

Follow Yvonne at www.yvonnekohano.com, on Facebook as Yvonne Kohano, and on Twitter @yvonnekohano to learn what tickles her about being a writer, and at www.GooseYourMuse.com for creativity tips.

WINE INTO WATER

Prologue – The Witch

She peeked out from behind the stout trunk, its red bark smooth against her cheek. She liked this kind of tree. Rubbing against its sun-baked contours reminded her of comfort, something she hadn't felt in a long time. Even hiding in the brush, she remembered the clean smell of herbs and flowers from warm, delicate skin. An echo of laughter in her distant memory made her stomach jitter like it was full of ants and tears pricked so sharply that she closed her eyes.

The sudden sharp crack forced her to abandon the sensations and startled her eyes open. The tall man at the edge of the clearing brought the large thing in his hands down on the tree lying in front of him, hard enough to make little pieces of wood fly in every direction. One more resonating whack and the log on the ground severed into a length as tall as he was. He glanced over his shoulder in her direction, and she froze, the same stillness deer used to hide in plain sight. His lips pulled into a tight line as he shook his head and hefted the log on to his shoulder.

She followed him up the hillside. Though he carried a load and she only needed to creep along behind him, out of sight and stealthy, her breathing labored and her heart fluttered as hard as a rabbit's. Near the top of the mountain, the man stopped in a clearing and stacked the log on the rest. He was too near her water, the only place where she'd been able to settle. The day he'd examined her bed, nestled in the torn roots of a long-dead pine tree, she'd run so deep into the forest that it took her long hours to find her way out again. When she crept back to the cool spring, the man was gone.

Since then, he'd returned periodically and continued to stack logs. The shape was vaguely familiar to her. A house? But why would he build here, when he already had a house, a much bigger house, down at the bottom of the hill? This was her place. It was the only place she still felt safe.

The man had skin like hers, but that didn't make her trust him. The first ones had skin like hers too, but they talked funny. And her mama and papa were covered with blood and unmoving as the strangers dragged her sister and brother away. She hid in the woods for a long time after that, learning how the small animals escaped detection and surviving on forage. She made their habits her own until the voices of her family faded into a blurry memory.

"Où es-tu?"

The man's voice, coarse but gentle, perked her ears to attention. The words were familiar but lost to her. A musical quality in his tone soothed her. She raised her gaze to find him staring straight at her, as if he could see her hiding in the tall grasses. He moved slowly now, laying down the tool in his hand and staying in a low crouch as he approached.

"Où es-tu?" He called it again in a singsong tone. But he was looking right at her. He knew exactly where she was.

Her heart fluttered again, her body yearning to creep out of her hiding place and move towards that lovely sound. He was close enough now for her to see kindness in his gray-green eyes and sadness cut into the deep lines of his face even as he wore a small smile.

"Nous allons prendre soin de vous, ma petite fille."

Her mind struggled to understand his words. Little one. Care for her. But others had said something like this, and it made her anxious. She shrank further into the grasses but couldn't help the nervous twitches of her body.

"*Venir.* Come. Little girl – food."

She knew these words. The last brought a rumble to her belly and a longing to reach out a hand to him. She watched his face screw up in concentration as he continued to crawl towards her slowly.

"*De famille.*"

Family.

She cried out, her vision blinded by memory of the red shooting from her father's neck, her ears filled with her mother's screams to run, run as fast and as hard as she could. The men laughed and grabbed *Maman*, throwing her to the ground as they pulled at her dress and apron. She kicked them, her pointy-toed boot crunching into bone and flesh, and soon the men were yelling in anger. Then they held her mother down and she covered the swell of her belly as they cursed and raised a knife in the air.

She screamed like the wild thing she had become and crashed backwards through the undergrowth, the tall man's curses ringing in her ears as she bounded into the forest. Running on instinct, she burrowed deeper into densest shrubs, tearing at her dress and scratching her arms so that she was bleeding too, just like her parents. She stopped only when she could no longer move, when her legs had no strength and scalding tears blinded her eyes. And there she lay, wishing that she too could die.

Chapter 1

The pale memory lingered at the edge of her mind. She didn't believe in ghosts or witches. Even so, she couldn't explain what she'd seen.

"Hey, it's only a small cut, not deep, and it won't even leave a scar. Why so morose?"

Marguerite Devereaux looked into the concerned faces of her two best friends and almost squirmed. Their sincere caring saved her day after day. She treasured them and considered herself lucky to find such warmth in her life.

Pasting on a smooth smile, she said, "It is nothing. I am only thinking that I had hoped to age more gracefully than this. Clumsiness is not in my genes. But instead, you are patching up *mon ineptie*."

Roxy LaFollette looked back down at the hand she was wrapping in gauze. "I don't know what you just called yourself, but accidents do happen." She glanced back up, and Marguerite had to grin at the mischief evident on her face. "I know what your problem is. You keep watching that young cellar rat instead of keeping an eye on what you're doing. You need to keep your eye on the prize, or in this case, the wine. And you need to get laid, girlfriend."

Marguerite gave a bark of laughter. The idea that she would be in the least bit drawn to the youngster, fresh out of school and cherub-faced, was outrageous. And the sentiment was exactly what she needed to shake off her residual unease.

It had been there, in the corner of the tank room, almost hidden by the tall steel cylinders. The vapor of a woman had appeared, not too different in age from Marguerite herself but in clothes from another era. The worn garments spoke of hard times, while the expression on the woman's face bore sadness and a touch of hysteria.

Marguerite froze, mesmerized by the plea she could see in the woman's eyes. How she could tell it was a plea, she was not sure. The vision faded to wisps and then reformed, closer now. When the figure put out a hand, palm up and entreating, Marguerite squeezed the hose fitting to stop from reaching out. She only realized how tightly she gripped it when the burn of pain from the slice to her palm brought her back to herself. When she glanced from the blood already oozing back to where she'd last seen the vision, it was gone.

Was it the famous witch? From time to time, the workers reported seeing her, a shadowy female form, particularly when they tended the grapes. They claimed she followed them, reaching out occasionally to caress a vine or test the plumpness of a cluster of fruit. Marguerite laughed off their comments, saying that they'd been in the sun too long. But the men and women in the vineyard had been sure.

The spirit world was not real, of this, she was certain. And menacing? *Non*, it was caused by overactive imagination.

"Have you had a tetanus shot?" DK McGiven handed Roxy a pair of scissors to cut the gauze as she quizzed Marguerite. "Because you know that metal slices like this can be fatal."

"I know, I know. I promise you I've had all of my shots, just like your dog." Marguerite grinned to take the sting out of her words. "Leave it to the two of you to be the ones to come to my rescue."

Of course, they wouldn't have had to rescue her if she'd been paying attention to what she was doing instead of becoming distracted by tricks of light and shadow. When they came to pick her up for a night out with the girl tribe, they'd found her in her office, trying to wrap her hand to stop the bleeding.

"You could have done worse, you know. Who better to fix your boo-boo than Roxy, who's tended more knife slices in her chef years than she can count, and me? I've never met a piece of metal that didn't do me some injustice while I try to bend it." DK flexed her arms, strong despite her pixie size.

"Yes, this was my undoubted good luck to have you find me, rather than say, Serena, who has appeared more than once with cuts and bruises from her construction hobby, or Tess, who has been known to tangle with a rose bush or two, or Gabby, with two hyper-active little boys who keep the wound care industry in business. They would know nothing about how to bandage a mere scratch on my hand."

Her friends laughed. They were all capable and independent and talented, each in their own way. The girl tribe provided an anchor Marguerite wasn't aware she needed until they had crossed her path.

"Come, the others will be waiting. Where are we going tonight? That restaurant Gold, or someplace else? I feel a need for wine after this."

*****

"How did you do this?" Tess Willowspring set a gentle hand on Marguerite's, soothing what little sting was left with her concern. "You are always the picture of concentration, so focused that it's scary sometimes. I'm in awe of your intensity."

Marguerite shrugged and gave Tess's hand a light squeeze in return. "It is not intensity, I keep telling you. But I do have a strong need for control."

Tess burst out laughing at this. "Yes, that you do. But really, what happened?"

Roxy pulled up a barstool and sat on Marguerite's other side. "I say she's distracted by that youngster she hired, the new cellar rat. We need to find an eligible man for our friend. Her hormones are out of control." And she spun around to face away from the bar, seeming to peruse the men behind them.

Marguerite felt a flash of embarrassment. True, she focused on her work. She wasn't interested in being tied down to anything other than her job.

But that didn't mean that her friends needed to fix her up.

She spun Roxy's stool back towards the bar, just as DK returned with a huge grin on her face. "This place always makes me feel nostalgic. Vince and I came here on our very first date and look how well we turned out. Maybe there's someone for you here. Or we could go meet the guys. They're at Mallory's, and it sounded like the whole wolf pack would be there. What do you say? Single men, anyone?"

Marguerite stared into the mirrored wall behind colorful bottles, meeting her own eyes. The faint throb of new age music competed with voices rising and falling, the occasional clink of glass, and the ting of silverware on plates from the restaurant. Decorated in muted wood and stone, both the dining area and bar in Gold were designed to be soothing. Usually she liked this place. But tonight, the dark corners drew her hasty attention. It had been a figment of her over-active mind, she was sure of it.

"Your face is priceless right now, I have to say. Is the idea of spending a couple of hours with the men folk so scary?" DK stared at her reflection intently, avid curiosity and affection making the look less invasive.

Shaking off her recollection, Marguerite sat up straighter and made a production out of setting her glass just so. "With those men? Pah – none of them interest me. Besides, you and the others have most of them wrapped around your little fingers already. No, staying here is fine with me. I do not need a man to distract me or to fill my life. I am and always will be happiest on my own."

Even as she finished the words, Marguerite stared back into her own eyes and saw the lingering unease. On her own, as the ghost was said to have been. Alone on the mountain until her passing. Why this suddenly seemed like her own unlikely end, she wasn't sure.

DK caught her eye again. "Yeah, well just you wait. One of these days, you're going to find yourself in the same predicament as the rest of us. They'll be a man in your life, someone you can't resist. And you'll find that your precious control won't stand a chance."

Chapter 2

"That new bull is proving himself to be a fine investment."

When his uncle spat his wad of chewing tobacco into the gravel road and scratched the crotch of his stained coveralls, Deke Kermarrec winced. He loved the old man, but some of his habits had become more than a little disgusting.

"Yes, he covered those heifers and seemed to hit on every single one. Never saw him busy, but the calves are dropping one right after the other." Deke made sure to smile at the old man as he replied.

"Yup, he sure had hisself a fine time." The old man spit again and chuckled.

"So, Uncle Royan, what are your plans for this winter?"

Deke tried to act casual as he asked the question. With his uncle, he was never sure if he was going to get the real truth, or the truth of the moment. Once, just once, he'd like to feel that he knew what was going on in the man's head.

Scratching himself in a way that made Deke flinch again, the old man took off his floppy fishing hat and scrubbed a filthy hand over the bristly gray hair that stuck every which way off his head. The contrast to his own neat ginger-colored ponytail made the difference in their ages even more obvious. Still, at seventy years of age, his uncle worked his land as if he was Deke's contemporary.

"Haven't quite decided myself on anything yet. You know that the girls ain't interested in the land and want me to sell it and come live in one of those fancy communities for old people. But hell, I ain't old yet!" And he spit again.

Despite the crudeness, Deke found himself grinning at the sentiment. Just because the man didn't see himself as old didn't mean that he shouldn't slow down, though. He didn't want to receive a phone call someday, saying that a horse wandered home without its rider, meaning the old man was on the ground someplace in the middle of his thousands of northern California acres.

Searching umpteen square miles of rough and scrubby foothill crags and canyons was not something he wanted to consider. Losing his uncle, the last of his generation working the land, even less.

Turning back toward their two trucks, their age and shininess another sharp life contrast, Deke made his case for what seemed like the hundredth time.

"When you're ready, I'd like to discuss buying your land from you."

"Aww, Deke, now why would you want to add more to what you got already? You got plenty of land, and for a guy to handle all this by hisself, well, it's plain ridiculous."

But it was family land, or at least it had been for generations. There was precious little of it he could still add to his own. Just Uncle Royan's spread and the three thousand owned by his aunt and her new husband. And they didn't have any kids or kin who were remotely interested in ranching.

Hell, his own siblings didn't feel tied to the land either. It was only Deke left in his generation. But preserving as much of the old Kermarrec homestead of Three Rivers Ranch as possible was his destiny, one he accepted gladly. And he'd made protecting it his life's work.

"Hell, you used to be one of them easy-going types. Now all you got is stress, and you know what they say on the news. Stress'll kill ya. What you need, son, is a wife." And the old man's yellowed teeth shone in his big ugly smile.

Deke found himself digging the toe of his dusty boot into even dustier ground at the words, denial spurting up and almost leaving his lips. There was no time, not when he had thousands of acres to manage and horses to train and livestock to raise. Would a wife repair the fences any better than his hired help did? Could she select the right breeding stock to cross or the best new heritage animals to add? What exactly would he gain in having a wife?

He knew Royan was right on one count though, and it wasn't a need for a partner to work the land. No matter how hard he worked or how long the hours stretched, the nights were empty. Did he want to be that old himself someday, alone on land that no one else cared about? That was a damned scary thought.

Stretching to ease the tightness in his shoulders, he changed the direction of their conversation. "You know that the hands would object to hearing they don't do anything around here."

The old man chuckled, winced and rubbed his back, and spat again. "Yeah, but none of them can keep your bed warm at night, or give you children, or bring you peace of spirit at the end of the day."

The loneliness in his tone drew Deke to search his face. He forgot, in the busy race that was their work from before sunrise to past sunset, how much Uncle Royan might miss Aunt Debby. She'd been dead for six years now, and with each passing month, Uncle Royan let himself go a little more, throwing himself into his ranch to the point of exhaustion.

Just like Deke did, if he was honest with himself. Was he looking in the mirror of at some future version of himself? That idea was more than terrifying.

Covering his concern with a sharp whistle for the dogs, he turned towards his pick-up. "Royan, I appreciate the sentiment, I really do. But you know as well as I do that there is too much going on for me to think about dating, much less marrying."

He heard his uncle behind him haul his truck door open with a shriek of metal on metal and figured the conversation was over, at least for now. And he was no closer to learning if he ever would have a chance to acquire the old man's property. Dogs yipped in happiness and jumped into the bed of his truck, and he turned back, intending to say goodbye and be on his way.

Instead of finding Royan ready to leave, though, the man stood only scant feet away, a frown carving even deeper crags in his face.

"I know you're worried, son. I hear things too, ya know." He paused as if trying to find the right words. "If things get bad, you know you can bring the stock over to my place."

Ready to contradict his uncle's words, Deke reconsidered as they sank in. He'd kept it quiet, and few people knew how dire things were. His hands were getting curious, though, and the secrecy couldn't go on much longer. Soon he would have to act.

*****

Only the faint hint of a breeze pushed through the open window. While the heat hadn't abated from the day, he hated to sit in the noise of the swamp cooler as he took care of the books. The sounds of crickets and tree frogs chirping their symphony outside and three dogs snoring in various keys and cadences at his feet should accompany these kinds of reflections.

Deke leaned back in his chair, the squeak of the springs barely registering on the dogs' radar as he stretched. Their snores continued, Dolly twitching in pursuit of an imaginary foe while Jenny gave a loud huff and rolled to expose her belly, all four paws in the air.

He smiled. This is what ranch life was supposed to be about. Hard work during the day, comfort at the end of it, and the only worry in between about how many head of cattle to sell or whether it was time to move a herd to the next pasture.

Dropping his feet to the floor, his boots echoed against the old reclaimed wood. He'd built this place, log by plank by stone. It had taken him years of work, long hours after working beside his father on the ranch. He'd planned it for his future family, not that any such thing seemed to be on the close or distant horizon.

He started when Dolly placed her black and white head on his leg, her big blue eyes regarding him thoughtfully. When he only stared back, she added a paw and a happy smile that allowed her pink tongue to loll to one side.

"Oh yeah? What do you think you need?"

She cocked her head to the side, her ears perking up in the universal sign of intense interest in doggie-dom. Behind her, Jenny shrugged to her feet and shook herself mightily, while Dozer continued to snore on the floor.

"I swear your brother is deaf, or dumber than a log." Deke reached out to ruffle the fur on the border collie's head, giving the lab mix the same attention when she pushed forward. The sleepy dog finally raised his head, a huge yawn showing the backs of his teeth and the full length of his tongue.

"Finally up, eh boy? The girls have you beat, you know. Someday, you're going to miss out on kibble."

That brought the dog to his feet in a flash, pushing his way between the girls and trying to jump into his master's lap.

"Hey – off, you goon. It's almost bedtime. Time to go out?"

All three dogs headed for the front door, their yips nearly drowning out the click of toenails against the hardwood. Deke stood, switching off the desk light as he shut the laptop lid, ready now to call it a night.

There were never enough hours. He worked alongside the hands during the day, leaving the chores and tasks to them, but filling in where he was needed. They liked his level of involvement. It gave them the freedom to work without someone breathing over their shoulder. And yet, if they wanted him to make a final decision, he was there.

Three wiggling bodies stood eager and whining at the carved door. Impatience at how long it took him to cross the living room was obvious when their noise grew louder, the closer he got. It was the same dance every night. Something normal and regular and real. He smiled at that.

"Now don't go too far, and come back when I call, okay?"

The wall of fur erupted across the porch and down the steps as soon as the door was wide enough for passage. Noses to the ground and tails in the air, they spun off in three different directions until darkness swallowed them up.

He had longer conversations with his dogs than he did with most people. Even on days when he drove into Flynn's Crossing for supplies or food, or when he worked with the hands, those discussions typically dealt with the ranch or the weather or the latest on livestock sales and pricing.

Deke strolled across the porch at a more leisurely pace, inhaling the cooler night air gratefully. Here, the cacophony of night creature noises was louder, and a city dweller would probably complain about it. But for him, it was the lullaby he'd grown up with.

And now, if he wasn't careful, it was one he'd lose for no fault of his own.

Chapter 3

"Come on, come on. I told you there's nothing more relaxing than a game of darts, a beer in hand, with your compadres gathered around you."

Deke lifted the beer in salute, more to avoid responding to his brother Jake than because he was thirsty. When he lowered the glass, his gaze met the humor-filled eyes of his sibling. Something was up, and he didn't like the smug prankish grin his brother sported.

"The only thing better is being in the arms of a beautiful woman, I tell you." Vince Cassidy, self-proclaimed leader of the wolf pack, slapped Jake on the back, toasting Deke with his bottle of ale. "And I, my friends, am lucky that way. You guys, not so frickin' much."

Jake turned to give Vince an evil eye, and Deke was glad for the shift in attention. His brother, younger than him by a year and a half, got their mother's good looks. Favoring their father, Deke's stockier build was honed by years of ranch work. Not that he could call his brother a weakling, given that he was a sheriff's deputy and no slouch when it came to physical activity, but he wasn't close to the land and its daily tending the way that Deke was.

No, he and only he cared about the land. Legacy aside, it was what he'd been drawn to since he was a boy. His life was their family's ranch. And that made the latest report from the hydrologist all the more concerning. Wishing that he could extricate his brother from the camaraderie of the growing group, he wondered again if he was overreacting. If he was, it would be a blessing. If he wasn't, he didn't want to contemplate the battle to come.

"Luck has nothing to do with it."

Realizing that the teasing had continued while his mind wandered, Deke tuned back just as their cousin Dave Preston sauntered in, followed by Steve Cartwright, another county worker. Like Deke and Jake, they were single. The rest of the wolf pack was being picked off like mice by the hawks.

"Who got lucky? Jake, have you been holding out on us?"

Deke took a step back away from the table, hoping to step out of the spotlight as easily. But Jake seemed to be on to him.

"Nah, not me. But Deke might."

What the hell?

Shaking his head in denial, Deke let Jake pull him back into the fray with a hard hand on his shoulder.

"I doubt it. The last time Deke talked about a date, he was in college." Dave elbowed Steve in the ribs and they both laughed.

"Just because he doesn't kiss and tell, which, I might remind a few of you, there seems to be a lot of going around these days, doesn't mean he isn't seeing someone." Jake's rapid move from clown to champion didn't fool Deke. He was up to something.

"I am not seeing anyone."

"What about fixing him up with that winemaker, Marguerite?" Dave addressed the question to Vince, who appeared give it serious thought.

Deke felt the situation spiraling out of his control. He was usually the most easy-going of guys, but this continued attention on his dating situation or lack thereof was getting on his last nerve. All of his other nerves were worn thin with worry about the ranch.

Vince shook his head slowly. "She is one exotic lady, that's for sure." He made a big show out of shivering.

"But controlling? Oh shit yeah. No offense, Deke, but I don't think you and Marguerite have a chance in hell. She's all ice princess and sophisticated and chic, and that's just not you."

Okay, it was hard not to take offense at that. Vince had a way of putting his size eleven feet into a pile, even when he had the best of intentions. But before Deke could respond, Jake's teasing tone returned.

"Not his type at all. Nothing in common, nothing at all. But I know how to match him up with women who are his type."

Peppered with questions from the rest of the group, Jake grinned like he'd won the lottery, and Deke had the urge to grab his arm and drag him outside before he could get into more mischief.

Jake slapped him on the back and lowered his head confidentially, causing the rest of their group to lean forward with expectant grins.

"I took care of it for you."

"You took care of what, exactly, for me?" He might have to do his brother bodily harm this time, because this didn't sound good.

"I signed you up."

Jake was enjoying this. In the pause that followed, the thunk of darts on cork, sharper clatters of glasses set on wooden tables, and smell of beer and peanuts rose around Deke. Undoubtedly, whatever this would turn out to be would be ingrained forever into his memory. He didn't want to ask, but Jake seemed to be hell-bent on telling the rest of his story no matter what he did.

"You signed me up for what?"

Jake's grin grew even broader, and Vince murmured that this was going to be good to anyone who bothered to listen. Deke winced. It wasn't the first time he'd been on the receiving end of one of Jake's pranks.

"I signed you up for that dating site, the one for farmers and ranchers. Put a profile in for you and everything. You've got at least a dozen women interested in you already, bro. All you have to do is open up their emails."

It was hard to hear the resulting catcalls and laughter from his so-called friends over the roar in his ears. He closed his eyes, wishing he could teleport back to the ranch, where the only things he needed to worry about were water and grazing and stock production. When he opened them again, the first thing he saw was Jake's big grin.

"Congratulations, big brother. You're going to have a date."

*****

"Seriously, I think it's a great idea."

Deke considered the possibility of slugging Jake, cop or not. The story had been retold with the new arrival of each wolf pack member, until Deke was sure that the whole damn bar knew that he was supposedly the hot guy on an Internet dating website. This was not funny.

"I mean, how else are you going to meet women? You work twenty hours a day, seven days a week. You have no social life other than what the guys and I drag you out to. Hell, if a single woman expressed any interest in you at all, you'd miss it because your only passion, your constant passion, is the ranch. Man, it is not healthy."

"Is that any different from your commitment to being a cop?"

Deke noticed Jake recoil, and he was glad he'd hit a nerve. It didn't seem to slow his brother for long, though.

"At least I meet women in my line of work. And I work with single ladies too. Tell me, does the feed lot even have any eligible females left, or are they all underage or married and pregnant?"

Deke waved off the question, digging in his jeans pocket for his keys. Trying to discuss anything serious with Jake today seemed to be a waste of time. When his brother continued on in the same teasing tone as he followed in the direction of their vehicles, Deke spun on him.

"Not that it's any of your business, but I date when I want to date, when I have time and inclination to date. And right now, I have much more important things on my mind than women. I have a crisis on my hands."

When he turned towards his truck once more, Jake fell into step beside him saying nothing. Inhaling the dry summer air did little to calm his anger or ease his frustration. The headache lurking in the background almost constantly these days, stealing away his good nature, pounded once more. Deke beeped the truck unlocked and reached for the door's handle. A strong hand closed on his arm when he tried to yank it open.

"Hey, I'm sorry. I was just funning with you. You know, like when we were kids. You used to be able to take it better."

Deke swung around to look directly into his brother's eyes. They were the mirror of his, the one family feature they undeniably shared. They looked apologetic and troubled, the color a turbulent gray-green.

Letting out a sigh and allowing the chip to fall off his shoulder was hard. He longed for those simple days when they were both easy-going hellions their mother chased after with a broom for their latest misadventure. Their tight bond lasted through high school and through the addition of three more Kermarrec boys.

Jake said, "I'm sorry. I was kidding. I didn't really set you up on that dating site. But maybe you should think about it. You know, meet some women who are as interested in ranching as you are?" He arched his eyebrows and tilted his head as he raised the question.

Deke rubbed his hand across his eyes. Coming out tonight had been a bust, a mistake. He could have been doing more research or thinking about a strategy. Anything but getting ribbed about something that mattered so little.

His butt hit the side of the truck as he leaned back, staring at Jake with a face that he was sure shared all of the bleak worry he was feeling.

"Apology accepted. I have a lot on my mind, Jake. Right now, women don't even rate in the top one hundred of why I'm worrying."

Jake turned and leaned back against the front quarter panel and kicked a booted foot up on the tire. His crossed arms matched Deke's. Mirroring again, that cop trick to encourage someone to talk. Deke almost let the edge of his lip curl in recognition. Jake probably wasn't even aware he'd slipped into investigative mode.

"So what is at the top of your worry list?"

Deke examined the parking lot of Mallory's, his eyes sliding from car to truck to SUV, recognizing more than a few. He'd lived in this county since the day he'd been born on the ranch, other than some of his college years. He knew all of the old families in the ranching world of their region, and most of the new ones as well.

"At the top of the hit parade is water."

He saw Jake's surprised gaze snap to him out of the corner of his eye.

"Are the wells drying up? That's never been a problem in history." He frowned, and Deke turned to look at him more fully. Jake opened his mouth, seemed to reconsider, and closed it again. Then he shook his head and started over.

"I've heard plenty of stories recently about wells going dry because other users need a lot. For example, that winery you're next to. They have to irrigate, and I bet they're drawing out of the same aquifer."

Deke shook his head in the negative as Jake's voice faded off. "It's not the amount of water. We have plenty. I don't think that the winery draws from the same place as we do anyway. No, it's not that."

"So what is it?" The puzzlement on his brother's face was genuine.

Deke sighed again. He'd wanted to discuss this with Jake, but somehow, it now felt like he was dumping his burden on shoulders that hadn't made the same choices he had. But he needed an impartial sounding board, and for that, Jake was great.

"I think something's poisoning the wells."

Jake's frown deepened and he stood up straighter. "Poison? How do you know? Something or someone? "

Squeezing the back of his neck did little to release the tension or the headache rapping at his temples. Jake might not be a big part of the ranch, but he'd protect it as if he was.

"I've lost some livestock over the last few months, more than what I would consider normal. The last two seemed so bizarre that I took them to the vet school for analysis. And they came back with toxicology that was through the roof. Residues of herbicides at high levels. Things that we don't use on the ranch."

"Could it be something natural?"

Deke shook his head before Jake had a chance to finish the sentence.

"No, it's not natural. And I think I know what's causing it. Or rather, who."

Chapter 4

She had blurted out the first thing that came to her mind as he'd reached out his wine glass.

'Your eyes are like the sea.'

Merde, how embarrassing was that?

"You met someone?"

Marguerite's frown at her memory changed to a grimace at the astonishment in her friend's voice. It wasn't like she was a nun, after all.

She turned from the kitchen table to avoid Tess's wide-eyed gaze.

"He is a neighbor of the winery. His family has been on that land for a long time. He is…intriguing." Her French accent rose on the last word, and she flinched when she realized that it gave the term an erotic tone.

"Ah, then it's Deke Kermarrec. Yes indeed. He would definitely put that blush on your cheeks," Tess teased.

Marguerite shook her head, letting long black curls hide her expression as she busied her hands with the food on the table. "He came into the winery the other day, saying he had watched us grow for quite a while but had never taken the time to visit. We chatted. He is very charming."

And sexy as a rich Cab, almost making her forget that she had yet to encounter a man who could meet her expectations.

When Tess didn't respond, Marguerite felt compelled to fill the silence. "His ancestors were French, from Brittany. They have been on their land for seven generations."

Tess deposited the washed vegetables next to Marguerite's cutting board and wiped her hands in a towel. "Yes, I know. His brother Jake is a sheriff's deputy. The three younger boys left the area. It's a shame. Their ranch is supposed to be amazing, rich in history and amazingly productive. I know that Larry at the charcuterie shop is always delighted to get his hands on any of the fresh game or domestic meat Deke provides. He said that the quality is unlike anything else he's tasted, even among organic grass fed stock."

A man as committed to excellence on his land as she was to quality at the winery. It could make their future conversations very lively. Maybe he would be a nice distraction for a time.

Until he said the wrong thing or bored her to tears.

"Are you going out with him?" Tess's quiet question contrasted with the lively scrutiny on her face. "I mean, you don't seem any more inclined to date than I am."

Happy to be able to shift the spotlight, Marguerite wiggled her fingers in an all-encompassing circle in response. "Ah yes, but you are enmeshed with that brother of Dane's, Powers, are you not?"

"Powers and I have – issues," Tess replied, waving off the idea.

"This Deke and I will probably have – issues – too," Marguerite countered, tossing aside the offending word as if none of it mattered.

"I think that you should give it a chance," Tess countered.

"And I, you," Marguerite shot back, letting her smile mirror Tess's, even as the other woman shook her head.

"Someday, you'll explain to me why you are so resistant to the idea of dating."

No, Marguerite wanted to reply. Men didn't live up to her high expectations over the long term, and it was better not to waste her time.

Instead, she flipped her hair over her shoulder and gave Tess a wicked grin. "Maybe it's the witch in me, just like the mountain."

When a shiver washed over her, she realized that perhaps she was tempting the fates too much.

*****

The sun barely set below the western ridges when Marguerite pulled up to her house. It had been home to the previous landowners, and for a time, it had belonged to Drs. Davinia and Marcus Dawson as their new place near the top of Witch Hill was constructed. When it was finished, they offered the cabin to Marguerite as one of the benefits of being the Witch Hill Winery winemaker.

Even two years later, the sight of the place in the dimming light of dusk usually brought a smile to her face. Designed to mimic an old log cabin, it was the contemporary and more spacious version of the kind that early settlers and miners alike built when they laid claim to their land. Of course, it also included all of the modern amenities, a fact that Marguerite appreciated as much as the secluded setting.

Tonight, though, she was too distracted to savor the wide covered porch or the soft murmurs of the surrounding woods. The girl tribe dinner had been interesting to say the least. Between urging Tess to give Powers a chance, discussions about possible nuptial sites for their artist friend DK and fiancé Vince, and similar prodding for writer Gabby Cooley-Burke and her Rick, the night had been stimulating. The fact that she was able to escape any further poking into her own business was even better.

She was single and loving it, she assured them whenever they asked. Independent, self-sufficient, and owned by no one, she still treasured her friends, even as time became harder to carve out for their time together. One by one, each member of the girl tribe was meeting her match, and each woman seemed to be willing to endure what Marguerite saw as the very noticeable and unfortunate flaws in their men. Even Serena Williamson, now Serena Ashland, had accepted that her husband Dane might never fully recover from the tragedies he'd experienced in Afghanistan.

Settling, that is what her friends were doing. She, on the other hand, would never settle. If the man was not perfect, and did not meet every one of her long list of required traits and characteristics, he was not for her. Better to be alone than to settle.

Shaking her head, Marguerite reached for the phone she'd plugged into her dash charger when she'd arrived at Tess's home. There would be no emergencies needing her attention that couldn't wait until she and her friends had enjoyed an evening of laughter together.

And honestly, since every one of their phones except Tess's had rung with a call from their men at some point in the evening, she didn't want it underscored that there was no man wondering when she would be home, settling or not. A part of her, a part she'd never admit to in public, was envious. Just because she enjoyed being on her own didn't mean that she was never lonely.

'Your eyes are like the sea.'

Her own words echoed back to her again. His eyes, the color a mixture of green and gray and blue, had startled her then. There was a Breton word for it – *glacé*. The eyes would change based on the mood and temperament of their owner. Her native French compatriots said that reading the color of those eyes would only scratch the surface of emotions underneath.

That day, she'd nearly boggled the wine thief as she lifted it from the barrel, intent on showing off the futures of Cabernet Sauvignon on a busy Sunday afternoon. The crowd had been steady, and when she looked up to give her welcome and standard explanation about the wine, his direct gaze stopped her mid-pour.

He smiled, a lazy grin that spread slowly across a face that was too rugged to be called handsome and too transcendent to be anything but intriguing.

"Since they caught your attention, I suppose I should thank my grandparents five times removed on my Dad's side."

Recovering her composure with effort, she remembered what she was doing and closed the distance between the wine thief and his proffered glass.

"Indeed you should. I have not seen eyes like yours since I was last in France."

He swirled the wine in its deep bowl, took an appreciative sniff, and sipped, his eyes closing as if to focus on the experience. It gave her a chance to stare as the muscles in his throat worked around the swallow. His hair was the color of lightly oaked Chardonnay, and waves that ran just past his shoulders undoubtedly made many women weep in envy.

Not her, of course.

Those amazing eyes opened slowly, and he met her gaze with stillness. Obviously, he was used to being examined so closely by the women he met.

"I can tell from your accent that France isn't a distant ancestor to you like it is to me. I know you're Marguerite, the winemaker. I'm Deke Kermarrec. My family owns the ranch to the south of this mountain."

She ignored the red wine staining her fingers and put her hand in his outstretched grasp. The shake was warm, his larger hand engulfing hers and the rough calluses sweeping over her palm like a caress, making her shiver before she caught herself. The almost playful quality of his deep quiet voice drew her closer, and she couldn't help the teasing note in her reply.

"And before then? Because you know, it only matters who your people were at least ten generations ago."

He chuckled, a musical sound as delightful as new wine hitting a fresh glass, making the skin on the back of her neck tingle.

"Eight generations, ten, or twenty, it would have been Bretagne. Some time back then, though, I think it was a Celtic nation, not French."

She wanted to continue this interesting conversation with this intriguing man, yearning at a level she hadn't experienced in a long time. But other guests were standing with glasses outstretched and waiting.

"Mr. Kermarrec, I hope that we have a chance to discuss in more detail how the French merely allowed imposters to borrow part of our country for a time. But now, I must continue to work. If you'd like to return to the tasting room, there are more wines to experience. It has been a pleasure meeting you."

He nodded and moved to the side, and she felt a stab of disappointment, sharp enough to create an unfamiliar ache. It had been a long time since she'd had a worthy adversary with whom she could trade barbs, and she sensed that it was likely this man would have been a skillful opponent. As busy as it was today, she would not be free any time soon.

But he surprised her, rounding the barrel to lean against a steel tank a few feet away. With one boot crossing the other at his ankles and a hip cocked to the side, he looked the picture of ease. That appreciative gaze lit his face again, slowly building from glow to mega-wattage, and she couldn't help but grin in return.

"I can see that you're busy. It's okay. I'm in no hurry. A good debate is always something worth waiting for." A genuine smile crept across his face and turned his eyes a fathomless rich blue, the color reminding her of tropical seas and hot sands, as he added, "And it's Deke."

She rubbed the phone in her hand like a talisman at the memory. In small tastings, they'd begun to get to know one another. She baited him with ancestral slights, but he surprised her once more by changing the course of their discussion completely as he asked about her winemaking process. That eventually led to her inquiries about his ranching business during another brief lull in customers.

And after two hours of random conversation, she remained intrigued. She was almost done with barrel tasting for the day. But by then, he'd looked at his watch and excused himself, saying that livestock needed feeding.

"I hope we have an opportunity to continue to explore Franco-American relations," he'd said, with a wink and a squeeze of her hand. Taking two steps back, he turned and walked out the barrel room door, giving her a fine view of his well-toned physical attributes. Marguerite felt that full-body shiver once more, even as she told herself she didn't care if she saw him again.

The cell's energetic ringing in her hand made her jump in the driver's seat and nearly hit the car's horn. It was the public ringtone, so the person on the other end wasn't someone she knew well. It was tempting to let it go to voicemail and deal with it tomorrow, but years of training in the polite niceties of world society wouldn't allow her to. With an ever-useful deep breath, she focused.

Sliding a finger across the screen, she waited a couple of seconds for the call to engage before saying, "This is Marguerite Devereaux."

In the pause on the other end, she heard light steady breathing before a deep male voice chuckled and replied, "Your name sounds much better when you say it than when it's massacred by an American accent. Marguerite, this is Deke."

Chapter 5

"Are you sure this is all right with you?"

Deke felt the tension below the surface in his words, and grimaced inwardly with the emotion. He'd told Jake he needed to do some digging, but he hadn't expected it to backfire on him. Nothing about the winemaker was what he had expected.

He'd picked a Sunday to visit the winery because he expected them to be busy and any questions he posed would be lost in general discussions. No one would give a second thought to his queries.

The tasting room staffers were harried but friendly, more than happy to volley back and forth with the many inquiries of guests stacked three deep at the bar. If this was a usual Sunday, they must be doing well. And yes, they said, weekends were always busy. But he learned what had upped the interest that day, a barrel tasting of upcoming releases. Taste the nascent wine still aging in oak and get an idea of how it would continue to mature with time. You had the opportunity to buy the product in advance at a price below its eventual retail rate. Of course, you had to wait a few months until the wine was bottled, but the discount was worth an early investment.

When he asked about vineyard management practices as subtly as he could, the young woman behind the counter smiled apologetically and said, "I don't want to give you the wrong information. It would be best for you to talk with Marguerite Devereaux about that. She's our winemaker, and she's out in the barrel room. You can't miss her. She's the one with all of that lovely dark hair."

He'd turned and headed towards the doorway the woman indicated, figuring that he could blend in there too.

The transition from light airy tasting room to darker and cooler interior only made him pause for a minute. The crowd here was thinner, aligned in front of single barrels set forward from large racks stacked high. An individual he assumed to work for the winery chatted with the crowd at each one. An arrow pointed to the left behind rope stanchions, and Deke moved towards the queue, scanning the workers to find his target.

When his eyes came to rest on the winemaker, he was glad he was hidden by the crowd in between. The woman did indeed have a mass of dark wavy hair, pulled up in some kind of knot at her neck that only emphasized her regal posture and haughty bearing. Then she laughed gently at something a guest said, and the sound rippled over his skin before diving to embed itself past easy extraction.

He was mesmerized. He felt drawn forward in the line, listening to the words describing each wine without any notion of what they meant. Sipping mechanically, he tasted nothing. This was not going as planned.

By the time he arrived at her barrel, he thought he had himself under control. He put his laziest grin on his face, the one that a woman or two over the years had said was a very engaging smirk. Drawing so close that he could see the unexpected flashing color of her eyes, he'd stretched out his wine glass before she'd turned to look at him. And when she stared at him in surprise, he was grateful that he'd had the time to hide his disquiet.

'Your eyes are like the sea.'

The statement almost made him laugh out loud, but the stunned expression on her face was such a contrast to the cool aloofness of a moment before that he opted for a quip instead, one that she returned with one of her own almost as quickly. Her surprise changed to calm control within only a minute. Their exchange was unlike anything he had anticipated, and he assured himself that he could afford to spend an extra couple of hours doing research.

Digging was both easier and harder than his preconceived notions.

She was like a witch, casting a spell over him. He found himself thinking about her at unlikely times since then, like when he was checking the condition of his heirloom cattle. It almost earned him a black eye and broken nose when the object of what should have been his attention raised its head to butt him.

This would just be more research, he assured himself. He hadn't had time to get the answers he needed to confirm or deny what might be happening. That, and only that, was the reason he needed to see the charming Marguerite again.

What better way to learn more from her than to ask her out? When he'd called Marguerite for a date, he intended to take her to Roxy's restaurant in an effort to showcase his ranch beef on the menu. It wasn't like the idea of showing off was intentional. It was only a casual opportunity to educate her about his ranch.

When she countered with a proposal that they first walk the vineyard so that she could explain more about her vines and he could point out parts of his ranch visible from those heights, he was both fascinated and astonished. Most women he met didn't want to have a first date walking rough and uneven ground in the baking heat of a foothills summer afternoon. When she generously agreed that dinner would be a good idea after all of that exercise, he made reservations and kept his feelings to himself. After all, she'd played right into his hands.

And she continued to surprise him.

"I'd like to hear the stories your family tells about what this land was like before all of this," her arm swept in a graceful arc to take in the vines next to them and the winery buildings at a distance, "came to be."

He halted in his tracks, wondering where to start. But this was part of why he wanted to talk with her, after all. Impressing her with the fragility of the land – along with its economic importance – was his goal. If he enjoyed himself with an attractive woman in the process, all the better, as long as the end game, his end game, was the goal he kept in sight.

It was a damn fine view from where he was standing now too. She was tall, almost as tall as he was, and not slender, but not overly voluptuous. She would be an armful, but the right kind of armful. Today her raven hair hung loose down her back, and he speculated that it probably would make it to her denim-clad waist if the curls hadn't taken up so much slack. Her bare arms were toned, and clearly she was no stranger to physical work anymore than he was. Her boots were as scuffed as his and almost as dusty. And still, she carried herself like a princess.

When she realized he was no longer walking behind her, she stopped and glanced over her shoulder. Her eyes twinkled at him, full of mischief and sparkling in a purple violet, the color of flowers his Ma used to grow. It was like she knew the effect she had on men in general, and she was testing him to see if he was any different.

"Deke, is this too – energetic for you?"

The question, delivered with a hint of amusement, made him smile.

"No, just trying to figure out where in the history of seven generations and over a hundred and fifty years you'd like me to start my story."

She laughed then, a throaty sound that reminded him of those rare summer storms that blew in from the Sierras. That thunder had the same tempestuous tone, like the best and the worst you can expect out of life rolled into one.

"Let's start with how your family came to settle the land."

He resumed walking, at her side now with his shoulder occasionally brushing grape leaves to avoid knocking into her. He resisted the urge to put a hand under her elbow to steady her over the more uneven patches. She didn't appear to need the help, but he had a sudden overwhelming urge to touch her.

"If you remember your French history lessons, all of Brittany was in a deep economic recession for most of the early to mid-1800's during the French Revolution. Social unrest and brutality ruled. The Breton language was banned, and its citizens were treated as chattels, or worse, cattle."

It was a dark period, one of many in France's long and complicated re-alliances and restructurings, something that still brought shame to those who took their history seriously. He'd studied it out of curiosity to know more about his roots.

"My ancestors suffered as most did. Those who could, emigrated to Paris or other parts of the country and attempted to start over. But my family lived off the land, and moving to a city to take poor laborer jobs wasn't an option."

"It must have been difficult for your people at that time. My people struggled as well, though they lived in the city and worked in the trades until this century." Her serious tone matched his, though he wasn't sure she fully grasped exactly how hard things had been.

He pondered how to respond to this. "In the country, they often had greater freedoms than city dwellers. After all, they could survive on what they grew or raised, and they were free within the confines of their land and their community to continue to practice their traditions and culture, though in secret. They could choose to withdraw from local society and keep their children from school and their animals from market. But even that wasn't enough to guarantee their safety, and too often they were threatened or their livestock killed to send what today we would consider a message."

She remained silent as her steps slowed, her hand reaching out now and then to brush back a leaf or examine a cluster of green grapes beginning to show slight tinges of lavender color. He wasn't sure what he liked more, walking next to her and watching the contemplative expression on her face, or striding along in back of her and studying her other fine features.

Steady boy, no need to take things where they had no business going. But it was impossible not to consider. Strolling next to a beautiful woman on a summer's afternoon was an invitation to something. The fact that this woman could be the one causing all of his problems was not an idea he relished.

Clearing the sudden harshness in his throat, he took off his hat and put it on her, drawing her eyes to him in surprise. Then she smiled and settled the wide brim more securely on her head.

"Let me guess," she said, the teasing notes back in her voice. "They decided they would become rich in the New World."

He grinned back at her as they resumed their casual pace. "Yes, 1849 was a magical year as word spread around the world. As the story goes, my grandfather seven generations ago had eight brothers and sisters. I forget how many of each exactly, but in the end, three of the boys and one of the girls and their respective spouses and children all headed around the world to find their fortunes here in California during the Gold Rush. It took them a year, sometimes more, but they finally made it."

She watched his face with what he took for rapt attention. He enjoyed telling the family stories, and he had a good sense of how to keep an audience engaged. For once, he was especially grateful for the talent. If this violet-eyed witch continued to look at him this way, he might forget about dinner in a public restaurant and ask her how she felt about steaks on his grill at home. Followed by dessert, and not the baked kind either. Over the scents of sun and earth, her fragrance was intoxicating.

They stopped at the end of the trellised row, boots crunching in unison on the dry rocks and parched midsummer dirt. He thought about taking her hand for the walk back, only a casual gesture. His actions followed his thoughts without conscious prompting as his fingers and eyes followed the line of her tanned arm down to tangle his fingers with hers. Then he blinked and froze.

*****

She found she loved the way he told his stories, the gentle cadence of his voice and the meaning of his words equally mesmerizing. In fact, they'd walked a lot further than she intended. This stroll was meant to ease those awkward first few moments when they each decided if they did in fact like each other as much as their first meeting indicated.

In the process, they'd traveled to the far side of the vineyard and the heat of the day was only now starting to dissipate with a late afternoon breeze. The fact that he gave her his hat to shield her eyes from the lowering sun only added to his charm. His hair hung loose, tangling in his shirt collar and brushing over his shoulders. His arms were tanned in a way that made her guess he wasn't hiding a farmer's tan, pale-shouldered and white. There was something about him that made her think he was comfortable working in his jeans and boots, and those alone. She considered slipping a hand into his as they walked, but she could afford to wait. It looked like she was about to be rewarded for her patience.

But he stopped, and from his current posture, she wasn't sure what was wrong. Every easygoing muscle in his body froze tight, and he stared at her hand like it had grown into a second head. His face grew serious and wrinkled in concentration.

"Deke? What happened to your family then?"

He didn't appear to hear her, and she wondered if the sudden heat of sun on his bare head had caused a stroke. Even for an American and a cowboy, he was acting oddly.

He licked his lips slowly and let out a steady breath. His hands came up, grabbing her wrists and gliding slowly but firmly up her arms, harder than a caress. He didn't look at her, though, and it pissed her off. What was this, some kind of cowboy foreplay?

She didn't like being manhandled unless she was ready for a little playtime. They still barely knew each other. And here she was, out of sight and hidden by the grapes with a man who might be a lunatic, and –

"Marguerite," his voice commanded, low but purposeful, "do as I tell you to."

She opened her mouth to argue, more pissed off than ever since he was staring at her feet instead of her face.

"Follow my lead."

Something in his firm tone made her pause before venting. *Merde*, what did this bastard think? That she was some submissive woman who wanted a man to –

He pushed her hard without warning, to the side and uphill a few feet until she was against the grapevines. His body followed hers, and when he pressed into her, his eyes finally filled her face.

She wanted to yell at him, to push him away at the very least. But his hardness, muscles toned to perfection by years of his daily routine, carved into her softness in all the right places, despite their similar heights. She was barely conscious of the vines jamming into her back as his hands came to rest on her hips, steadying her and keeping her upright.

At this distance, she could see the rapid color change in his eyes, the sea-swept green-gray altering to a more turbulent blue. His gaze traced over her features, and his nostrils flared as if he was memorizing her scent. When his stare came to rest on her lips, she couldn't help herself. Her tongue came out of its own accord and licked first her top lip, then the bottom.

He hissed again roughly, the sound ending in a harsh rattle. This wasn't what she expected, but the effect she had on him was turning her on too. Then he frowned and looked back to the end of the row of vines. This time, she recognized that the rough noise wasn't coming from him.

"What is it?" Her accent had grown thick on the question. She wished her voice wasn't so low and breathless, but she couldn't control it at the moment.

Deke remained in front of her but eased the pressure between them. His hands gave her hips a soft caress, like regret, before they dropped to his sides.

"Rattlers."

*****

He considered downing the shot of tequila in one gulp. Based on how quickly Marguerite lowered the level of her wine, she was as unsettled by the events of the afternoon as he was. Whether it was the snake scare or their close contact, he wasn't sure. For him, it was all Marguerite.

When her eyes followed his to lock on the rattlesnake almost hidden in the dappled shade of the grapes, its head raised in a position ready to strike, she'd shoved him away and leaped back a few more steps. The string of curses was recognizable from his high school and college French language courses, and he had to admire the inventive positions some of her words proposed. He doubted she even knew what she was saying, her face pale and her eyes staring at the writhing form on the ground, his hat knocked back on her head and in peril of dropping to the dirt.

Finally, she quieted, pulling in deep breaths and planting her feet like she was making a stand.

"That is one very long snake." Her words were soft but her voice was under control, barely a quaver left in it.

He thought to add to her knowledge but decided against it. Silently, he'd taken her arm and turned them back towards the security of her cabin. When his hand slid down her arm and his fingers twined with hers, she held on tightly. Neither of them said anything as they both stared carefully at the ground and stepped with consideration over rocks and furrows.

When he gently suggested that perhaps tonight was not a good night for a date, she denied it vehemently, grabbed her purse without even looking at her reflection and marched towards his truck.

The ride to Roxy's was accomplished with little more in terms of conversation, and when Roxy LaFollette herself made a point of coming from the kitchen to greet them, she'd examined them both closely like they were unusual new menu items. After a few pleasantries, she cut to the bone.

"So, you two, here together. Marguerite, I thought that you said that the two of you barely knew each other. Deke, you should have told me it was Marguerite you'd be bringing tonight." She didn't look the least bit sorry to be grilling them, and Deke was willing to let it go by. By the fixed smile on Marguerite's face, he guessed that she was feeling less generous about it. Once they'd been seated and ordered their drinks, they fell silent again.

"That was one very long snake."

He looked up from his glass on the words she repeated from the vineyard, watching her stare into the depths of her wine. The dining room buzzed around them with date night activity, but they were somewhat secluded from the bustle by the high back of their booth.

"Two snakes." He wondered if he would make a mistake with that piece of news.

"Two snakes?" She shuddered, then let one curse escape, this time in English.

"It's a bad year for snakes. I've run into a number of rattlers already this summer, along with gopher snakes and kingsnakes and a wide assortment of others. The kings are pretty, with rings of white and black and gold, and they eat rattlers."

She looked up at him then, the intense fire in her eyes making the violet almost iridescent. A fleeting thought that this is what she would look like when passion took her over rippled across his mind, and he took a longer steadying sip of his tequila without breaking eye contact.

"Two snakes? Why did you not kill the snakes? Don't you have some sort of cowboy gun in a hidden holster, or a big knife?" Her interrogation thickened her accent and made the words even more intense.

He smiled at that. "I'm a rancher and a businessman, not a cowboy. I don't carry a gun unless I'm culling a herd or hunting, and the only knife on me is this." He pulled a small pocketknife with various folded attachments from a jeans pocket.

She wrinkled her nose at it. "That will not do anything. Why did they not strike us? We were right on top of them." This time her tremble was faint, only a slight quake in her hand. Her accent was again thicker, though, an easy tell of her emotions.

Considering her tense expression, he realized that she had no idea what they'd witnessed. How would she take the news of that little spectacle?

"They were – otherwise occupied."

"Occupied? Doing what? They were sitting in the open in my vineyard, for god's sake. That one had its head in the air, ready to strike."

He let his grin grow wider and leaned back in a position of deliberate ease. Marguerite liked to come off as worldly and sophisticated, but there were some things she was remarkable ignorant about. And he got the pleasure of enlightening her.

He let out a chuckle and took a final sip of his shot, playing out the moment. She continued to stare at him like he was in cahoots with the snakes.

"They were busy making little snakes."

Her mouth dropped open and astonishment moved over her features, followed by realization and something that he thought was grudging respect. Then she took a long drink of wine and sat back to mirror his posture.

"Is this something you watch all the time? Are you a snake *voyeur*?" The hint of amusement was back in her voice, and color flooded back to fill her face.

Now it was his turn to feel astonished. Her recovery was remarkable, and he wondered if much threw her for a loop for very long.

"No, it's not something that most people ever notice. You see, mating season is usually in August around here, and many people never venture out into sunny parched areas in the heat of the day at this time of year." He paused again, aware that he had her rapt attention.

Suddenly he wished he hadn't brought this up. Her eyelids were heavy even as her gaze locked on him, and there was a gentle blush of color on her cheeks. Her lips parted, and the rise and fall of her breathing highlighted her form underneath a top that was now too revealing. He shifted on the padded bench and cursed the fact that his jeans were now uncomfortably tight.

Clearing his throat, he signaled the waiter for another round without consulting Marguerite. If she was going to complain about this, maybe that would take her mind off other things.

"Do they only do it," she put air quotes around the last two words, "in the sunshine?"

"Usually they avoid the hottest parts of the day. The mating dance is the culmination of a long courtship, where the male follows the female around and sometimes engages in battles with other males over the right to mate with her. When they finally do get it on, their dance is something to witness. They curl around each other like braids, and sometimes it looks almost – violent."

*****

She sat in silence, processing his description. Something about his delivery of the words left her hot and achy, wishing that the wine glass in front of her wasn't now empty.

"Do you love snakes?"

She felt a perverse satisfaction when he looked first confused at her question, then incredulous, before shifting in his seat. Her friends would call him antsy.

"No, I don't love them. I respect them. They fill an important niche in the ecosystem, keeping down a rodent population that would otherwise run rampant. They're a vital part of the complete life cycle of the land."

Deke was turning out to be a very unusual man. He had an answer for everything, coupled with the strangest bits of information.

"Are you afraid of snakes?" His gentle question was matched with a raised eyebrow, moving so high on his forehead that she wondered why it didn't disappear into the ginger hair drooping down over the space. Her fingers itched to push the hair back, wondering if it would feel as soft as it looked.

Now it was her turn to shift in discomfort.

"No, I am not afraid of them." But she heard the bravado in her voice and sat up straighter. Years of training in the art of conversation, drilled into her at a very young age and a habit that was hard to break, made her adept at turning the tables.

"Why do you know so much about snakes?" And, she wanted to add, centuries of French history, modern grape growing practices, the Gold Rush, and many other diverse topics. They hadn't dwelled on any one subject in their conversations to date, and he seemed to have an array of facts on the tip of his tongue about everything. That, or he was very adept at bullshit.

He moved closer to her side around the back of the small enclosure. He looked around the restaurant, his eyes stopping on different tables as he observed people with passive interest. When the waiter returned with their drinks, he thanked the young man warmly but declined the need to order their meals yet. Finally, when she was beginning to feel irritated with his lack of attention, he searched her face with such concentration that she sank back into the booth padding. His eyes pinned hers with their intensity.

"I like to read. I like to study things. I like to know about people and what makes them tick, even decades ago. Same goes for animals and birds and reptiles and all of nature. I get curious about something, so I learn all I can. Most times, I never use that knowledge again, but it makes for great party conversation if things get slow." He gave her a small grin to go with the shrug of his shoulders.

She could appreciate the sentiment, since she too had an arsenal of topics that she pulled out when the situation called for it. His lazy smile at the end of his statement passed his full lips and lit up his eyes, now smoldering in a cross between gray and blue. She didn't know what to make of his mood. His tone was playful, and she almost forgot what they had been discussing.

Shrugging and swirling her new glass of wine before she took a sip, she leaned back in a careless posture and gazed around the room with studied nonchalance. When her eyes returned to his, he was giving her a speculative stare that carried more than a little humor. And along with the humor, sympathy.

"You know, it's all right to be afraid of snakes. They're not for everyone."

"I am not afraid of them! I merely do not like them, and I don't see why they aren't exterminated." She heard her volume rise and made a conscious effort to shift into her best cool and haughty expression.

His smile disappeared, and he hovered forward over the table as if he was sharing a big secret.

"Like everything, they have a purpose. Without them, something would be out of balance. Sometimes, they need to be destroyed, just like sometimes, things that seem to be right are wrong for a variety of reasons."

Marguerite frowned at his words. He stared at her like he was sending her a hidden message, but for the life of her, she had no idea what it could be. This man was confusing and beguiling at the same time. Then he grinned again, that smirk raising one corner of his mouth higher than the other.

She matched the smile, determined that he wouldn't know how much he intrigued her. *Il en confondant son* – confounding her and mixing her up along with the captivation.

Still, it would not last, so it was better to enjoy the experience while she could. Somehow, though, she had a feeling that Deke Kermarrec wouldn't be dissuaded until he was satisfied that things between them were at an end. And she wasn't sure if she liked that level of self-confidence or not.

Chapter 6

"I enjoy doing this, Ms. Devereaux, I really do."

His young face was so childishly earnest, Marguerite had to remind herself that he had, in fact, graduated from college with a Master's degree in enology, and he was also old enough to drink. David had been with her for only a month and a half, and he showed promise, even if some of his skills were – how best to put it – undeveloped.

"David, if you feel that you would rather greet the public than work behind the scenes, of course you can pour for events like today. Just remember that you need to learn all aspects of the business to be successful as a winemaker of the future. And that means cleaning tanks and barrels and hauling cases too."

When he smiled so hard that she thought she could see his molars, Marguerite sighed. It wouldn't hurt for him to serve at today's tastings. He had learned about the wine he was responsible for, an award-winning Zinfandel, down to the finest detail. He couldn't do any damage, and it would help him to grow a little bit.

And growth was something that David needed. Or maybe it wasn't growth. Maybe it was more like maturation.

"So you're giving the kid a chance with the customers, eh Margie?"

The short squat figure of Fernando appeared at her side. When the vineyard manager started using this nickname for her, with a hard G in the middle that mimicked her full name, she'd chastised him. When he kept using it, his gravelly voice teasing, she yelled at him. All he did was grin at her even more. Over the past few years, it had become part of their running repartee.

"Ah yes, he will learn. I suspect that giving him chances like this, when he can do no real damage, will go a long way towards building his self-confidence."

Fernando played with the paper stick in his teeth, the only remnant of the lollipop he'd been sucking on earlier. He said it kept him from smoking around the grapes, which he maintained would ruin the resulting wine's flavors. The couple of times she'd visited the vineyard manager at the small cabin reserved for his use at the base of the property, she'd felt the need to shower off the stale smell of cigars as soon as she left. At least he didn't bring that stink around the winery.

"Yup, he could certainly do with a little more backbone. What are you going to do when I retire, Margie? Think the kid will be able to stand up to you by then?" His laughter brought on a fit of coughing.

She'd had too much time to think about that recently, with Fernando planning to leave at the end of the year. He said it was because he was ready for the next adventure in his life, whatever that meant, but in reality, she suspected it was because his lifelong addiction to big cigars had resulted in failing health and he didn't want to be a burden to anyone.

Damned cigars.

"Now, my friend, you know that no one, not matter how skilled, will ever be able to replace you. Why, you probably know this land better than the ghost of the witch does."

She was rewarded by a cackle of laughter that grew in volume, even as a coughing spasm made him back out of the tank room and into the sunshine. Before she followed, she glanced back to make sure that David seemed to have his station under control.

Fernando ran the back of his hand across his eyes, leaving behind a trail of tears as his chuckles continued. He stuck the sucker stick back in his mouth as his gaze wandered over the vineyard rolling down the hill in almost every direction. When he'd calmed himself down, he smiled with satisfaction and shook his head agreeably.

"Yup, I do know this mountain reasonably well. I was mystified by what happened to the grapes when the place was deserted, how they thrived with no water and no care. The ghost of the witch, or maybe the witch reincarnated? I doubt it. More like hardy rootstock and ideal growing conditions and Mother Nature taking her due. But yeah, I do know this land."

His expression saddened, and she wondered for the umpteenth time why he felt he had to retire now. After all, wouldn't he be better off with health insurance, staying close to people who knew him, in a place where he wouldn't be alone? And he had children nearby, did he not?

She swallowed around the unexpected tightness in her throat. She'd grown quite fond of the old man. "You don't have to retire, you know. You're a healthy old goat, and you could prance around this mountain for as long as you like. And you would give David – how should I put this – seasoning."

He rewarded her with a big grin. "Yeah, and you want him to pick up my bad habits as much as you want him to start calling you Margie too, right? Nah, it's okay. It's time. I've done just about everything I want to do here. The bright lights of Las Vegas are calling my name."

He tossed the stick, now reduced to shreds, into a nearby garbage can, and gave her a wave. "Have a good afternoon, Margie, and keep an eye on that boy. God only knows what kind of mischief he could get himself into on his own."

*****

He learned quickly, Marguerite noted. If he heard an explanation once, he could make it his own and engage the prospective wine buyers with information about the wine, without making it sound like a college lecture. If his freckled face grew ruddy from some off-color remark or teasing, so be it. He had to grow some *boules*, correct?

"And if you'd like to taste next year's vintage, still in the barrel, our winemaker is ready to serve you some for comparison." David waved an arm in her direction, and Marguerite smiled at him as their guests walked her way.

"How are you today? You tasted this same Zinfandel from David, only that one was a year older. This new Zin promises to be our best yet from the grapes in this vineyard."

She could do this on autopilot, though she tried not to. She also tried not to get too distracted, glancing up every time someone entered the tank room, hoping that a certain cowboy walked in for a taste too. So far, the afternoon had been disappointing in that regard.

What was it about Deke Kermarrec that was so intriguing? It wasn't his looks alone. He was different. She could sense it in his acute attention to all things. At dinner, he missed nothing of their server's explanations of the various preparations, and when their selections arrived, he'd been able to enlighten her on what was included on her plate when she herself could barely remember what dish she ordered. His piercing gaze seemed to miss little and take in everything. In it, she believed she could see what he was thinking, and artifice wasn't part of the equation.

Dinner and dessert passed too quickly, and by the time they were outside, the uncomfortable heat of the day had faded completely and Marguerite wished she'd thought to bring a sweater. Running her hands up and down her arms didn't alleviate the goosebumps or the chill, but when Deke followed her movements with his own hard fingers, she felt a rise in temperature that made the earlier midday sun pale in comparison.

She was a sophisticated woman of the world, and yet in the presence of this cowboy, she had to concentrate so she didn't lose track of his lightning-quick changes. It was like the magic of aging wine. One day is tasted rough and uncharted, and the next it was smooth and rich. One minute he pissed her off, and the next, he charmed her.

"This was a very interesting day, Marguerite."

Dieu, but she could get used to the sound of her name rolling off his tongue. He'd taken her hand to help her down from the truck, and he kept it tucked in his as he walked her up her cabin steps. Turning to face her and capturing her other hand, his glowing eyes met hers. He lifted first one hand, then the other to his lips, and with slow deliberateness, lightly brushing a kiss across the backs of each. The air heated even more, to the point that she thought the sun must surely be crashing into the Earth.

"I hope that we can do this again, very soon." He paused and watched her carefully. "Minus the snakes, of course."

His quirk of a smile brought an answering laugh from her, and he leaned forward, put a knuckle under her chin, and stared into her eyes. His deep azure blue gaze arrested any thoughts she had, any words she meant to say. The smile on his lips settled into something richer, and he leaned forward. When he brushed his lips across hers as lightly as he had her hands before, her toes curled inside her boots.

So much for sophistication.

It was what it was. She'd had no serious relationships to speak of for years, and the casual sex with friends far away who shared her need to keep things vague scratched the occasional itch, even if it did nothing for her soul. But she was fine the way things were. It was best to keep her standards high, even if her sex life and deeper emotions had been suffering from a long drought of late. That way, she wouldn't be hurt.

Realizing she'd been musing for too long, she glanced around the barrel room to see David standing at the ready, his eyes fixed on the doorway. Two men and two women walked in, talking among themselves. They looked like young professionals, dressed down in casual chic for a weekend of wine-tasting and good food. It was a growing market, the Millennial generation that David was a part of. At least this was a group he should relate to easily.

"Welcome to Witch Hill Winery! Have you visited us before? Great – today you get to try our new release, and you're in for a treat! I'm pouring our most recent bottled Zinfandel release for you to try..."

David rattled on about the source of the grapes, the unique aromas and flavors they could expect on their palates, and the sugar and alcohol ratios. Yes, he was developing good seasoning. Perhaps it was time to allow him to pour for a few events on his own.

"I definitely get the berries in this – it's ideal." The other man in front of David agreed with his friend's pronouncement. The women lingered in front of a display of pictures taken during last year's crush, one finishing a white poured in the tasting room. As the men wandered in the direction of the photos to finish their sips, the women took their place in front of David.

"So I know you've been here before, which means you're probably familiar with our old vine Zin. In this vintage, you'll taste..."

The young women each tilted their glasses for a pour, and Marguerite noted that David was flashing his best smile at them, the little flirt, despite the rings on their fingers. Too bad he didn't realize that it would do him little good with these two. Marguerite smiled, enjoying the dynamics.

"...and berries. Do you get those?" He looked from one woman to the other.

"Ah, no, no berries here." Her friend shook her head to agree, and they both looked at David.

"Yes, berries are a dominant flavor characteristic. Have a cracker, perhaps the white wine is still on your palate. Your husbands both got the berries right off the bat, but everyone's palette is different."

Merde, but look what he stepped into now. Marguerite meant to intervene and invite the women – and the men – to taste the futures. David still looked at the young women expectantly, his face getting a little red around the ears as he waited.

The two women looked at each other, then over their shoulders at the men across the room. When they returned their stares to David, they both burst out laughing. One woman choked off her peals of mirth long enough to call over to the guys. "Hey, he thinks you're our husbands!"

*****

"I can't believe I did that."

Marguerite put a fresh bottle of water in David's hand and patted his shoulder. His face was still red. In fact, when it turned the color of fresh red grape juice at the joint laughter of the four guests, Marguerite felt very sorry for him. And old beyond her years.

Seating herself behind her office desk and waiting for David to open the bottle's twist top and drink deeply, she felt a pang of guilt. He was just a boy. She would have thought that after school in a major California university, David would have picked up on it.

The fact that the young four-some were not traditional couples hadn't escape Marguerite's attention. Not that it mattered to her. She was French, after all. Such things were common in more mature countries, even if it was still a topic of great controversy here in the U.S.

"What you did was not awful, David. Tell me, have you no gaydar?"

He looked up at her, confused. "Gaydar?"

She softened her words. "Yes, gaydar. You know, so you can tell who is straight and who is gay."

He flushed again, dark red, and stared at the floor. "I thought I did. I guess maybe I don't." He threw the empty bottle at the trash with enough force to knock the can on its side, papers in it now skittering across the floor.

"Damn – I mean, darn it. Sorry, Ms. Devereaux." He launched himself out of the chair and began picking up papers and pushing them back into the wastebasket with more deliberation than necessary.

"David, we can't be perfect." Well, she was pretty close to it, but then she'd had years to develop the skill and practice it around the world. "I too had to learn this, and I will tell you a secret few people know."

He settled on the edge of the chair, the red in his face receding further even as he continued to stare at the trashcan.

"I learned it the hard way. My ex-husband was gay, though I never knew until I caught him with his young man lover. What an uproar! I felt so stupid at the time, but I learned. You too will learn. You are still young."

He leaned back into the chair and finally met her eyes. "Sometimes I think that all I will ever do is learn, learn, learn. Someday, I'd like to be able to teach someone else a thing or two." The seriousness of his thoughts reflected on his face, and Marguerite couldn't help smiling back at him. He was always so very intense.

"I doubt I'll ever be as worldly as you, no matter how hard I work. My parents sheltered us, and I was always a geeky kid. I guess I have a lot of learning left to do." The deep sigh, delivered in the direction of his running shoes, punctuated his personal disappointment.

She leaned forward in her chair, folding her hands on her desk. "David, some things can be learned from a book. Some things take experience, and for that, time must pass and you must be exposed to things. You will do fine, believe me. Don't let what happened today discourage you."

He rose, even as he gave her a doubtful glance. "I don't know. They say experience changes you. I don't feel changed. I just feel – humiliated."

He gave a wave at the door and wished her a pleasant evening. She smiled at him, her trademark public look of cool reserve in place until she heard the outside door swing closed. Then she let her shoulders fall and put her head in her hands, knocking her forehead into the desk.

Yes, experience changed you, and not always for the better. She was not always the best judge of what was below the surface with people. She would do well to remember that, particularly when it came to guarding attraction for one rugged cowboy with flowing blond locks.

Chapter 7

Lining up his shot on the green baize, Deke tuned out the noise blaring from the flat screens lining Mallory's walls, along with the crests of conversation that rose around him. If he made this shot – and it was a tricky one – his brother bought the next round.

And it was about damn time, too.

Pulling back the perfectly aligned cue to give the ball a gentle spin, Deke knew he had the outcome in the bag.

"So, did you get a chance to settle anything with Uncle Royan?" Jake's voice was all innocence as Deke stopped the cue a fraction of an inch before it made contact. He raised his head to put an evil eye on his younger sibling.

"You're doing this on purpose, aren't you?"

Jake grinned and took a sip of his ale in response.

Deke scowled at him.

"Nah, he wouldn't be trying to distract you, Deke. But Steve over here, on the other hand, might try it, based on the bribe Jake gave him."

Cousin Dave finished his statement with a wink to Steve. Steve looked around the room, an expression of rapt interest on his face as he examined a deer head hung high on the rock wall above the fireplace.

Around him, Deke heard chuckles and jeers from his other friends. He pulled in a big breath and got into position again. And he waited.

"Com'on. How long do you plan to hold that shot, Deke?"

"Oh, leave him be. All the man wants is a little peace, right?" Steve tapped him on the shoulder as set his glass down on the tall table in the corner. "Did you know that Dave is planning on doing some big game hunting so he can bag himself a buck as large as that old fleabag on the wall?"

Deke took that moment of distraction around him to hit the ball. Side pocket. Perfect.

"Oh, damn, not again. You're hustling me, I swear you are. Did you put a pool table in your living room or something?" Jake threw money on the table in disgust and signaled for the waitress. The circle of men around him clapped or groaned, with a little money exchanging hands.

Taking a second to enjoy the victory, Deke tapped his brother on the shoulder with the cue.

"I'm a single guy with nothing but time on my hands. What would I do, other than practice my game?"

Jake guffawed and shook his head. "Yeah, and I'm the king of France. With so much going on, I'm surprised you have time to join us for a beer."

Deke felt the moment of lightness dim again. Yeah, he had little time for frivolity. Hell, he was struggling to cover the basics when it came to his operations. And the news on the well wasn't good.

His brother read the loss of a smile and backpedaled. "Hey, I'm pulling your leg, you know? I wish I could do more. Rock wishes he could do more, and maybe he will once he gets out. Who knows with him? About the others, I'm not so sure." No one had heard from the twins in a while.

Five brothers. No wonder his mother took her worn out self and retired to Arizona the year after the twins were grown. Life had been hard on her as a widow.

He still missed Dad, even if they never truly got along. Two master's degrees in animal science and in business didn't convince his father that Deke was any more prepared to take over the operations of their extensive ranch holdings, and working side by side for almost ten years hadn't softened him. The old man died without ever acknowledging Deke's capability to do anything more than cause trouble.

Jake had no interest in the land beyond a vague pleasure in riding it on occasion and limited ranch work when his schedule allowed it. Spread across a big geography and suffering from tight budget cuts, Jake was more likely to be riding in his big sheriff's SUV, patrolling the long county roads, than sitting a horse.

And the rest of the boys were far away, drawn to things in their lives other than heirloom cattle, specialty deer, and an assortment of high quality, high cost animals and feed that Deke spent days juggling and nights worrying about, even in his sleep.

Recent testing confirmed the problem with the main agricultural well. He believed he knew the cause. He just didn't know how to prove it.

And he didn't want to believe that someone as amazing and intelligent as Marguerite was responsible for it.

*****

"Seriously, you should hire more help. You can't keep doing so much yourself. There's only one of you, and much as I'd like to tell you you're superman," here Jake paused and gave a significant dance of his eyebrows, "you're not."

Deke stretched against the bumper of his truck, grateful for the cool night air. The only way it would have been better is if there was a rich damp smell meaning the ground was absorbing a wonderful gift of Mother Nature, rain. Giving Ma Nature a break for the long dry spell was part of his daily routine. Giving his brother the gift of a smile was harder.

"Things keep up the way they are, I won't need to be worrying about hiring more help. I'll be worrying about finding a townie job."

Jake's eyebrows shot up to his hairline at that comment.

"I was wondering how things were going on your research. You haven't said anything further. What have you learned?" Jake, ever watchful in cop mode, swung from scanning the parking lot as patrons wandered out the bar's door into the night to examining his brother.

Deke didn't bother to hide his grimace. What to say, and how much to say? He didn't want Jake to feel pressure to get involved. And truthfully, he didn't want to confront the winemaker. Or at least, not yet, not until he'd had a chance to get to know her better. Then maybe he would understand why.

"I don't have any more information, and it may all be a wild goose chase. And Uncle Royan fiddling around with his will-sell, won't-sell mindset isn't helping me."

Shaking his head, Deke met his brother's eyes, hating the sympathy there.

"You need a partner, someone as tied to the land as you are."

Jake's words brought up a sharp pang of anger. He'd tried to find investors, people who were committed to keeping the ranch intact and operational, with pockets deep enough to hire more hands and expand their holdings. But ranching and farming were risky businesses, and no one was crazy enough – or wealthy enough – to take the gamble.

"Yes, I tried that. No one wants to trust that the rains will come and the grass will grow." His lopsided smile didn't hide his hurt.

"Not that kind of partner. I mean a woman. As in, a wife. And I'm serious this time."

The idea was so ludicrous that Deke couldn't help himself. He burst out laughing, so hard and for so long that he had to bend at the waist to hold his gut in. If that wasn't the craziest idea, he wasn't sure what was. Other than that dinner he'd had with Marguerite, there'd been so little action in his life that his body probably forgot how things worked. He'd only been trying to learn more about her winery operations, and look where that landed him.

Interested despite the undercurrents, too interested in a violet-eyed witch.

The thought sobered him, and waiting for Jake's punch line, he wiped a couple of tears from his face as his final chuckle stopped abruptly. But when Jake was silent, he glanced at his brother sharply.

The guy was serious.

And the expression of pity on his face made Deke want to deck him, just for the satisfaction.

Chapter 8

Marguerite knocked on the scarred door, wondering, not for the first time, if the old cabin would one day fall over under such an onslaught. They'd offered Fernando better accommodations, a trailer or doublewide on this same site if he wanted it. But he'd said he was content with the simple nature of the one room structure.

Thinking he must be outside, since there was nowhere to miss the noise in the shack, Marguerite turned to let her eyes wash over the clearing. The cabin was near the top of the mountain, and legend had it that it was the original cabin the witch used. Pines grew tight around it, the variety that only thrived at higher elevations. And the top of Witch Hill was one of the highest points around.

She'd heard all of the stories, of course, about the young woman who grew old and crazy on this mountain. At the time, the locals thought she had the power to throw curses and hex unsuspecting trespassers, hence the mountain's name. That was generations ago. More recently, people, mostly young and with no business tracking around in woods where roads were an oddity, swore they saw her ghost flitting around, with its strange maniacal laugh and shiver of cold as it passed by. Most of the reports involved alcohol of a distilled kind and smoking of an illegal nature, so she was sure that they were all only hallucinating.

That was, until her encounter in the tank room.

Ready to shout again in case Fernando was within calling distance, Marguerite stopped as the trees at the edge of the clearing began to rustle. There wasn't any hint of a breeze, and with her recent musings, she felt her heart rate pick up a little with the possibilities. Just as quickly, she dismissed them. After all, sane people didn't believe in ghosts.

She realized that she had the door handle gripped in her fingers, ready to push open for a place to hide. This was stupid. What would her parents think of her behavior? And she didn't want Fernando to think that she would enter his home uninvited. Pulling in a deep breath, she forced her fingers free and shook herself to her full height. If a ghost was going to make an appearance, she would not cower like a child.

When the trees parted to reveal Fernando, she let her shoulders drop in relief.

"Marguerite, what are you doing here?" He stopped within the sanctuary of the trees and dropped what he was carrying out of view. Too relieved to care what he was doing, she leaned against the doorframe and smiled.

"I came for a visit, and to discuss things about the winery. Do I need an engraved invitation?"

When her teasing tone didn't bring a smile to Fernando's face, she was puzzled. He wiped his hands on his stained jeans, light brown mud being the predominant marking, and pulled out a cigar from his shirt pocket. It looked like he'd started it a few times already, an end burnt and the point he set to his lips stained. His hands shook as he brought up a lighter and turned the cigar to build up a satisfactory glow.

By the time he finished his ritual, Marguerite could see that only a fine tremble quivered his hands. He breathed in the smoke deeply, coughed a couple of times, and pronounced, "Smooth."

"Yes, and life-ending as well. Why don't you quit? Then you can truly enjoy old age."

He grinned at her, his usual demeanor finally returning. "Naw, I like it too much. Besides, I got to look like a high roller when I get to Vegas."

"You won't live long enough to spend the spare change in your pocket at the rate you're going, my friend. Besides, with what those things cost, you could have savings that would support you and a ladyfriend." Damn, but she was really going to miss the old man. Who would she tease like this?

And she worried about him.

He laughed at that, a sound that mixed with coughs and drags hard enough to make the cigar's embers bright red. Glancing over his shoulder into the trees, he laughed harder. When he turned back, he carefully ground out the end of the cigar against a rock, crushed the life out of any sparks with a muddy boot, and stepped forward in a haze of smoke.

"Don't you worry about my savings, Margie. No, you don't have to worry about me at all."

*****

It wasn't until she was back in the office that the oddity struck her. Mud, in the middle of August? That didn't make any sense. True, she'd heard rumors about a spring somewhere on the mountaintop. But supposedly it dried up in the summer, and they'd had a long parched spell beginning in spring.

When Fernando invited her to sit and have their discussion outside the cabin, she'd been momentarily confused. On the few occasions she'd visited him, he'd always invited her in. The stink of old cigars, an odor as putrid as unwashed socks, made her visits brief. She thought he was being respectful this time.

When she began to describe the ideas she had to delay his upcoming retirement, he'd glanced again at the woods and rushed her along.

"Tomorrow's soon enough for talks like these. I promise to come in early so you can talk all you want on the subject." He'd walked her to the top of the pitted gravel road with his pronouncement, patted her on the back, and waved her into her car. He stood in the road next to his beat-up sedan, a model so old that parts could be found only in junkyards, and watched her until she was out of sight.

But where did the mud come from? It had even smelled strange, dank and moldy like it had been rotting for a long time.

The knock at her door distracted her from her curiosity. The frame was filled with the one man she least expected to see there.

"Why, hello Deke. This is a pleasant surprise." She fought the urge to run a hand over the clip holding her hair and straighten the old winery t-shirt. If he didn't like to see her in her usual working attire, so be it. She sat up straighter.

He shifted the folder from his right hand to his left and stared at her. The smile he gave her was close to that lazy grin he favored, but there was nothing relaxed about his posture.

"Am I interrupting? I can come back another time." But he stood his ground, and she couldn't help running her eyes quickly from his face to his boots and back again. The jangle this produced on her nerves quieted her voice.

"No, you're not interrupting. There isn't anything here that can't be done later, and there is no end to the list of things to do anyway."

He nodded. "I hear you. It's the same at the ranch. If one thing gets crossed off my list, ten more jump in to fill the void." Moving forward, he sat in the facing chair and kept the folder in his left hand, tapping his right palm with its edge. "How are you?"

The deeper tone as he delivered his question made her breath catch. It brought her eyes to his lips. What would he taste like? A well-aged red wine? A tart new white? Or maybe a deep and disturbing port? She hadn't had a chance to savor his flavor fully when his lips brushed hers a couple of weeks ago.

Marguerite blinked to focus and looked up, right into eyes that were rapidly changing from green-gray to blue. He was smiling now, the real thing, and she marveled that his teeth could be so straight and white and she'd never noticed before.

"I'm fine, fine. How are you?" She was an idiot, stuttering like a child and in front of a cowboy, no less.

"I'm good. I'll be grateful when the rains come. I've had to cull some of the game because grass is so sparse. Luckily, the market for premium meat is good right now, so there's no real financial downside." He paused, then pushed the folder across the desk. "I brought you some research I've been doing."

Deke and his precious research. She pulled the folder towards her. "Is this about snakes?" She expected him to laugh along with her, but when he stayed silent, she glanced up from the desk.

He was so serious now, no hint of the lazy smile or casual cowboy posture. What did he have to show her that was so damned important?

"I know nothing about ranching, so I am probably not the best person to review whatever it is you have." Frowning at him, she noted the change again, his eyes now more gray than anything else while his expression turned formal. The shifts were fascinating.

He crossed one boot over the other knee and slid down in the seat a little. Eying her with speculation, he tipped his head towards the thin manila. "It's not about ranching." And he stared at her, a flash of uncertainty gone before she was sure it was there.

*****

"You brought me research on vineyard management practices? Why?"

Okay, he'd gone about this the wrong way. But he'd been curious, after their discussion about the Witch Hill processes at dinner, what it meant for the land. It all came down to sustainability, in his opinion. There were many ways to do things, each of them with benefits and risks. In this case, any risk flowed down hill, specifically, to his holdings.

Her violet eyes flashed a neon message that she was more than a little pissed off at him. The softness he'd noticed when she looked up to see him earlier, the quick delighted smile that she schooled so quickly into a more controlled air, had him thinking about taking her hand in greeting, pulling her out of the chair, and finding out if she tasted as good as the wines she made.

That was long gone now.

Still, he was committed. And he had to be. The future of his land depended on it.

"I got curious the other day after we talked about current viticulture practices. After all, we share the same watershed. I wanted to learn more about the impacts on the land, both yours and mine."

Of course, that wasn't completely true. He'd only added to what he'd already gathered about the herbicides and pesticides and insecticides that were commonplace in the wine grape industry. Frankly, he was amazed that so many chemicals were used on something that people ended up drinking. It didn't mean that Witch Hill used them all, but it only took one really bad actor to spoil it for everyone within range.

"Deke, I can assure you that we are very up-to-date here at Witch Hill. I study the latest research myself – continuously. I have a young man working for me who just graduated from one of the finest viticulture and enology programs in the world. And Fernando knows this land better than anyone. He wouldn't let any harm come to it."

Marguerite folded her hands in a posture that reminded him of what the nuns required in Catholic school when he was growing up. Her face held no beatification, though. Instead, he detected more than a little anger simmering behind the mask of schooled patience.

"I'm sure that you aren't intentionally doing any harm. But there are many different ways to accomplish the same goal, and I thought I'd share some of the latest ideas on how to grow grapes sustainably, so that – "

He bit off his words in surprise where she all but reared up out of her chair, knocking it back to roll against the wall behind her. When it clattered into the credenza, she didn't even blink. Instead, she fixed him with a glare.

"There is only one way to do things here at Witch Hill, and that is my way. My way is the correct way for these grapes, for this *terroir*, for my wines. I will thank you to remember that." She slammed a fist on the folder's edge sending pages flying. *"C'est vraiment des conneries!"*

Whoa, that was rough. He didn't think it was bullshit. He rose as she continued to stare at him, giving him what his mother would have called a death stare. Maybe some charm would help.

Smiling and tapping the folder under her now-splayed fingers, he drew his face close to hers. He sensed her surprise in the widening of her eyes, but she didn't back down. Letting his eyes slip to her mouth, he watched in fascination as the tip of her tongue peeked out and brushed across her full bottom lip. He couldn't help it when he raised a hand and allowed his thumb to follow it path.

"Marguerite, I don't know what to say." And he realized that he wasn't sure anymore what he was referring to, their impasse over some research or the wave of attraction that he couldn't keep at bay. The sudden thrumming of desire flashed from hair pulled back in the band at his neck down to the soles of his feet in his dusty boots.

She watched him, eyes barely blinking and breath coming faster. His was too, and to stay this close to her meant a sure recipe for trouble. He'd act on his emotions next. And that would only complicate things further.

He paced back once, then again, feeling the doorframe at his back. She hadn't moved. He didn't want to leave.

Clearing his throat, he tried again. "Read the articles when you have a chance. Then maybe we can talk about how those ideas might help both of us, your land – and mine."

And he got the hell out the door before he did something – or maybe it was something else – stupid.

Chapter 9

"Can you believe that he brought me articles that he expects me to study? Like I have no idea what I'm doing? *Casse-toi!*"

When the walk from one end of DK's pool to the other wasn't long enough, Marguerite marched out into the grass and back, ignoring DK's dog Fusion dancing happily at her feet.

"Marguerite, you're making us dizzy. Please, sit." DK waved at a chaise by the pool, and looked to the rest of the girl tribe for help when she was ignored. She didn't lower her voice when she added, "What did she just say?"

She knew she should not have come. It wasn't that the women wouldn't understand, but to be subjected to watching the men, or rather, one specific man, play ball across the yard was doing unfortunate things to her mood. And to her body.

He flustered her. The attraction he held for her probably wasn't healthy, at least not for her psyche. Sexual tension made her feverish with only a glance at him. And yet she couldn't ignore him, nor could she avoid him. And in truth, she did not want to.

Flopping into the appointed chaise with little grace, as unnatural a thing as she'd probably ever done in public, she met the eyes of her friends. Tess was curious, DK more avid, and Serena questioning.

"I apologize. What I said was unforgivable and also not something that can even be translated. I am letting my bad humor ruin your party. Perhaps I should leave." And escape while she still had her pride intact.

Serena leaned forward in her chair, her earnest counselor's expression sending a message that she was going to try to reason with her. *Bonne chance* with that.

"Maybe he didn't mean to question your ability." Serena paused, looking around at the other women with significance, before she smiled and continued. "Maybe he wanted an excuse to see you again. Maybe he wants another date."

Marguerite felt herself blush, a condition so unusual that she realized she was fanning her face without a conscious thought. As DK murmured in agreement, Tess added, "I think he's perfect for you."

"*Non, non, non!* I will never go out with that – " Marguerite bit off the sentence as that man, along with the others, headed in their direction.

All of the men were shirtless, so there was no reason for her eyes to stray to only one fine physique as the informal teams broke apart, heading for the stash of beer and water bottles. But like a magnet, her eyes locked on Deke's torso, appreciating the ripple of tight muscles on his abdomen as he stretched to reach for dark glass handed across the crowd. When he tilted it back and drank deeply, her insides started to fizzle, as effervescent as a glass full of Champagne.

Curse the man, he did not have a farmer's tan. Every *béni* inch of skin he was showing was the same rich dark hue, reminding her of the toast color of a new French oak barrel. His hair was pulled back into his traditional ponytail, and she had the urge to cross to him, rip out the band, and run her fingers through it, then continue until she'd touched every sculpted muscle in his body.

Oh mon dieu, she was going to get herself into trouble. Suddenly, the articles didn't seem like such *un important sujet*, and her thoughts strayed to the many ways they could better use their time than debate the merits of various vineyard methods.

When he emptied the bottle, Deke turned and leaned over to toss it in a trashcan, and as he bent, she had too good a look at the tight pull of denim across his thighs and butt. She inhaled sharply, and he seemed to hear her across the expanse, because his eyes immediately fastened on hers when he stood.

He regarded her solemnly, his eyes hidden by sunglasses. That easygoing quirk of a smile appeared, and he drew off the glasses as slowly as a striptease. Marguerite realized she was fanning herself again and stilled her hand with effort.

Just then, Deke winked at her.

"I, ah, I need to leave. I am sorry. I just realized that I left some of the tank cooling systems off and I don't want the wine to spoil." She stood up so fast her head spun, but she soldiered on over the protests of her friends. The men approached them, and luckily for her, that kept the other women momentarily distracted. She slipped around the corner of the house and bolted for her car.

*****

He felt her eyes on him from the moment she arrived, making concentration on the pick-up game harder and harder to manage. When it got hot, he had no qualms about stripping off the t-shirt and tossing it in the pile with everyone else's. Maybe the sight of flesh would inspire her.

Because he was definitely inspired. He knew she would be here, hanging out with her girl tribe friends. When Vince Issued an invitation to the wolf pack, he didn't need to think about it for more than a second. More time in Marguerite's casual company was exactly what he wanted, and a hum of pleasure ran through him each time he looked at her. And look at her frequently he did.

He hadn't been disappointed. Unlike the other women, Marguerite hadn't chosen a swimsuit for today's party. Instead, she wore a tie-dyed blouse that billowed as she strode away from the group, a brightly colored bird in flight. It reminded Deke of his mother's kind of hippie clothes, god forbid. Even with that memory, it was like waving a red flag in front of a bull. He had to charge after her when she grabbed her purse and all but ran around the house towards the driveway.

Taking off at a jog, he heard some ribald comments from the other men. Undoubtedly, he'd hear all about this the next time the wolf pack got together. All of the guys would give him grief for heading after Marguerite like a buck after a doe in heat.

To hell with them.

He heard a car door slam as he rounded the corner, pulling his shirt on as he jogged along. It was a tough call – head for his truck and follow her, or try to cut her off by standing in front of her car before she roared down the gravel. Either way, he was going to look like a fool and eat a lot of dust.

To hell with that too.

But he slowed when he noticed that Marguerite hadn't started the engine of her shiny sports car. Instead, she sat in the driver's seat and faced forward, and from the limited amount he could see through the reflective glass, grim determination warred with heightened confusion on her face. The contrast was so unlike what he'd come to anticipate from her that he almost stopped before thinking that he'd better take advantage of her delay.

By the time he reached the car, she still hadn't make any move to start the ignition. When he tapped on the window, she jumped before giving him a glare that would have made the legendary witch proud. Engaging the electronics with her key, she sent the window humming down and continued to scowl at him.

Even angry, she was gorgeous. The fire in her eyes made them shine like gemstones. Tightness pulled her lips into a thick bow, and he wondered how many licks of his tongue it would take across the crease to get her to open for him. Below his belt, he felt his body stir, making the snug denim suddenly tighten to match her mien.

"So, am I ever going to be forgiven?" He leaned down to bring his face inches from hers and was rewarded when her mouth softened as she watched the words form on his lips.

Her eyes snapped to his, confusion and anger warring in those violet depths, then she turned forward so fast that he wondered how she avoided whiplash.

"I am not sure. I do things my way, not anyone else's. When do you plan to apologize?" While her words were brittle, she made no move to start the engine. The rapid rise and fall of that filmy top gave her away.

Deke kept his smile to himself. So he was under her skin like she'd settled under his, digging deeper than barbed wire. There were plenty of ways to win her over without enraging her further.

"How about over dinner tonight?"

Chapter 10

Why she had agreed to this, Marguerite wasn't exactly sure. In fact, everything from the moment she'd zeroed in on his naked chest and the fine line of blond hair running down his abdomen to now was something of a blur. *Elle était malade*, here was no doubt about it. Sick in the head, and fighting a desire so bold that she was surprised she hadn't jumped his body yet.

Following him down the dusty driveway and on to the main road, she had plenty of time to try to marshal her thoughts into action that made sense. She was no young virgin, and she knew men and enjoyed them. Upon occasion, she used them to her satisfaction and gave it little consideration past her personal pleasure. But Deke was different.

Trying to rationalize her actions, Marguerite argued the merits of turning her car towards her cabin instead of continuing to follow him to his ranch. He wanted a shower, he said, before taking her out to a wonderful place that featured fine tequilas. When she protested that she didn't like tequila, he merely smiled and assured her that they had fine wine too. He even offered to drive, saying she could then partake of as many different choices as she wanted, an offer she declined.

She didn't even glance left at her turnoff, her eyes glued to the back bumper of the shiny dark truck in front of her. There had to be something she could pick on, something to bolster her need to stop and turn around before she got herself into trouble. Scowling at the California Native sticker on the bumper didn't help. He had more right to it than most, she supposed.

When his left blinker came on and he slowed, she mimicked his actions and focused on the large gate with a sign arched overhead. Three Rivers Ranch. There was no sign of water anywhere nearby, but she had only a vague idea of the topography in this valley.

Pavement rolled under her wheels, and on either side of the blacktop, fencing stretched for the mile or so it took them to reach buildings. On one side, she could see horses grazing and lazily swishing their tails in the late afternoon sun. The strangest looking cows occupied the pasture on the opposite side, their red and white faces turning in unison to watch the truck and car pass by.

When Deke slowed in front of her once more, she anticipated stopping at the two-story building to the left of the drive. It looked like a house, and while it had obviously been sitting in place for decades, the wood sides were bright with care and the porch was clean and welcoming. It faced a series of barns and other outbuildings. With a casual wave to a group of men clustered around the front of the largest barn, Deke continued on, and Marguerite felt curious eyes follow her down the drive as it switched from pavement to gravel.

She expected that the ranch was large, based on what Deke told her about his acreage. But she wasn't prepared for the vast expanses that stretched the eye in every direction. To the north, Witch Hill rose abruptly, and from this vantage point, she could see the vines extending in straight lines across the lower vineyard. Oaks and other tall trees provided a horizon mountain view to the east, while to the south, large meadows filled with different breeds of animals reached to yet another band of trees.

"What do you think?"

She hadn't been aware of stopping until Deke stood by her open window. She'd been staring at the distant forms of deer, her hand on the ignition as the engine continued to hum.

"You do have cows. You are a cowboy."

Foolish woman. She couldn't believe what kinds of nonsense came out of her mouth when she was around this man. If she were smart, she would make her excuses about dinner, turn around, and drive as fast as her peppy little European racer would carry her down the driveway and away from his gravitational pull.

When he burst out laughing, she glared at him. "What is so funny? You have cows, or at least that's what I thought those strange things were." She heard it in her voice, the annoyance aggravating her accent.

He chuckled again, running a hand absently down his torso to hook his fingers in the pocket of his jeans. Grateful for her sunglasses, she realized she'd followed his hand and her eyes were now resting on the zipper holding worn denim together. She swallowed and thought of her friends. What would they say right now?

Maybe they'd cheer her on with a simple go for it. *Saisir l'opportunité*, though of course, this opportunity was currently at eye level but not nearly close enough as she barely remembered to breathe.

"Yes, those are cows. Heirloom cattle, to be exact. They're part of our special breeding program to re-introduce diversity into the meat industry. You had some of that steak at Roxy's." He put a hand through the window, popped the lock, and opened her door wide. "Care to come in and cool off while I shower?"

The man would be the destruction of her yet. She could easily imagine his heavily muscled body with water coursing down perfectly tanned skin, the aroma of his honest sweat and subtler fragrances of pine soap and aftershave making her head spin.

Shoving past him with more force than was polite, she tried not to breathe in his bouquet. She willed her accent to hide as she said, "Yes, perhaps cooling off would be a good idea."

*****

He read the surprise in Marguerite's face when he pushed open the front door and led her inside the vaulted main room of the house. On the outside, it looked like a log cabin, but inside, he'd designed it for spacious living.

"This is not at all what I expected." Marguerite's head tilted back as she followed the room's lines to the high ceiling, and all Deke could think about was running his teeth along the ridge of her long neck, taking little bites to please them both along the way. The lust currently ruling his thinking would get him in trouble. He shook his head to clear it, intent on playing the premier host.

"I built it a few years ago, when it seemed that my father would live forever. He and Ma and the younger boys lived in the house you saw across from the barns. That's where I grew up. They had no interest in moving, and I wanted space of my own away from the rest of the crowd. I'd been planning to use this site for years."

His eyes swept around the great room critically, trying to see it as she did for the first time. The set of open stairs leading to the second story and its wraparound walkway opening to bedrooms was to one side, with the kitchen tucked under the opposite. The tall stone chimney spanned both levels, and next to it, equally tall windows took in the view out to the meadows and to the Sierras beyond.

"This is stunning, Deke. I mean it. Who would have thought that a plain log cabin would be this *fantastique*." She walked slowly into the middle of the room, eyes glued to the view.

His view at the moment was pretty incredible too, though he couldn't say that to her. The light from the windows shone through the gauzy material of her blouse, outlining her body better than any x-ray. The residual heat from the game was nothing compared to the rage of desire burning through him.

"Not everything is what it appears on the surface, Marguerite." When she turned to look at him in puzzlement, he shook his head to clear the vision of running his hands down those curves and waved towards the kitchen. "Help yourself to something in the fridge. I won't be long."

He strode to the stairs and took them two at a time, eager to jump into a cold shower before his body's signals were noticed by her too-observant eyes. Kicking shut the door to his bedroom, he wondered what she made of his last remark. Her expression hadn't changed. Either he confused the hell out her, or she wasn't sure if he was crazy or not.

He tried to empty his mind as he cranked through a shower and dressing in record time. It was better not to speculate why she'd agreed to dinner with him. And it was much better not to consider what might happen after dinner, if they were both lucky.

Deke knew it was only a matter of time. He wanted her, and she didn't seem to be immune from reciprocating those feelings either. Two forces of nature were going to clash, not unlike those snakes, and he wasn't sure if either one of them would survive the onslaught.

Chapter 11

Deke was a man full of surprises. He smiled across the table at her as the waiter set two flights of tequila in front of them. One was a rich amber color, and the other a more muted oaky tone.

She wasn't sure why she'd let him talk her into this. She didn't like distilled liquor for the most part, preferring the mellower flavors of wines in their various forms as her drink of choice. But he insisted, almost daring her to try something different. The manner was so like a flight of wines, she was intrigued.

"Artisan tequilas like these before us are not meant to be mixed into icy beverages, any more than your fine wines should be destined for spritzers." He moved the placemats with their notations about the specific tequilas more closely together and leaned across the table.

At this range, the myriad colors swimming in his eyes captivated her. Blue-green at the moment, they were outlined by lashes that were thicker than any man's had a right to be. The crinkles at the edges made him look years younger, the broad grin on his face lighting up everything about him. She had to look away. Otherwise, she'd do something stupid like lean across the table and lock her lips on his.

Playing with the first glass as if she was reading the notations and studying the color, Marguerite wondered what the hell had gotten into her. Her reaction to this man was so far from her usual cool that she was lost about what to do. His mere presence overloaded her brain. She'd never felt this adrift.

"Take a small sip, let it rest on your tongue, and inhale just like you would for wine. Then tell me what you think." He demonstrated, and she inhaled sharply when he pursed his lips to suck in air. She was staring again. She grabbed a glass and took a large sip. At first, the assault made speech impossible.

"Oh, *mon dieu* but that's like fire!" She reached for the water, stopping in shock when he grabbed her wrist. Moving a beer he'd ordered earlier into her hand, he released her, letting the tips of his fingers slide slowly off her skin.

Suddenly her skin was hotter than the drink she'd consumed. His fingers burned, branding her, and she wanted to put her wrist back in his hand so that he would close them tightly around it. Then she wanted those fingers to –

She had to stop this at once. What would her parents say about her complete lack of control? They'd raised her to be regal, artful in the ways of conversation, and fittingly sedate and composed in any kind of company. She would do well to remember those lessons now.

Sitting back, she spread her arms on the chair's rails and made a studied appraisal of the restaurant. Deke didn't say anything, though he did sip a glass of tequila and shift in his seat. When she thought she had herself under control, Marguerite met his steady gaze with one of her own.

"Tell me more about your family. How did they come to settle your particular piece of land?"

*****

The last thing he cared about right now was his family story. With over-bright eyes glowing across the table and deep deliberate breaths, Marguerite had transformed from the flustered creature that took that first lengthy taste to a seemingly serene statue. It was only her breathing that gave her away, causing a rapid rise and fall of her chest that he was trying hard not to examine too closely.

Using a sip to regain his composure, Deke sat back in a posture of ease. Two could play at this game. The fact that he wanted to slide his chair around the table and wedge it close to hers, taking her in his arms to explore plump lips now held in a tight line, meant nothing. He was in a pretty deep manure pile at this point, and he knew it.

"You'll recall I mentioned the brothers and sister and their families started out for the new world. Freedom and a better life called them, as well as gold. The oppression in France killed off so many that they were often buried in mass graves. But my ancestors didn't fare well on their journeys either. None of the families survived intact."

He had her interest, and despite himself, Deke leaned forward. Her subtle fragrance, sophisticated and rustic at the same time and reminding him of old gardens and racing rivers, reached across the table to grab him. He took another small taste of the tequila in his hand, then passed the glass to her with a nod. "Try some."

She tipped her head in thanks as her fingers brushed his when the glass changed hands. He froze, and she did as well. Then she blinked twice and shifted her eyes away, taking a cautious sip.

"Ah, this is better, richer, I think. It is not like fire, as the last one was."

"The first one was a *reposado*, rested less than a year. This one is an *añejo*, aged up to three years. Like wine, it becomes more mellow with age." Like attraction does, aging into something so perfect that there is no turning away from its allure.

Now where the hell had that thought come from?

Taking a sip of the next tequila in line, he reached across the table and slipped Marguerite's hand into his, playing with her fingers. She had long fingers, sturdy and strong, and he wondered what they would feel like caressing his body and building a need in him unlike that any other woman ever had.

The idea froze his movements until Marguerite squeezed his hand gently. "What happened to the ones who settled your land?"

Breathing deeply, he tried to focus on his story. "One of the brothers died during the sea passage, and one of the wives didn't make it across the Isthmus of Panama. There was no canal then, only a long trek through the rainforest that could take months. When they reached the other side, passages on ships going north to the gold fields were scarce. They were able to get as far as what is now southern California, but they were stranded there."

The next sip made caressing her fingers lighter, easier, and he continued on. "The brother who was now a widower and the wife now a widow hated each other, according to family legend. But they had five surviving kids between them, and in an untamed land, that was as good as gold too. Finding a ship to carry them all was proving to be so difficult that they considered settling for southern land. Finding new spouses was also proving to be impossible, and at that time, people didn't usually raise their children and settle their land alone. Finally, the two married, though they fought like hellcats until the day they died."

"Sometimes those marriages last the longest." Her quiet words startled him, and he looked up to find her staring at their linked hands. When he didn't speak, she raised her eyes. "My parents are like that. They are diplomats, and they travel all over the world to work. But in the privacy of their own home, they fight like heathens." She shuddered.

It was the first glimpse she'd given him of her own background, and he was instantly riveted. What other mysteries did she hide behind her prickly exterior and black-and-white perspective?

Resuming his story, he laced his fingers more tightly with hers and was happy to find her leaning closer as well. "A ship's captain took pity on them and gave them some advice. Maritime ethics wouldn't allow any captain to ignore a boat that was adrift. He told them all they had to do was row away from shore in a dingy at least a mile out and into the shipping channel, then heave their oars overboard and wait for a ship to rescue them. They would then be guaranteed passage on that ship."

Her eyes widened in shock, her pupils lightening to a lilac color for an instant. "But that is foolishness. They would be afloat at the mercy of the ocean. What if no ship came by, or it could not see them? What if the ship was going someplace they did not want to go?" Shaking her head, she put her other hand on top of their joined fingers and gripped tightly. "They were either very stupid, or very brave."

It only took the clench of her fingers to make his body boil. The voice delivering her words had lowered to almost a whisper.

"We're lucky people, my ancestors included. The ship that happened to pick them up was captained by the same man who gave them their advice, and he was heading for San Francisco. They buried one child at sea during the voyage, but they made it. Bartering for horses and a wagon and the supplies they thought they would need, they started along the wagon trail route to the gold fields. On the way, they stumbled into a valley of three rivers. They buried another child there, and were preparing to birth one as well. The land was fertile, the water plentiful, and easy gold was harder and harder to find. Great-grandpa decided that the valley was where they needed to stay."

*****

His family story was much more interesting than hers. Such bravery, such courage, and such heartbreak was something she was not immune to. Her own family had it easy by comparison, if you called the courts of France and their devilishness and malicious destruction easy.

When dinner arrived, he let go of her hands with seeming reluctance, and Marguerite instantly felt the loss. Deke didn't continue his story, and their conversation rambled across disagreements about what they liked to read, agreements on music, and comparisons of places that they wished to travel. Deke's bucket list was much longer than hers, though he'd spent significant time around the world. It surprised her until she found out that the heirloom livestock breeds the ranch raised were from four continents.

"What did you think of our tequila adventure?" His hand had reached out naturally as they left the restaurant, and she let him close warm rough fingers around hers as they approached her car in the parking lot. "Want me to drive?"

Laughing, she shook her head. While she'd enjoyed the novel experience, she'd stopped once she'd enjoyed the flight. In the couple of hours since, she'd mellowed to match the tequila, though she was no longer buzzed.

"Where are we going to now?" She started the engine and backed slowly out of the parking stall, intent on getting out of the lot and into traffic. "Deke?"

He was staring at her, the brilliant blue of his eyes a distraction that she couldn't manage while driving. Eyes front again, she waited in silence. When they came to the freeway entrance ramp, she took is automatically and headed east for the mountains.

A gentle hand invaded her space, tunneling under her hair and cupping her neck. Her foot came off the accelerator before she caught herself and resumed the posted speed. His fingers caressed her skin, tangling in her hair and combing through it as if he had all the time in the world.

"Deke?" She hated the faint breathless sound of her voice, but it seemed to be all she was capable of at the moment.

"I want to take you home, Marguerite, to my home. And I want to get to know you a whole lot better."

Chapter 12

She stared at the eastern sky, the peaks of the Sierras outlined in relief against the dawn's glow. What the hell had she jumped into?

The heavy weight of an arm across her waist and splay of fingers on her belly made her heart beat faster. She intended a meaningless night of shared pleasure. If she did not move now, she would turn and kiss the stubble-roughened cheek, trace his lips, and waken him as she wished.

As it was, she tried to lift his arm without rousing him and slide across the vast expanse of the king-sized bed. Twisted sheets were evidence of the intensity of the night. A modest light in the bathroom guided her as she gathered her clothes as quietly as she could. Even the clink of a belt buckle could give her away.

Elle était un imbécile. And she was the worst kind of fool, too. One who knows better but follows the path of destruction anyway. She had thought she could enjoy a night of mutual gratification and walk away unscathed. That joke had backfired.

Last night was nothing short of *très étonnant.* But amazing didn't even cover it. She had not expected fire and gentleness, playful fun with heart-stopping intensity. Deke could never be dismissed as a fling. She would never forget these few hours.

She had too much pride. It hurt to think about she'd almost begged him last night. He bewitched her with such force that there was no turning back.

Realizing she was mesmerized by his snore, a gentle cork pop on each exhale, she ached to reach out and touch him. Maybe they could compromise. He would come to see that her way was the right way to do things, and then she could contemplate something more with him. Perhaps with time, she could learn to trust him fully.

By the time they'd returned to his house last night, she'd been shaking with desire. It wasn't the simple brush of his fingers or the trail they followed down her arm as she drove, concentrating hard to avoid hitting anything in her agitation. He built a crazy energy in her, and she could do nothing in the ensuing silence to stop needs that grew so fast. She was amazed she could still function.

Maybe it was only the lack of truly great sex in her life. But sex with any man would not make her feel like this.

Last night, she'd driven down the county road on autopilot, her hands and feet guiding the car while her mind raced between the ramifications of what she was about to do, ultimately saying what the hell. When he pointed to a parking spot next to his truck, she fought to keep her breathing from being an audible pant in their small confines. Deke had said few words once they'd left the freeway, and he released the seatbelt and turned towards her while she let the engine idle.

Running a light hand down her right arm, he gently pried her fingers off the vibration of the steering wheel and closed them in his. A sandpaper thumb ran across her knuckles. Her eyes locked front, she sensed his gaze on her profile as they continued to sit in silence.

The steady cadence of his stroke calmed her. He lifted her hand and kissed the back of each finger, and the punch of lust this simple gesture brought made her turn in her seat. He watched her, not with glee at arousing her, but with patience. She suspected she wasn't the first creature to be on the receiving end of his seemingly limitless deep well of control.

"Will you come in?" The gravel in his voice was the only indication she had that he was unnerved by their situation. If she placed a hand on his jeans, would she find him rock hard and ready? His eyes burned a brilliant blue, giving her all the answer she needed.

By the time he'd kicked closed the front door, she'd wrapped herself around him tighter than a vine on a guideline, marveling that every part of him was as sturdy as a tree and he didn't bend with her pressure. They'd kissed on every stair. By the time they reached the landing, his shirt buttons were long gone and her blouse hung off her shoulders.

The sight of comfortable ranch chic in his bedroom halted her. She expected a utilitarian space, but this was full of creature comforts, warm tones, soft-looking fabrics, and ease. A large fireplace sat at an angle in the corner, with windows on either side taking in the dark mountain view. A deep leather sofa, large enough for two people to recline side by side, stood in front of it. Across the room, the bed rose like a ledge on the side of a cliff, full of fluffed pillows and a deeply pleated duvet. And the whole room smelled like Deke, like pinesap and deep woods and the sage-like flowers she often crushed underfoot in summer.

She hesitated, struggling to decipher the messages he was sending. His breath was deep and fast, but his hands were steady on her shoulders, holding her blouse in place as she looked around. His arousal pressed against her back, but he wasn't rushing her. He waited, patient as usual, and that made her more than a little crazy.

Turning in his arms, she examined his face for signs of triumph, a victor claiming his spoils as he'd gotten her this far. But instead, there was quiet acceptance in the brilliant blue eyes and a trace of a smile on his lips. She was only beginning to know the hard planes of his body, and she sensed no tension in the taunt muscles.

If she was on fire with this *truc de fou*, this crazy thing between them, why wasn't he?

"I can back off. You can stay, and we can simply talk. Or you can leave."

Frowning at his words, Marguerite muttered a string of expletives that left no doubt as to what she thought of his parentage, then smiled sweetly.

"I understood that, you know," he said, his hands squeezing her shoulders once before dropping and stepping back.

Her eyes ran down his body, and the evidence of his continuing desire for her was there, straining against his jeans. When she realized she'd been staring, her eyes lifted quickly. Now he was smiling. He shook his head, holding her gaze.

"Know this, Marguerite. I want you. I usually get what I want. And I believe you want me too." His eyes flicked to her nipples, outlined against her bra in the dim fading light of evening. "But you call the shots here. I can be patient."

His quiet self-assurance, delivered without a trace of bravado, pissed her off to no end. She wanted him to be as crazed as she was, contemplating a night of passion that she had no doubt would satisfy her dry spell for quite some time. Driving him as insane as she felt at the moment became her mission.

Shrugging a shoulder, she allowed the blouse to billow to the floor. It landed like a colorful butterfly on the bark tones of the rug. Bending at her waist, she leaned over, slowly, oh so slowly, and finger-brushed her hair until it hung in waves, hiding her face. Swinging it up and standing straight again, her fingers reached for the button on her jeans.

She noted with satisfaction that his nostrils flared. All traces of his smile were gone, replaced with a concentrated focus that made her breathe in fast. That was a mistake, bringing in more of his unique bouquet, and she wished for once that she didn't feel so compelled to be the one in control. She wanted, in this moment, simply to feel.

"Allow me," he said in a whisper, and stepped forward, kneeling in front of her. His fingers closed around the back of her sandal, and she put a hand on his shoulder to steady herself. Even through the shirt, she could feel the intense heat pouring off him. When he tossed the sandal aside, she had already shifted to allow him access to its mate. Then he stood, and without touching her elsewhere, put his lips to hers.

She nearly boggled her belt now as she thought back, the same belt he'd removed so gently last night along with her jeans. When she stood in front of him in bra and panties alone, she thought she might explode with the energy coursing through her. His shirt was tossed into the darkness as he toed off his boots, then he unbuckled his belt and slid down the zipper, each move deliberate. If she couldn't see his arousal pressing against the fabric of his briefs, she would have thought he was unmoved by their actions.

Things happened so fast after that, they were almost a blur. Almost, because each move he made became indelibly marked on her psyche. His gentle touch, almost reverent as his fingers closed around the clasp on her back and removed her bra, traced her spine. The wisp of silk against her skin made every nerve-ending tingle as her panties joined the growing pile on the floor.

"You are *magnifique, riche convoitise personnifiée, voluptueuse et sensuelle.*"

Rich lust personified? Voluptuous? The meaning in his words wasn't lost on her. He was playing her, and in her own language, but the drumbeat of her blood meant she didn't really care.

Marguerite sighed on that memory, and Deke shifted on the bed, his pattern of sleep interrupted. She held her breath before he settled again, facing towards her on his side, his face peaceful in repose as dark blond stubble covered his chin and cheeks. She needed to get the hell out of here before she distracted herself with the many ways he'd pleasured her last night. His unbreakable control was still in evidence when she'd slipped a condom on him with shaking fingers, fingers he gripped in his own around his hard length before he sank inside her. She almost gasped out loud at the memory of coming, for the third time and the longest she could ever recall feeling, before he'd whispered her name and followed her.

She crept across the room, turning at the door to run her eyes down a strong naked body she wouldn't forget. It wasn't just the muscles, but the man. Then she opened the door on silent hinges, slipped through, and, leaving it ajar, crept down the stairs.

*****

It was the creak of the third stair that confirmed it. He'd meant to fix it, and now he was glad that he hadn't. It alerted him that Marguerite was leaving. Not that she would get very far, since her keys were in his jeans pocket, and his jeans were on the bedroom floor.

He stretched, reaching his fingers for the wall and his toes for the doorway, content and replete in a way he didn't remember being. Sex was sex, a nice distraction, a pleasant exercise. But with Marguerite, it blew him into a thousand tiny pieces.

Her body was that of a goddess, each soft curve covering a form that was made for loving, and a lot of it. He teased her at dinner as she gobbled up her large steak. What had she replied? She was a woman of large appetites. Evidently it wasn't just what she consumed, but what consumed her.

And they had consumed each other last night, falling asleep only a couple of hours ago. The breaking dawn through his window was his usual alarm clock. Despite the short hours, he felt oddly rested and peaceful.

Today he had to tell her that he knew. Things weren't all as they seemed to be on her mountain, and it was having an impact, a bad one, on his valley. He didn't relish the conversation, even more so now that he'd tasted her lips, her skin, and all the dark and private places that made her cry out in pleasure. He'd nearly lost his mind and any semblance of control when she engulfed him in one stroke, so fast that they both gasped. Then they raced for a conclusion that left him stunned, speechless, and unable to do more than roll and shift her to drape her body across his chest, and sooth her back with a hand that shook.

Rolling his feet to the floor, he surveyed the damage to the room. Clothes, only his, were in various corners, his jeans in a heap near his boots. She would discover soon enough that her car keys were missing, and unless she had another set in her purse, she wasn't going anywhere. Still, it wasn't polite to keep a lady waiting.

Pulling on his jeans commando-style, he grinned to himself. Maybe he could convince her to come back to bed for a little while. He'd found a particularly tender spot, one that made her gasp and laugh when he tickled it, and he wanted to explore it further.

He wanted to explore everything about her further, her lush body and her over-active mind. But first, they needed to clear the air. And then maybe he could convince her that there was plenty of room for two in his shower.

Chapter 13

Damn, where were the keys? She remembered sitting in the idling car last night, watching the trees sway in the evening breeze as she decided her next step. When Deke reached across her and turned off the ignition, she was too consumed with the expression in his eyes, the patient stalking presence of him, to think anything more.

He had her keys. Damn the man, she would either need to find them herself or wake him. And she couldn't face him this morning, not when she all but laid herself out like a raunchy feast for him to enjoy last night.

Not that there hadn't been feasting on her part too. What would it take to break his patient control?

The first shaft of sun crossed the floor, darting through an open curtain in the living room. It lit a path back to the stairs, back up to Deke. She didn't need a sign. She needed her keys, and she needed to get out.

Pulling her blouse more firmly around her, she tried to twist her hair into a bun to get it out of the way. It was knotted and snagged in so many places that she doubted anything other than a lot of cream rinse would untangle it. She hissed in frustration, then stilled, thinking that she heard something. When nothing more than bird calls reached her ears, she let go a breath and started searching the living room.

Merde, not on the entry table next to his set, and not on any surface that she could see. She yanked at her purse, thinking perhaps he'd given them back and she dropped them inside without conscious thought as he distracted her. Her grab at both handles failed and the contents spilled on the floor, and she swore with more fervor. Kneeling, she attempted to retrieve the business card case that slid under a couch.

When a warning creak sounded like a rifle blast, she froze. A warm chuckle drew her eyes to the stairs. He stood a couple of steps from the bottom, dangling her keys off his too-clever fingers, a teasing smile on his face.

"Now that is an incredibly pretty sight," he said, his eyes on her behind sticking up in the air. His jeans were open, riding low on his hips, and it was obvious that he had nothing else on. Nothing at all. He was too damned rugged and sexy as sin standing there, one ankle crossed nonchalantly over the other as he leaned back against the railing. She gave him an angry bristle as her fingers returned to groping for the case. Maybe she should leave it, make a grab for the keys and head out the door. A fingernail snagged the edge, and she pulled it towards her.

He was still smiling at her when a quick series of knocks sounded on the front door. It was followed by a turn of the handle and the big wooden frame swung inward. And a petite woman of gentle older age crossed the threshold.

*****

She had the prettiest heart-shaped backside he could recall seeing, and set up in the air like it was made him suddenly wish he'd zipped his jeans, or at least found his underwear. He was going to give himself away, and what they needed now was discussion, not desire.

The tight frown she shot him over her shoulder only made the blood surge faster in his veins, moving from trot to gallop by the mere suggestion of emotion on her face. He could tell she was embarrassed. And she was pissed with him for having the keys, of that he was certain.

He contemplated his next move. Forward, and help her up? Or wait, and let her come to him? She wasn't getting the keys yet in either case.

The rapid staccato knock stopped him, his mouth open to invite Marguerite to stay for breakfast, and when the door swung open and he saw his unannounced visitor, he wasn't sure if he should laugh or cry.

"Well, hello dear. What are you doing down on the floor? Did I startle you? I guess I should have knocked harder, or maybe waited longer. But whatever. Can I help you up?"

The red hair was almost the same, only a shade lighter where more gray had taken root. The sparkling green eyes were full of mischief as she raised her head and found him across the room, her grin saying she knew exactly what they'd been up. Her lips pouted, a finger there as if making a decision, then she clapped her hands and advanced across the space.

The desire that a few seconds before seemed to be heading for a full hard-on wilted in a heartbeat. What in the hell did he do now?

"Hello Deke honey. How are you? Why don't you get more clothes on? And zip your fly. I didn't raise you to be an animal."

She patted his cheek, pulling him down the last two steps and reversing their positions, so that she was eye to eye with him. She pinched his chin and shoved his mouth closed, none too gently either, and gave him a hard buss of a kiss on the lips. Then she turned him back towards Marguerite, and as if this was the normal way she met people, put an arm around Deke's shoulders as she stuck out her hand.

"Where are my manners? I should introduce myself. I'm Emileen, but everyone calls me Emie. And I guess I have to claim this boy with no manners as my son."

He watched Marguerite's eyes widen in surprise. A light flush colored her cheeks as she shoved something back in her purse and stood up slowly. She squared her shoulders, and he watched years of training take hold and a polite smile come to her face.

"Edouard Kermarrec the third, your zipper," his mother said reprovingly, and gave him a small push in the direction of the kitchen. "Go make this nice young woman some coffee. I'll have herbal tea. I'd like to hear what's been going on here, though I can probably tell that for myself. And then you can enlighten me about something I heard from Royan. Something about the winery poisoning our wells, and the winemaker being the cause of it?"

He froze on the ball of one foot and the heel of the other, mid-step, as he'd been reaching to pull up the offending zipper before inviting another pointed remark by his mother. She was a hippie from a generation long on opinions and short on decorum, and she'd ruled their household with a firm but loving hand, making five rambunctious sons, a gruff husband, and a multitude of hands toe the line over the years. And she was never afraid to say exactly what she wanted to, either, all four feet and eleven inches of her.

That was what he was afraid of.

Her last words finally registered over the shock of her turning up unannounced. She had obviously heard the news already and was more than ready to discuss it. But he wasn't, at least not until he and Marguerite could talk about it and he could hear her side.

His eyes on Marguerite, he saw the transformations as each word penetrated. Her son – her polite mask was slipping into place. Going on here – a flash of embarrassment. Puzzlement at Royan's name.

And then the worst of it. Anger followed confusion at the words winery and winemaker. The anger shifted to betrayal as she looked at Deke, her eyes strangely shiny. Then the anger returned, and with it, a haughtiness that would have been appropriate for the queen of France. The gaze she gave him was as icy as the north wind in January.

He watched in disbelief as the woman who had been such a supple and demanding lover throughout the night turned into a statue, albeit one that moved with deliberate steps.

Marguerite stopped in front of Emie on the steps, raised a hand, and accepted a brief handshake. Her accent was thick when she said, "I am Marguerite Devereaux, Mrs. Kermarrec. It is a pleasure to meet you. Deke has told me nothing about you," here she paused as if to add significance to the words, "so please forgive me if I am at a loss." The French drawl was so thick that he doubted the final words were even comprehensible to his mother.

"Why dear, you have an accent. French, isn't it? How absolutely beautiful. Did Deke tell you that he comes from French stock? Though it was a long time ago. Come, tell me all about yourself. I love meeting my boys' friends." She tucked her hand into Marguerite's elbow and turned them both towards the kitchen.

The anger on Marguerite's face was now a feral thing. He doubted anyone else would see it, but he knew. It was there in the tightening of her eyes and the grim set to her lips, even with a polite smile pasted in place.

His mother's disapproving ahem grabbed his attention, and she rolled her eyes before looking pointedly at his zipper one more time. He yanked it into place, certain he'd pay for the short hairs now lodged in its firm grip. But that was nothing when compared to the pain he knew he had caused Marguerite.

When the two closed in on him, he watched the woman he'd made intense and incredible love with last night turn, pat his mother's hand on her arm, and disengage herself.

"Thank you so much for the lovely offer of coffee, Mrs. Kermarrec. I do appreciate it. But I must go. I'm sure you and your son have – much – to talk about."

At her deliberate pause, she looked him the eye, and without saying a word, put her hand on the keys still clutched in his hand, digging her nails sharply into his palm. He released the metal, not because of pain, but because the hurt he saw reflected in violet was so deep, her eyes were almost black. Then she spun on her heel, grabbing her purse as she passed it, and strode out of his home.

*****

"Well why didn't you tell me who she was?" His mother blew on her tea and stirred the spoon. "I would have waited."

There was no point in noting that she'd barely taken a breath when she'd come in the door, blurting out what was on her mind as usual.

Deke swore he could still see dirt swirling in a stiff wind from Marguerite racing down his gravel drive. He'd gotten as far as the grass verge at the bottom of the cabin's steps when she'd backed around his truck. She met his eyes, the expression in hers hidden by the window's tint. But there was no confusing the message she sent as she gave him a stiff middle finger, revved the engine, and accelerated hard enough to ping rocks against the side and tailgate of his pick-up.

He couldn't even flinch. He watched her hurl along the road, fast enough to have the animals on either side raise their heads and watch too. After she was out of sight, he still stood. Then with a feeling of resignation that his life was never really his to control, he turned back to the house.

His mother had made her own tea, started the coffee, and rummaged around in the cabinets until she came up with a box of forgotten cookies. She was crunching one and examining it with a frown when the coffeemaker chimed with the completion of its task. She bustled over to it, poured a big mug, and set it down at the place next to hers at the table, patting the chair.

Deke sighed.

"Now dear, come tell me all about it."

Chapter 14

Shifting the bottles of wine in her arms, Marguerite lifted a hand to knock on the big oak door. Her hosts always insisted that she should come in without announcing herself, but years of diplomatic manners ingrained by her parents wouldn't allow it. Waiting on the stoop, she stepped back and turned to appreciate the view.

From this elevation, the fall-tinted vines of Witch Hill draped gently over the undulations of the mountain. The winery itself was out of view over the crest, but that suited the owners. It wasn't as if the doctors wanted wine-sampling visitors to be peeking into their living room windows.

It was amazing what a few years and significant hard labor could do to improve a vista, and she gave the vines a satisfied nod. When the Dawsons had asked her to consult with them on the property, she'd nearly refused. On paper, it seemed to be a total loss. The previous owners had abandoned the vineyards years before, and the grapes hadn't been so much as watered during their neglect. In this climate with months of no rain and intense summer heat, the vines should all be dead.

But Davinia and Marcus convinced her to walk the land with them. They were sure that the property had value. They'd already purchased it, along with the ramshackle house they'd turned into her home and the small cabin Fernando used.

"You must see it, Ms. Devereaux, before you say no. By some miracle, the grapes continue to flourish."

Five years ago, they'd pulled on their boots and walked the long lines of vines together. Marguerite was amazed. Not only were the grapes alive, despite the neglect, but they were sturdy and showing every sign of producing a great crop that very year.

"Who has taken care of them while the bank owned the property?" Marguerite directed her question to tall, broad-shouldered Marcus, since Davinia's diminutive stature was hidden completely in the next row by the enthusiastic thrust of new bright green shoots.

The good doctor, his bald black head shining in the sun, stopped to examine a tiny cluster that would one day be Petite Sirah wine, as gentle with it as he was with his emergency room patients.

"That's the mystery, or some say, the magic, Ms. Devereaux." He paused, meeting her eyes with a mixture of laughter and awe. "No one."

She'd blinked at that, staring again at the abundance of clusters and the semi-wild nature of the vines. Granted, a good pruning was required, but the fact that they were alive at all proved their heartiness. And hearty vines produced fine wines.

If she hadn't been completely convinced by their stroll up and down the hills, the next big reveal decided her.

"I would like you to look at the business plan we put together. We are going to call it Witch Hill Winery, after the legend, you know. And we believe that we can be at full production in five years."

They sat in a small dining room of a restaurant called Roxy's, their server assuring them that there was no hurry. The lunch crowd had lightened and they had the place to themselves, as Davinia brought out a design for the logo and labels, estimates of yields and tonnage, financial projections, and an operating plan. Rough drawings captured their vision for the winery building itself, perched on top of the mountain.

A thrill of excitement ran through her that day. To have an opportunity to start with this undeniable diamond in the rough, with owners who had the smarts – and the money – to develop the winery and vineyards fully, was a dream she thought she'd have to wait years to fulfill.

And it was hers to run. As the thought crossed her mind now, a chill like the brush of a cold hand ran down her spine. She couldn't stop the shiver in the warm afternoon.

"Marguerite, there you are. Why didn't you just come in?"

The business professor took two of the bottles out of her arms and rose on her tiptoes to give Marguerite a kiss on each cheek, French style. Davinia insisted that she liked to add that little touch of the homeland to her winemaker's life.

"I'm sorry, I was just admiring the view of the vines. The colors make them seem to glow, wouldn't you agree?"

Davinia paused long enough to smile with contented satisfaction at the view, then patted Marguerite's arm.

"Yes, my dear, when they look like this, they look like magic. Makes you believe in the tales of the witch, don't you think?" And her straight teeth shone brightly as the smile cut across her dark face.

*****

"I can't believe it's been five years already, and a full year since you opened the winery." DK McGiven nudged her in the arm, gesturing with her wine glass. "And this was the first vintage, wasn't it?"

Marguerite grinned at her girl tribe friend. DK was like family to her since they'd bonded over the difficulties the metal artist had finding a muse for the passionate centerpiece placed in the winery's front drive. The woman's inspiration had taken the form of lifestyle writer Vince Cassidy, now talking with great animation with two wine critics across the room. When he turned towards them, he waved at his fiancée and saluted her with his own wineglass.

It was good to see her friends finding love in their lives. All of the girl tribe were now settled.

She considered herself settled too, after all. She was married to her work. When her mind wandered to a certain patient cowboy, she pruned her thoughts with the same ruthless precision she used for her vines.

"Yes, it was the first year, the grapes we picked from those wild vines. I can tell you, the workers were not pleased that year. To have to hunt and search for the clusters had them cursing in very colorful ways." She laughed at the memory.

"All that hard work paid off. This is an amazing wine. Vince says that the one critic – the one he knows well – is so impressed that he wants Vince to do a story on the legend."

Not again. Enough about the witch. She stretched her neck at the sudden knot of tension.

"It is just that, a story. There is no witch, no ghost, and no legend. It is all a myth."

If one more person brought up this fictional character, she would be forced to curse them in her native French. That only happened when she was really pissed off, and she was *en pétard.*

"Come on, don't get in a snit. You know Vince is going to bug you about it until you let him interview you. You know," here DK rolled her eyes for emphasis, "what he's like when he's convinced something will make a great story."

Yes, she knew. After the past few years, she was well aware that everyone, everyone but her that is, believed that there was truth to the legend. Whatever she'd seen in the tank room that day was a trick of the lights.

"I do not understand why everyone is so convinced there is a ghost responsible for this wine. In fact, I may take offense at this." She smiled, but she was only partially kidding. "The vines come from excellent stock, and much hard work goes into the production of these wines."

"Marguerite, don't be a – let's say witch – about this. Honestly, you are the most black and white person I know."

That is what a man she preferred not to think about called her as well. Black and white, unwilling to explore other options.

Deke had called her. When she hung up without saying a word, he called again. It took a few more times, when the phone rang with what she could sense was his increasing impatience, before he stopped calling.

He'd shown up at the winery repeatedly, where she couldn't order him away without inciting a riotous amount of attention, with papers in hand and a determined look on his face. She pawned him off, first on David, much to the young man's confusion, and the next time, on Fernando, who'd only given her a quizzical look. When he came to her house, she demanded that he leave before she called the sheriff. His face had reddened at that.

Where was his precious control then? The thought gave her a glimmer of ill-feeling glee. Black and white was right when she was right. And she was right. In the intervening weeks, he'd broken off contact altogether, and she couldn't be happier about it.

Even if she did wake up with sheets in a tangle and brilliant blue eyes pinning her soul in her dreams.

*****

"That went well, don't you think?" Davinia accepted the dirty wineglasses and turned to stack them in the dishwasher.

"Yes, I agree. Everyone is very satisfied with your success. Witch Hill Winery will be on every wine visitor's map as the place they must try in the area."

Davinia stopped her stacking long enough to give her a measured stare. Was this how she looked at her university students when they came up lacking?

"Allow me to say tsk-tsk, my dear. Without your winemaking skill, none of this would be possible." The older woman smiled with assurance, no doubt or concern in her face.

Being polite, she did the only thing she was raised to do – she waved off the compliment and turned away to pick up more dishes that needed clearing.

"DK and Vince certainly are an unlikely couple, and yet they are so happy."

Marguerite agreed with a nod, passing over the stack of plates.

"All of your friends seem to be finding interesting partners. I hear that even Tess has met someone. But, my dear, why is there no special man in your life?"

Marguerite's thoughts flashed to broad shoulders, long golden hair, and captivating eyes. The sweep of attraction was there and had been from the first moment she'd inspected him across the wine barrel. Not that they would have a relationship.

"I do not have time for dating. We are very busy at the winery, and crush is coming up, making things even crazier. There are never enough hours in any day." That was truth enough.

The petite woman shook her head before the protest tumbled from Marguerite's lips. Then a fond reminiscent smile lit her features.

"You remind me of me at your age, my dear. Really, you do. I too kept insisting that there was never enough time. I was busy building my career and my professional reputation. And Marcus, dear Marcus, was even busier, making his way up through the ranks of the hospital. But one look at him, and I was hooked and never even knew it."

It was Marguerite's turn to shake her head, though she smiled at the pure joy that radiated from her boss. "There is no one who has – how did you put it – hooked me." She gave a polite shrug as if it was no major concern.

"That's not what I hear. Roxy mentioned that you and Deke Kermarrec were at the restaurant a while back, and Fernando said that Deke was asking Carl – he's Fernando's son who works for Deke, you know – about you. And I've seen the way your eyes linger on the view of his ranch, now and then." She leaned forward conspiratorially. "I can keep a secret, but I don't think I have to when everyone else is noticing this too."

Chapter 15

He shook his head to clear it of the memories. Her skin flowed like velvet under his fingers. Witty conversation and lively debates mirrored their spirited tangling under the sheets. Her appetites meshed with his at every turn.

That didn't mean they were a good match, though. Turning him away had become her habit. She didn't want to see the science, the test results, or the research. Her righteousness drove her so strongly that she ignored him.

Even more bitter was the fact that she didn't want to see him – at all.

It stung him in a major way that she could stand across this party and act like he wasn't there. The deliberateness of her stance, maintaining her back to him no matter where he moved, let Deke know that she was as aware of him as he was of her.

Fine, two could play this game. He could ignore her just as well.

Glancing at the crowd across the patio, Vince took a long sip of beer, watching him with a considering expression. Deke straightened in his chair and mimicked the pose. And he waited, because one thing a rancher got good at was patience and waiting.

Taking a final sip and draining his bottle, Vince stared into the beer like he couldn't quite believe it was empty already.

"I've got an assignment for a story about the witch of Witch Hill. Major magazine, big spread, complete with pictures." He paused, frowning deeply.

Deke would frown too, if it was his job.

"How do you take a picture of a ghost?" He kept his drawl serious, baiting Vince.

"Yeah, funny, ha-ha. Dane's taking the pictures, so he can figure out how to find the ghost. Me, I'm just doing the words. Which is why I need you."

Knowing what was probably coming, Deke began to shake his head, then stopped with a sudden thought. Why not talk about the old tales of the ghost? Maybe it would make people think before they tore down another story-laden treasure.

Vince plowed on as usual. "I set up some time to talk with the Dawsons too, since they own the hill now. But it was once in your family, wasn't it, Deke?"

Yes, it had been, until an aunt a couple of generations back had a fight with an uncle, and when her husband died and her kids were all gone, she'd sold it without a word to the family. Served her right that she died not long after moving off the mountain. Deke hated to take any satisfaction in someone else's misery, but still.

"I'm planning to interview Marguerite too. I've heard that the workers at the winery swear they've seen the witch a few times, and maybe even felt her hand or something. I don't know. I was thinking that you could join us. Maybe next Tuesday?"

Shaking his head to say without any doubt that he would absolutely not be available, Deke drained the last of his beer.

And she picked that moment to laugh. That rich deep rumble made him think of wild nature, or doing wild things together. The sound ran across his skin and tunneled into his bones. The chair was suddenly too confining and the patio too small. He stood before he realized he'd moved.

"Okay, so Tuesday won't work. When will work? I'll see if Marguerite's available at the same time."

He had to get out of here. His thoughts were suddenly chaotic and all he could remember was her infectious laugh – when she still laughed with him – and the bright sparkle in her violet eyes as she challenged him across the dinner table and in bed. She stirred him up, and there wasn't a thing he could do about it. Sleeping with her had been a mistake, a distraction, albeit a mind-bending one. They'd tumbled together as easily as a rock rolled downhill. But he had to remember what mattered.

He was halfway to his truck before he registered that Vince was asking him what was wrong.

"Nothing, nothing at all. Listen, I can meet with you sometime next week, but I'm not sure when. My schedule's," he tried to think of the right word, "unpredictable. But I'll call you, or you call me."

Deke felt Vince clap a big hand on his shoulder and give a squeeze.

"What is it with you two? We were all sure that they two of you were going to become an item, like the next ones in line, particularly after you chased after her that day. The way Roxy tells it, you two were very cozy at the restaurant even before that. But mention her to you or you to her, and you both go off like rockets. Come back to the party, man. Later, you can tell me what gives."

*****

"I wonder what they're discussing so intently over there." DK tilted her head towards Vince and Deke at the patio's edge. "Vince needs to get over here so we can get the party started."

Marguerite wondered what more the party needed. There was wine and beer and food – lots of it. And the patio with its inviting pool, though no one seemed to be inclined to dip into it on this slightly chilly evening. And music, loud and raucous with a beat that forced her to move her hips.

Grands appétits, oui. Big appetites and much passion. She loved to dance, propelled to move her body to a beat, any kind of beat. It was the one type of joyous abandon that her parents had allowed in her childhood. And it was a language universally understood, no matter what nation they were in.

"I didn't know you liked country music."

Marguerite turned to DK, bumping and grinding alongside her. Together, they shimmied and shook until they were both laughing. It felt good to laugh for a change, even if the cause of her worries lingered not too far away.

"Is this a private party, or can anyone join?" Serena's long hair flipped along with the bobs of her head, and pretty soon, all three of them were singing along to the song with varying degrees of success.

"Aw, look at them. I think they're ready for the road. What do you think, Dane?"

Marguerite smiled, ready to give Vince some grief. He, of all of her girlfriends' men, was the fastest when it came to sharp repartee. And Serena's husband Dane, when he wasn't being the strong silent type, was a close second.

When she turned, though, she looked right into the face of the one man she didn't want to see. Her step faltered before she spun around quickly and found herself facing a window that reflected back the dusky backyard perfectly. He was staring into her eyes in the mirroring glass.

Deke. The shadows on his face partially hid his expression, though what she could see looked grim and stubborn. Loose long hair flowed like golden wine in the torches on the patio. The eyes she couldn't help staring into were shaded as well, though she could feel the burn of them on her.

"Honey, what were the two of you cooking up?" DK wrapped her arms around her fiancé's waist as he gave her a quick kiss.

"And where were you in the mean time?" Serena put an arm around Dane and gave him a questioning stare.

That left her staring again at the one lone man in the group. The fact that he was staring back didn't help. In fact, she wished that she could escape to avoid his penetrating attention.

"I don't know what they were cooking up. I just met them coming back from taking shots of the sunset. See? Working here." Dane held up his camera for explanation.

"We were just catching up, talking about work and stuff. Deke was filling me in on some of the local gossip." Vince glanced around until he stared at her, opening his mouth to continue. "Deke was convinced he had to be someplace else. I convinced him otherwise."

"Leave it alone, Vince." DK gave Vince's arm a warning yank for emphasis. Worry colored her tone as she flashed looks between Marguerite and Deke.

She wasn't sure if she should stand or sit, stay or leave. And she certainly wasn't sure what to make of Deke's refusal to share what had happened between them. It would be the perfect opportunity, since the men ribbed him unceasingly about his lack of a date for the evening. The women, thankfully, were willing to let the story sleep for the time being. But the expressions on their faces told her she was going to be quizzed about this later.

If they knew how easily she jumped into his bed, there would be no end to the teasing.

"Much as I hate to give up a good story, and I know there's a doozy in there somewhere, you're right, as always, my love. We have more important things to discuss." Vince dropped a kiss on DK's head as he turned her towards their house. Still chattering, their friends disappeared through the doors.

That gave her time to examine the man standing next to her out of the corner of her eye. He hadn't moved since he'd followed Vince and Dane to the patio.

Thinking back, the pain of that day was still fresh and crisp, harsh as a new paper cut and just as surprising. Now would be the perfect time for him to lay it all out to people who would undoubtedly take his side. And yet, he said nothing. Did he still believe she was deliberately poisoning the land?

His quick glance in her direction turned into a more pronounced fixation as their eyes met. His were the color of glass washed up by the waves on some far away beach, gray and giving away nothing.

"Deke, Marguerite? Are you with us? Because we have an announcement to make." Vince's raspy voice cut between them from the French doors.

She closed her eyes, unwilling to let Deke see how much his accusations still hurt her. Shaking her head slowly to clear it, she made sure she turned towards the others before she opened them again.

*****

She drove him absolutely nuts. That is, when she wasn't making him fucking crazy with need. His big brain and his little brain were in a constant state of disagreement on which should rule his actions. Following her inside the house meant he had an opportunity to watch the gentle sway of her hair down her graceful back, ending just above her belt. He itched to keep walking when she stopped and wrap his arms around her, pressing her tight against him.

Vince handed around champagne glasses, giving Deke two. He knew what his friend was trying to do. Marguerite's hands were empty.

Her fingers touching his as he handed her a glass, long enough to send a shot of electricity up his arm and numb him, was child's play when compared to the doe-eyed plumy softness that heated her eyes. Shock showed on her face before she turned back to their friends, the fast movement no less deliberate. He knew his heart was still working because its rate picked up to a jungle beat.

She had no right to turn him inside out and then hurt him with her distortions. It was up to him to protect his land, and she'd been willing to destroy everything he worked for. He couldn't help that surge of new disappointment, tart and bitter on his tongue.

He still wanted to know why. What would make her so obtuse when it came to protecting the earth they both farmed? And how could she ignore the heat between them? It nearly melted him in his boots.

"We have an announcement to make. Vince and I have set a date and a place, and we hope that you can all join us for the celebration."

"She means, we hope that you'll all work – for free, I might add – to pull the event together for us."

"Vince, honestly!" DK's elbow landed squarely in Vince's belly and he blew out surprised air, then had the nerve to look chagrined.

"What?"

Deke laughed with everyone else, but inside he carried a hollow feeling. One by one, every man around him was finding the love of his life and linking to them, promising to cherish and honor them.

And what did he have to cherish and honor? Dirt, cows, and a legacy that mattered to no one, it seemed, but him.

Chapter 16

The noise around the patio that night built to a big crescendo, then ebbed a little to exclamations. She'd stood frozen, the automatic words of congratulations leaving her mouth, fighting back impending tears. And she'd felt frozen ever since.

There was no reason for this, she lectured herself sternly. Another of her wonderful friends was getting married. It wasn't like it was a big surprise. They'd been engaged for months now and had been secretively hinting for the past few weeks that they'd formulated their wedding plans.

And just because she was conflicted about her own attraction to a man who seemed carved from the earth himself, she'd been in torment ever since the news came out. She slapped a hand on the counter in frustration, the whiteboard with its notes monitoring wine progress blurring. When she whirled to face the barrels, all she could think about was the news DK and Vince shared.

DK and Vince were getting married at the winery, next to the metal sculpture that first brought them together. It was so damned romantic, she had to fight back tears at the idea.

"Um, Ms. Marguerite? What would you like me to do next?"

David's earnest young face appeared in her line of sight, standing behind a stack of barrels so that only his nose and mouth were visible. He ducked down, and all she could see were his eyes and a tousle of hair.

He was like an eager young puppy, as disarming as big paws and floppy ears and a cold nose would be. He was almost housebroken and knew basic commands now too. Pretty soon, he would be able to walk off leash.

When had she become so catty?

Shaking her head to clear the uncharitable thoughts, she assured herself it was only because she'd been thinking about – him.

"In three days' time, we'll begin crushing. Have you moved the bins into the vineyard?" At his affirmative shake, made along with another head bob so that she could again see only mouth or eyes, she sighed and continued. "We'll need to move the empty bins out of the way on the crush pad." She looked at her watch. Almost four. "But that can wait until tomorrow. Why don't you call it a day, David?"

"If you're sure, Ms. Marguerite. I mean, I can stay longer and do something else if you like." He stepped out from around the barrels now, looking uncertain.

Shaking her head and waving him off, she couldn't help but grin a little when he backed up and nearly stumbled on the drain cover in the floor, blushing beet red. He brushed off his hands on his jeans, gave her a resigned shrug, and made it out the door without further mishap.

The moment of levity gave her a welcomed sense of relief. Her friends were happy, and her staff were, if not exactly thriving, at least developing at a pace that meant the future could be positive. The only lingering shadows were in the papers now in her back pocket. That, and the memory of her blond cowboy and how he could tame her body throughout the night.

She pulled out the pages reluctantly. A delivery service brought the three sheets of paper to her, signature required, and pointed out the notation in large block letters across the front of the envelope. *'Please read immediately.'* She didn't need to read the return address to know who sent it.

They were reports, fresh tests on the water quality of Deke's wells and the dirt that held run-off during the rainy season. The levels of residual herbicides, along with metals and a variety of other alphabet soup chemicals, were off the chart, rating so high that every single graph was marked in red, well above the danger level. They made no sense, and she'd checked the logs of chemical applications herself to be sure. The timing and rates of application were her responsibility and done at her direction.

The figures hadn't changed, and soon they too began to dance in front of her eyes. She fought the tears that stung the corners of her eyes. When had things gotten so out of her control?

She understood Deke's concern. This wasn't an accident, and it wasn't naturally occurring.

'Something about the winery poisoning our wells, and the winemaker being the probable cause of it?'

Emie word's echoed back into her mind. It wasn't only Deke who thought this. How many other people convicted her behind her back, without ever confronting her with what they thought was the truth?

And Deke blamed her. That left her only one option. Figure out what was happening, and stop it.

The tasting room door opened, triggering the brief bell that let the staff know a visitor had arrived. She heard it only vaguely, intent on her examination. Even if they were over-spraying, the concentrations would not be anything like this. And the soil tests were no better. Something was leaching into the water and the soil.

"Boy, I'd hate to be those papers in your hands. If you frown any harder, they'll light on fire."

Marguerite lifted her head to meet Roxy's teasing blue eyes. Today the food entrepreneur was dressed more traditionally in checked chef's pants and a tank top, the kind she was sure to cover with her executive chef's coat every evening. The fact that she no longer had to work so hard, her reputation secured by years of intense labor, didn't mean she was any more inclined to step aside.

Marguerite smiled at her, thankful for another distraction that would allow her to set the papers aside and perhaps forget about their existence until tomorrow. Doubtful, but even so –

"What brings you to the mountain top today, my friend? Is the restaurant out of wine? You know I would deliver it myself." Pulling Roxy into a hard hug, she automatically grabbed a clean pair of glasses and selected a bottle of their newest release for her friend to sample.

"No, not out of wine. Just came for a visit in between shifts. The crews are working so well these days that I actually get a break now and then." Roxy smiled as the distinctive pop of the cork leaving the bottle. "Don't mind if I do."

Marguerite enjoyed watching her swirl, sniff and sip. Pulling the bottle towards her, Roxy nodded her approval. "Another wonderful wine, my friend. You are an artist, a magician, or – dare I say it – a witch!"

Despite the teasing tone, Marguerite felt herself jolt. It was one thing to be teased about it. It was another to have this thing, whatever it was, hanging over the winery. The fact that she hadn't seen the ghost in a couple of weeks did not make it less likely that it was still lurking in a corner, ready to pounce. If she even believed in it.

She shrugged with studied nonchalance instead, not willing to give any clue that there was a problem. But Roxy watched her closely, and at her assumed casual air, she shook her head.

"What's wrong? You might as well tell me. You haven't been yourself for weeks. Come to think of it, the tension level boils up to overflowing whenever Deke is in close proximity, like last weekend. So spill."

When the bottle clutched in her white fingers was replaced with the stem of the wineglass, she felt herself being propelled through the tasting room's door and out to the patio that invited guests to linger with views of the surrounding valleys. Roxy pushed her into a chair and poured more than a taste into the glass. Satisfied with her work, she dropped into the chair next to her and stretched out her legs, toying with the clogs on her feet.

"Talk."

From her vantage point, it was useless to try to look away. She was facing south, overlooking the vines that stretched down to the valley, Deke's valley. She could see gently rolling hills, two streambeds, and the random patterns of livestock, cattle or otherwise, wandering the brush. From here, the desolate dryness of September conditions was undeniable, parched, waiting for fire, or rain, or deliverance.

She sighed. Roxy wouldn't take no for an answer. She wouldn't accept that nothing was wrong.

"It is a man, *bien sûr*. Isn't it always about a man?" She wrinkled her nose in distaste, as if the conversation's subject displeased her greatly. "It is nothing. He is nothing. A speck of lint to be brushed away, of no consequence."

Roxy laughed. "Okay, that might work on someone who doesn't know you. But you forget who you're talking to here. I'm the same one who said that all men are scum, remember? And you so unequivocally agreed. You and I, we put on a big show of hating the men we met." Roxy leaned forward and placed a gentle hand over Marguerite's closed fist on the table. "You don't have to lie to me. Just tell me it's none of my business."

Marguerite forced her hand to relax. Roxy was correct, they were very much alike. However, Roxy had mended the fences with her man Mac, and he'd proved his devotion by dedicating the movie he produced locally to her, along with packing up his life in Los Angeles and moving everything to Flynn's Crossing. A happy ending dissolved the pain of the past into pleasure in the present.

Turning her hand over to give her friend a tight squeeze of acknowledgement, Marguerite let go and leaned back, shifting so that the southern exposure would be out of her view. "*Il n'en est pas de votre entreprise.*"

Leaning back in her own chair, Roxy stared at her, her face serious. "I think you just told me to blow off, right?" When Marguerite nodded, she sighed.

"Okay, know that I'm ready to listen any time you decide you need to spill it. Hell, any of us in the tribe are. Remember that you have friends." She tilted her head to one side, considering Marguerite carefully. For once, the examination was distinctly uncomfortable, maybe because this time, she had secrets to hide.

Slapping her hand on the table, Roxy pushed forward, her expression now impish. "As to why I'm here. You know that Mac bought the old Prescott place, up the road from the restaurant."

That wasn't news. The women had been discussing it for a couple of months, teasing Roxy incessantly because he'd bought it to be close to his ladylove. When she no longer swore at them in response and blushed instead, it was confirmed. She was in serious love. And whenever Mac could stay in town, he would be found as close to Roxy as possible, either trailing after her in her gourmet grocery, or wandering between kitchen and dining room at her restaurant, or camped out at her spacious apartment above it.

Marguerite waited, curious despite her own problems.

"So, the place needs a lot of work. Like, a whole ton of work. The inside of the main house is a mess, left to fall apart for the most part since the last owners couldn't pay their mortgage. There's a lot of land, about two hundred acres as a matter of fact."

Marguerite pulled back in surprise. "So much? I didn't realize that the property was still intact. I thought it had been divided long ago."

Roxy shook her head in agreement. "Mac bought back as much as he could, contiguous parcels, so we have one big mess-o-land now." She smiled, a look that conveyed love, hope and bewilderment all at once. "And now we need to know what to do with it."

*****

Deke eyed the growing storm clouds on the eastern horizon. The weather prognosticators had been singing about rain for days now, first on a ten-day forecast, then seven, and now imminently, though whether or not they would be accurate was yet to be seen. Still, this was the most promising build-ups of clouds in months.

And with rain, problems would be exacerbated once again. Each scientist he consulted said the same thing. Find the source of the chemicals and have them remediated. Otherwise, the run-off would continue to poison his water supplies and the land, building up more toxins in the grasses that he relied on for his livestock. Hell, even the streams, seasonal now and bone dry until the ground again became saturated, wouldn't survive a wet winter unscathed.

And he knew the source. He just didn't know how to prove it and then how to go about changing someone's intentions.

"Hey Deke? Do you mind if I take off a couple of hours early today? I want to check on Pop."

Deke shook off his reverie at the question. His hand Carl had been on the land since he could first ride. He came from a long line of hard workers who, over the generations, had a place on almost every major ranch, vineyard, and orchard in this part of the county.

"I hadn't heard. Is Fernando sick?"

"I don't know. He's been acting weird lately. Won't come to Sunday dinner. Doesn't have time for a friendly chat. Doesn't want anyone visiting him. And he's announced that he's retiring at the end of the year, and he's going to move to Las Vegas, of all places. He seems to have this idea that he's going to live the life of a high roller."

Deke chuckled, thinking of the old man who'd worked for Three Rivers occasionally over the years, when he wasn't committed to one vineyard or another. The fact that he planned to retire was something Marguerite had left out in their conversations.

"Frankly, Deke, I'm worried about him. He's got this cough that never seems to get better. He's turning into a hermit, and you know how gregarious he always was. I want to go to his cabin and check what's going on." What Carl described was a foreign picture of the vineyard manager.

"Sure, go on ahead. Let me know what you learn. If you think he needs medical care, I'm happy to help you tie him up and carry him into the doctor's office."

Carl's laugh and confirmation that he'd take Deke up on that offer faded as he moved away. A distant rumble of thunder replaced other sounds for a moment. And with it came a flood of thoughts about the one woman he appeared to want, even when circumstances said she was everything wrong.

If he could confront her with irrefutable proof, would Marguerite take his assertions seriously? What would make her believe that something very wrong was happening between their two properties?

The cell phone on his belt chirped, and he unbuckled the case and slid it to his ear.

"This is Deke."

"Deke, hey, glad I caught you. This is Vince. How are you?"

He returned the pleasantries, then waited. Vince always had a lot to say, and he didn't need any coaching to continue.

"Three things. First, the guys are going to meet at Mallory's tonight for a couple of beers. Can you make it? Mac's going to be there – you know, Roxy's boyfriend. And he has some questions he wants to ask you."

Weird, but not too strange. Deke had gotten used to the jet-set lifestyle that Mac lived, rushing between movie sets and director meetings and awards ceremonies. It all seemed to be okay with Roxy, and he wasn't one to judge.

And in truth, he'd gotten kind of used to the wolf pack, the erstwhile group of newcomers and old timers who were all somehow also related to the girl tribe. By proxy, he was included through an ever-growing friendship with Vince and Dane, engineer Rick who'd helped him with his water calculations, construction titan Powers, and the completed disassembled Mac. Add in his brother Jake, his cousin Dave, and friend Steve, and they were one big happy – wolf pack.

To Vince, he said, "Sounds good. Count me in. Next?"

The screech of a hawk overhead captured his momentary attention, wheeling and circling as two smaller birds chased it off from a nest or food source.

"Where are you, man?" Vince quizzed in his ear.

"On a horse."

The laughter on the other end was gruff and genuine. "I keep forgetting that you're a real cowboy, not the wannabe kind. On a horse, out on the open range, tending your cattle or sheep, or whatever the hell it is you have out there."

Deke chuckled, content. "Yeah, but the dogs are doing most of the work. Rain's coming, and I'm moving some of the cattle from a summer pasture to closer in. No point in losing some because they get spooked in a storm." He glanced at the clouds again.

"Well git along them little doggies, I guess. Anyway, second point. When do you want to schedule time to discuss the witch?"

Deke tightened his hands on his reins and his horse shimmied sideways, confused by the message. The only witch he could think of was a violet-eyed one, with long flowing black tresses and a body that made his own heat in response.

But he knew that wasn't what Vince meant.

"Maybe in a couple of weeks, if that works for you. If it does rain, and it's looking pretty promising, I'll be tied up moving stock and settling things for the seasonal change at the ranch. You can come out if you like, and we can talk there."

"Really? Perfect. Maybe I can get Dane to come with me and take some action shots, if that's all right with you. Any sign of the witch, by the way?"

The hint of teasing in his friend's voice was obvious, but his eyes were still blinded by his own private thoughts.

"And speaking of that," Vince continued, "anything new between you and Marguerite?"

Bingo. Vince couldn't have hit closer to his mark if he tried. And he probably was trying.

"Never mind, I shouldn't have said anything. It's just that DK keeps talking about it, says the girls are all up in arms, want the two of you to hook up, that sort of thing. I thought I'd warn you." Implied but not said outright was that if the women wanted them together, they would continue to throw them together no matter what.

Still, he didn't need to catch that toss, no matter how much he wanted to.

And that was just it. In the black hours when the night's darkness was complete and unwavering, he wanted to. He wanted to a lot. It was only in the light of day when he reminded himself of what was at stake that he could control his emotions.

Shaking his head, feeling the pull of his ponytail, and blaming it for the sudden headache, he focused in on the phone, determined to get Vince off the line so that he could again be alone with his thoughts.

"You said three things. What's number three?"

Vince was silent, though Deke could hear his breathing on the other end. It was so unlike Vince to have nothing to say, that Deke reined in his horse and stood still, savoring the experience. "You there, Vince?"

Clearing his throat on the other end, Vince finally answered. "I would like you to be my best man."

Chapter 17

"Best man? And at the winery? That's terrific. Man, this is going to be some party."

His friends' enthusiasm notwithstanding, Deke wasn't so sure. He'd gotten himself into something that was already taking on a life of its own. Why him?

Vince's reasons had been simple and direct. "You're the guy I'd ask last for a hand-out and first for a favor."

In an odd sort of way, he guessed it made sense. He took a sip of his beer and tried to focus on the discussion with Mac at its center.

"I bought the old Prescott ranch, or at least, as much of it as I could get my hands on. There were pieces of the original homestead available around the current house, if you can call it that. Personally, I'm not sure how much of it will be salvageable. Powers here is going to look it over and give me his expert opinion, and if it makes sense to renovate it, I will."

"Yeah, as in, if the place can be saved at all," Powers added. "You should see it, Deke. I've only reviewed pictures so far, and those alone would make you weep. The front porch is tilted to one side, the back porch to the other. Half of the roof leaks. I hate to think about the conditions inside."

He let the conversation debating the pros and cons of this major fixer-upper flow around him. Since he loved old places like this, he appreciated the fact that Mac wanted to try to save it. But some things couldn't be salvaged.

Like his relationship with Marguerite, if they could ever have even called it that. It pained him to think how things could have developed. As it was, there were secrets and anger words between them, and it would take an earthquake to shift the load.

Not wanting to go there, he focused on the current swing in the topic. Mac lamented his difficulty in finding people with skills to repair old treasures. Here at least he could help.

"You know, I have a friend who's a master carpenter, Geno Altimari. He specializes in old places like this. He uses old tools when it's practical, and the joints he cuts are done by hand and watertight. The guy's an artist." He paused, looking at the expectant faces around him. "He did some work for me on the old house."

When Mac enthusiastically agreed that an introduction would be perfect, he moved on to yet another question.

"As you know, it was once a working ranch. The thing is, many of the big old properties in that valley are now being converted to vineyards or other agricultural uses. There are even a couple of Christmas tree farms up the road. But I'd like to have a mixed use for the place." Mac paused, tilting his head and regarded Deke intently, before adding, "And that's where you come in."

*****

"Thanks for letting me come early, sweetie. I really wanted to talk with you before the others got here."

It had become something of a habit, the girl tribe getting together at one house or another, while the wolf pack met at the old restaurant and sports bar, Mallory's. Tonight was no different, except Marguerite counted herself lucky to be the host. With the sky beginning to cloud and the Sangiovese scheduled to be picked the next day, rain or shine, it would be easier to slip quietly into bed when she needed to, even if her friends were still talking.

Putting a dish on the counter, DK turned and examined her. The slight pinch of a frown meant she could see the circles under Marguerite's eyes that no amount of make-up seemed to hide. Just like Roxy, DK wouldn't be easily pushed aside when the questions started.

Directing the conversation came naturally to her, so instead she pulled the cork out of a bottle of wine, pointed a glass in DK's direction with a questioning tilt of her eyebrow, and waited.

"Yes, of course, you need to ask? If it's that lovely new wine you gave Roxy to try the other day, I can't wait."

Of course the others discussed everyone's business. She did the same. Still, she hoped that much of that conversation remained private.

"What did you want to discuss?"

"Well, you know that Vince and I are going to get married on the Saturday before Thanksgiving. Gosh, I can't believe it's going to be here before I know it, but that time will fly by."

"You know that everything will be perfect. I can assure you that I've planned many parties, and I will make yours a day to remember without, as you might say, breaking a sweat."

DK smiled at her, her pixie face sparkling with joy.

"I know you're a pro at this. Me, I'd rather run off to Tahoe and be married by a justice of the peace, but Vince has me convinced that this is the best way to keep my parents happy. And they are, happy I mean. Even if they still don't understand me and they really don't get Vince, I'm the last one who wasn't married or in a religious order. Next, they'll be asking about babies."

Marguerite chuckled. Her own parents were so different, convinced that she would never be one to wed again, never trusting that the right man would come along. And they were probably right.

"So, here's what I wanted to ask you." DK put down her wine glass and covered Marguerite's hands with hers. "Will you be my maid of honor?"

To be so trusted made her eyes fill. Marguerite wanted to laugh, just as she wanted to cry. Friends. She had good and wonderful friends. It made this place home.

Chapter 18

Startling in its power, the crash high up on the mountain reverberated like a thousand drums, echoing down the canyon and back up its granite face. The lightning strike was close, too close for comfort when grasses were already parched to a drought-induced crisp. But there was rain now, and a lot of it.

He lifted his face up into the pelting torrent. It massaged his eyes, released the tense wrinkles on his forehead, and brought the whisper of a smile to his lips. The relief was exquisite, unlike almost any other sensation. Throwing his hat into the front seat of his pick-up, he contemplated shedding his clothes to enjoy the full force of Mother Nature's blessing.

Wet again, thank god. They'd survived another hot dry summer.

The cattle didn't know what to do. Calm beasts most of the time and raised in summer's peace, they didn't take well to thunder and lightning. Bursts flew from one side of the sky to the other. The resulting wall of noise followed the same path. It herded them forward faster than any dog or human could for the protection of cover.

Sage and dry grass welcomed the rain, the scent a combination of rich spice and school glue that was the sign of fall each year of his lifetime, and all of the lifetimes around here before him. Seven generations back, they all recognized this as the beginning of the season when all would again be bountiful and lush.

But this season, it might not be something he could count on. If the evidence at his feet was any indication, there would be more trouble. Squinting against the sheets of water to the mountain to the north, he wondered what the rains would bring. Peace, or poison?

Because it must stop. It would, without any doubt, even if he had to take on the witch himself.

"Hey Deke? Whadya wanna do with that carcass?"

The surge of anger flashed through him as fast as the lightning above. Another dead animal. That made four in the past month, and if the necropsy results were the same on this one, it would be one more nail in the coffin.

Ignoring the rain as it ran down his face, he squinted through the torrent to his uncle. The old man had a longer oilskin on, and the hat on his head had seen better days a couple of decades ago. But Deke had noticed that his clothes were the cleanest they'd been in a quite a while. The old man seemed to be standing taller too. If he had any brainpower left juggling everything else, he might be curious about it.

"I'm trying to decide if it's even worth taking it to the vet school for testing like the others. I suspect I'll only hear the same response, so why pay the expense." The crack of thunder sounded closer now.

"Tell you what, I'll winch it into the back of my truck and take it up to the barns for you. I was going to stop in and see Emie, and maybe by the time we've visited for a while, you'll have decided."

That was the fifth time in the past ten days that Royan had stopped to spend time with Emie. His mother insisted on staying in the old house, despite its proximity to the noise of the barns and the bustle of the bunkhouse. She said she liked the craziness, enjoyed talking with the ranch workers, and even got back into cooking meals more often than not for the hardworking men and women. According to the gossip, Royan was showing up for supper on a regular basis too.

Whatever kept the two of them happy, he supposed. They'd both been single long enough, and while his mother never mentioned how she was doing and he didn't want to pry, he bet she was as lonely as Royan. It was nice that the two of them could be friends.

"Thanks Uncle Royan – I appreciate the help."

"Aww, it's no bother, none at all. I don't have the fancy cows you have, don't have all of the responsibility you got. All I got is time on my hands, so it's best I occupy myself so I don't get into trouble."

That made him smile. Royan having too much time on his hands was as ridiculous an idea as, well, as the idea of people seeing the ghost of the witch herself.

He knew what she'd look like, black flowing hair and violet eyes and a luscious rich body that –

Swearing out loud, he slammed the hat back on his head and slammed the door of the truck even harder. This was a different witch, a woman so stubborn and self-justified that she refused to consider the facts in front of her face. Maybe he should deliver the proof to her one more time.

"Hey Royan, hold on for a minute."

*****

"Merde!"

The next flash of lightning crossed the sky with an almost immediate cacophony of rumbling on top of it. They were directly under the center of the thunderstorm, and she was pissed.

Years spent recovering this vineyard, countless hours tending each individual grapevine to bring it back to its full potential, and an awesome series of accolades for their previously released vintages meant this could be their break-through year.

And now, as it was time to harvest, rain.

She cursed fiercely in her native tongue, even as the water coursed down the mountain over ground too parched to absorb more than a few drops. Electricity in the air raised the hairs on her arms while the vibrations of thunder in the ground jarred her bones.

The witch was a bitch today.

"Margie? How about we call it a day? The crew can't pick in the lightning, it's not safe. And we can't all stay huddled under this tent for the rest of the afternoon. We can start again tomorrow, God and Ma Nature willing."

Fernando stood next to her watching the rain continue to pummel the vines, his impatience only slightly less evident than hers. He chewed hard on the stick from his lollipop. Losing a day at this time of year was a curse. Picking crews were booked in advance, and now the grapes would need to come off as quickly as possible before they started to burst or rot.

But what he said was true. They couldn't risk the pickers on this mountain in a thunderstorm, and it didn't appear that it was going to stop any time soon.

"Yes, let's send everyone home. Schedule them again for tomorrow or as soon as you can."

The manager turned away and put an arm around the shoulders of the head of the crew, a man who had worked the vineyards in this region for decades. Together, the two men pushed worn hats on their gray heads and motioned the other workers out of the protection of the tent and towards waiting vehicles.

She'd had such great hopes for this vintage. She knew the Dawsons would be accepting of the results, no matter what. They were aware as well as she that they were at the whim of whatever the weather brought them. Snow on new buds, intense heat drying green grapes, or rain on ripe clusters. They never could count on the conditions, one year to the next. That's why they farmed grapes and made wine. They considered it part of their adventure.

She considered it her profession, and as such, one that she took seriously. She would make things perfect. But in this case, she was not the master.

Trucks and cars skidded down the track at the edge of the vineyard, and she watched them go. She had the ATV, and while it wouldn't protect her completely from the rain, it would get her down the hillside safely. The ground, unable to absorb the heavy deluge, was already carved into rivulets and gullies, and the ride would not be pleasant.

Staring at the sky one last time and railing against the witch that was Mother Nature, she almost missed the truck approaching her on the track. Over the noise of the storm, a dog barked as the engine quieted. And by then, her route of escape was cut off.

*****

"Deke, what are you doing here?"

She was stunning, even soaking wet. That's all he could think of. When the lightning flashed and lit her face in sharp contrast once more, he remembered his thoughts of the witch's appearance and almost grinned. He couldn't have been more accurate if he tried.

A black and white wet mass streaked past him as he stood next to his truck, and he called out a warning about a second too late as the dog jumped up on Marguerite.

"Oh, who are you? Does your master have you out in the rain? You poor thing."

"Dozer, down boy. God, you have no manners." He glanced inside the cab's open door to where Dolly waited to be released to join her brother. Her body quivered in anticipation, and he didn't have the heart to deny her.

Besides, Marguerite was already muddied.

When the second dog jumped in for a round of attention, Marguerite laughed at the antics of the two. Dozer jumped over Dolly, then Dolly shoved her brother aside. And they both gave Marguerite a whole lot of kisses when she bent down to pet them.

He wished she'd give him the same unbridled enthusiasm and attention. It had only been that one night, and he could still feel the passion. The irony of his dogs getting such affection while he stood out here and watched wasn't lost on him.

"What are their names? They are adorable. I don't remember seeing them in your house." Then she stopped as if realizing the night she was referring to, and she lifted a startled gaze to him.

"The one who nearly knocked you over is Dozer, and most of the time, that's what he is, a lazy dozer. His sister is Dolly, short for Dollar, since we knew when she was a pup that she was going to be a top-dollar herder. They sleep in the barns most of the time, since they like to be with the livestock they work. Of course, they also like to lay in front of the fire in the middle of winter. They're equal opportunity moochers, both of them."

"If you were mine, you would never sleep in a barn, would you now, *mes petits*." Marguerite dropped to her knees in the mud to hug the wiggling masses of wet fur and laughingly avoid slurping tongues.

If you were mine, I might never let you out of my bed. His silent words rang in his ears, louder than the thunder and drumming harder than the beat of the rain on the tent roof.

He'd changed his mind. He didn't want to do this. Revenge and shock value were nothing compared to mending fences with her.

She straightened, gathered up the braid of her hair, and tucked it into a thick oilskin hat. When that was firmly pushed on her head, she pulled her coat close around her.

The dogs, dancing around her feet, ignored Deke. Yeah, he knew how they felt too. She was a magnet.

"Is there something you needed?"

The temperature dropped about twenty degrees with her now-frosty tone. Evidently her lightness was only for four-footed creatures. She tapped a boot in impatience and glanced past his truck to her ATV.

"Why don't I give you a ride down? In this rain, you'll be soaked completely and bouncing like crazy on that thing." Not to mention, to get to it, she'd need to walk past his truck. To start the ATV, she'd be sitting in a seat that had a perfect view into the back of his truck.

What the hell had he been thinking?

She was already walking, minus dogs that were smart enough to get back into the pick-up's cab. His bright idea seemed like a dead bulb now. He obviously wasn't the brightest one in the marquee either. What was it about this woman that screwed with his reason?

"Marguerite, please stop."

He grabbed her arm, spinning her around towards him. Surprise showed on her face before she frowned at him and dropped her eyes to stare at his hand. She didn't say anything, and neither did he.

The cacophony of the storm was directly overhead, but that noise was nothing compared to the agony of screams he heard in his own mind. His senseless act of anger was now going to get him in big trouble. He was sorry he'd ever thought of it.

She shook off his hand without a word, and he felt powerless to stop her. Turning away from him, she straightened her shoulders and walked with deliberate ease towards the ATV. And as she passed the back of the pick-up, she glanced inside.

He knew exactly when her mind processed what her eyes were seeing. She halted, one foot barely on the ground. A hand came up to cover her mouth. She stood that way, staring, for what seemed like an eternity.

He had to move, to turn her away, to explain, but his feet felt like they'd sunk into mud. When he could finally make headway, she was already striding away.

Her steps were initially stilted, then more rapid. She turned and got on to the ATV, staring once again into the back of his truck. Again, forever passed before she moved. This time, she looked up at him as she pressed the ignition.

It wasn't rain coursing down her face, he was sure. It was tears.

Chapter 19

"This Sangio is a devil to crush. Those stems are like claws and they don't want to let go. You're going to have to move faster, son."

When the bin on the forklift tilted another few inches, the crusher whined in protest at the addition of more grape clusters. Swearing loudly, the old man shouted over its shriek at the young cellar rat to turn the damned thing off already. And shovel the damned stems away quicker too, as the tines of the pitchfork grating along the concrete added a metallic buzz saw screech to the cacophony.

Shaking her head, Marguerite watched the action from a distance. Poor young David wore ruby splotches on his pale freckled face, though she couldn't tell if it was because of how fast he was trying to work or a blush of dishonor at the ribbing he was receiving.

Fernando sat back on the forklift, glanced up at her with a wry little smirk, and shifted his lollipop from one side of his mouth to the other.

She had been grateful for the intense long hours of work in this past week. It almost made her forget, at times. But when she let her mind linger, the horror came back to her.

She thought she hid her feelings well that day in the rain. The dogs disarmed her, but she remembered all too quickly who she was facing. Deke was the one man who made her forget every better judgment.

When his hand wrapped around her arm, she felt the jolt like a stab of lightning, from her toes to the tips of her fingers. Her body warmed, and she willed herself not to throw herself at him and press lip to lip. Training won out.

He could have stopped her. He could have warned her. When she glanced into the truck, the colors catching the corner of her vision, she thought she might throw up.

It was one of those beautiful heirloom cows, its red and white coat still vibrant in the rain. But its body told the story. Contorted, its eyes rolled open and tongue hanging out, it was the picture of agony.

And she knew, without being told, why he brought this to show her. He thought she caused this.

When she felt the tears on her face, she wasn't sure why they were there. For the poor animal? Because this man believed that she would deliberately cause such agony? Or because he didn't trust her, and that hurt more than any pain she could ever imagine?

Thinking about it, examining it every night when there was nothing else to distract her, accomplished nothing. Wishing it was different now didn't produce a new outcome. Only work helped.

Shoving away from the doorjamb where she'd been leaning, she picked her way over the hoses and cords snaking across the crush pad. Working hard she could do.

"David, the stems coming out need somewhere to go. Rake the pile away and you can pick it up later. The bins are stacking up, and we need to keep crushing as fast as we can." Wrapping her long hair in a knot and tucking it under her cap, she grabbed another rake and worked clusters free of the bin, pushing them into the hopper of the crusher with ease.

"I'm sorry, ma'am. I thought I was keeping up." David shoved an arm across his sweaty brow, and reddened even more, if that was possible.

She would take pity on him, but not until they'd caught up to the pickers in the vineyard. They needed to finish crushing the Sangiovese grapes today, because the

Zinfandel was scheduled for tomorrow, the last of this year's harvest.

Squinting at the sky, she noted the clouds on the western horizon. The weather forecast for the next 48 hours was iffy at best. It might rain, it might not. They couldn't afford to wait any longer. The storms were completely unpredictable this year, and she didn't want a repeat of last week. It was hard to tell yet how much the rains had cost them in quality of those grapes.

David hosed the bin out as Fernando put the forklift in reverse, the trademark back-up beep-beep resonating in the metal roof over their heads. Where the sun hit the concrete, steam rose off the surface. Hotter than an oven today, and she knew it was even worse in the vines.

"Margie? How about we give the kid a little break? Besides, I could use a beer."

Fernando gave her an impish smile, the old scamp.

"Beer? Really? What will the pickers say when you pull up stinking of hops?" But she couldn't resist his winning smile, and she turned away so that he couldn't see the fond answering grin on her own face.

What would she do when he retired at the end of the year? Too many things were crashing around her at once.

"Ma'am? I could use a break too. I'll come back refreshed, you know? And then I can work faster." David's look was part hopeful puppy and part exhausted retriever. All that was missing was a lolling tongue.

She waved him off, and he dropped the rake on a pile of stems and turned for the cooler temperatures of the dark tank room. Counting the bins remaining, she calculated how much longer they would be working today. Into the evening, but by then, at least the work would be cooler.

Fernando eased off the forklift's high seat, his movements slow and cautious. Today he wore his age with less grace, the grimace of discomfort quickly hidden as he realized she was watching. When he caught her eye, he made a show of toying with the stick in his mouth.

"He's learning." He nodded towards David's retreating back. "Give him a few more months, and he'll figure out what all of those books and science experiments really mean."

She agreed. Too often, the degrees the young workers carried looked great on paper, but they didn't know how to put much of it into practice. Real life, working at a place like Witch Hill, put things in perspective.

It brought her own life into sharp focus as well. When she'd agreed to take the position, little did she know it would come with friends who became family, in a place where she too could send down roots. She didn't want to leave Flynn's Crossing, the closest thing to family and home that she'd ever felt.

It wasn't something she wanted to contemplate.

Instead, she trailed after Fernando as he followed David's path. In the shade offered by the interior, he reached into a cooler and pulled out two bottles of water, handing one to Marguerite without comment. As he sipped from his bottle, he gave into a coughing fit that turned his face burgundy red. When it subsided, he shrugged, easing a hand to his spine and rubbing his skinny frame. She watched him with concern.

"Fernando, perhaps you should go visit the doctor, eh? That cough seems like it is not getting better. This heat does not help, I am sure." Worry for him mixed with that continuing edge of concern. Managing without him for whatever the reason would not be easy.

"No, I'm fine. Just a little congestion is all. Nothing for you to worry about, Margie. Besides, pretty soon I'll be breathing that fine desert air." He winked at her before heading back into the sunshine. "Nothing but cigars and gamin' and fine showgirls to fill my days. That's Vegas baby."

*****

"Son, you look worried – again. It isn't good for you. You need to breathe deeply. Have you tried meditation?"

Deke sighed as Emie eyed him with more than gentle concern as she fluttered around the office, duster in hand. Meditation? When exactly would he have time to meditate, even if he believed in the value of it?

"That was one of the things that helped me the most, you know. Meditating at a vortex. It brought me answers to whatever my problems were that day. Why, when the young man who ran the bakery was so rude to me, telling me I was lingering with people too long and making customers wait, I was so angry. Madder that I think I ever was with your father, and that's saying a lot."

"Ma, why did it matter if you talked to other customers?" Her conversation veering across any number of different topics in seconds made his head ache even more.

"Not other customers, silly boy. My customers, when I was waiting on them."

His head pounded harder. The only advantage of being distracted by his mother was that it made him forget for a few seconds how he'd brought another strong woman to tears.

"Anyway, I was so mad that I just took off my apron and walked out of that place and went up the mountain. I loved that vortex by the airport, you can see for miles up there. And I meditated. And that's when I realized I needed to come home."

Deke twisted his neck, the resulting crack reverberating through his skull. Momentary relief made him blink, watching his mother swirl the yellow feathers around papers stacked on the small table by the window. He blinked again at her words.

"You decided to come home to Flynn's Crossing because you meditated on a mountain in Phoenix? And what were you doing working in a bakery?" There was so much in her previous statements that he didn't understand, and he wasn't completely sure he wanted to know.

"No, not Phoenix, Sedona. You know, Red Rocks country? Phoenix was boring, full of old people who wanted to play golf or tennis and gossip or were waiting to die. Not for me. So I took myself up to Sedona, and I found a job, and I had fun, for the most part. You meet the most interesting people there. They were just like me."

Not that he believed there were many people on the planet just like his mother, but how had she moved and he didn't know it?

"When did you move? And why didn't you tell me?" Something could have happened to her and he wouldn't even know where to look.

"Deke, you have a lot on your mind. I didn't want to bother you. Besides, we talked on the phone every week. I talked to Jake too. By the way, I invited him to dinner out here on Saturday. I told him to bring his girlfriend, but he told me he doesn't have one. What is it with you boys?"

Tears falling steadily out of violet eyes. He shouldn't have done it, shouldn't have given in to the feeling of righteous indignation. He had wanted her to see what her carelessness caused, up close and personal.

"Deke?" His mother's hand closed on his as he rubbed his temple, willing the vision away. His action would never be dismissed.

"Now son, you better tell me everything that's going on. First Royan was just about busting a gut to tell me about more animals dying and something about you dating the witch. Then you come home all shaken up with a dead cow in the back, heading straight for a shot of tequila, which is not like you. If you've got problems, you need to tell your mama so that she can help out."

The words were almost identical to the ones she'd used over the decades when one of the boys had skinned a knee or broken a bone, broke off with a girl in high school, or didn't achieve the best scores possible in college. Dad was liable to tell them to buck up, grow some and work harder. But Ma, with her tender heart and flighty ways, always seemed to find the kindness and caring in any situation.

The fact that she was talking about herself in the singsong voice like she was someone else – well, that was the same too. Some things you just never outgrew.

Lifting her hand to give her knuckles a quick kiss, he said, "Thanks Ma. You always know how to make us feel like we have a place to go with our problems." He stood and gave her a little hug. "But this time, I don't think that there's much that you can do. Kissing it won't make it feel better."

Instead of giggling as he expected, she frowned at him, and he noticed for the first time since she'd returned that there were deeper lines in her face, lines that he hadn't noticed when she moved away after his father died.

"Try me."

Chapter 20

"Ms. Marguerite, are you sure you don't want to do the inventory yourself? I'm not certified to apply these chemicals, and while I know we're not applying them, maybe I don't know enough yet to handle them properly."

No, she didn't want to inventory them. She wanted someone else, someone who had no idea what might have happened, to confirm or deny what she suspected. If there were herbicides missing, the only logical cause for the contamination of Deke's water supplies, she wanted an objective assessment of how bad the situation might be.

"You will be fine measuring the amounts. You can see the balances left inside through the sides of the containers. They are all sealed. Given that the volumes of the containers are labeled, you can calculate approximately how much you think is left in each one."

When the young man still eyed her uncertainly, she gave him an encouraging smile. "You will need to be certified to perform applications yourself before next spring. Once Fernando retires, I will otherwise be the only one who has taken the training and passed the test. You will be next."

That made him brighten, and he grabbed the clipboard with its printout of the chemicals inventory and took off from the office. Once he was gone, she slumped back into her chair and covered her eyes with a hand that wasn't completely steady.

What if it was true? Had she inadvertently directed Fernando to overspray herbicides? If she had, why had he not caught her error? She was in charge, and she was ultimately responsible. Still, it would be unlike Fernando not to take an opportunity to correct her.

"What's up, Margie? What do you have David doing?"

The questions made her drop her hand, thinking that perhaps she'd conjured him. The man in question stood in her office doorway, the lollipop in his hand as he spoke. Fernando looked unusually concerned, sucking again on the candy as if it was a lifeline.

She didn't bother to correct his use of her nickname today. "It is nothing, only an inventory of the chemicals we use. It is best to have him familiar with them, *non*? He will be attending his applicant's certification training soon."

Fernando shifted on his feet, his usual relaxed stance leaning against the doorframe not in evidence today. He glanced over his shoulder and frowned.

"Sure you don't want me to do it? I am trained, after all. I could take care of it in no time. Fact is, I know some of the balances in my head. You don't need to check them."

She waited for him to take his customary seat across the desk from her. It was his norm, coming in, as he put it, to shoot the shit with her so that he knew for sure she was on track. Normally the concept pissed her off a little bit, but today, she would welcome the distraction. When he stayed standing in the door, she gave him a puzzled glance, then continued the conversation.

"No, it is fine for him to do it. You and I, we work with them on a regular basis. David does not. He can take the inventory, and we know we have been objective."

Fernando scratched his grizzly chin, the lack of a shave today evident in the stubble covering his face. Before he could speak again, a rough coughing spell overtook him, and Marguerite wondered once again why he kept insisting he feeling fine. The man sounded like he had a death rattle.

"Have you been to the doctor? If you are sick, you should not be working, you should be home resting."

But the old man waved away her concern. The coughing subsided, and he pulled a remarkably white handkerchief from a back pocket and wiped at his streaming eyes.

"Nothing's wrong, I keep telling you. Just a whole bunch of mold and such in the air from the rain. Got me all worked up. That's why I need to move to Vegas, so I can breathe that clean desert air. Well, that, and the showgirls, of course." And he did his best to leer around a final quieter cough, sticking the candy back in his mouth.

His insistence did nothing to ease her concern.

"All right, if you're certain. Before you leave California, and before you no longer have health insurance through the winery, promise me that you will see your doctor, to be sure."

Fernando gave a wave of dismissal, turning towards the direction the cellar rat had taken. "Maybe I'd better check in on young David, just to make sure he's not having any troubles with those nasty chemicals. Wouldn't want him to get sick, you know? He's such a kid."

Before she could argue, he'd turned and walked away, and she didn't have the energy to stop him. He was acting strangely today. In fact, he had been acting out of character for the past couple of months, ever since he'd announced he was retiring at the end of the year.

That was the least of her problems now, though. She could rest easy if David's inventory revealed no discrepancies. No, she would think positive thoughts. When she had proven everything was accounted for, she would simply tell *Monsieur* Deke Kermarrec that he was wrong. Something else must be poisoning his animals. It was not her. It was not the winery.

She realized that she had a death grip on the pen in her hand when the phone rang, and she had to command her fingers to let go and pick up the handset. It rang twice more before she was able to negotiate the maneuver.

"Hello, Marguerite Devereaux."

"Marguerite, hi. It's Roxy. How are you?"

It was a standard question, and yet for once she felt like giving a truthful answer. If she said she was crazy with worry that she'd made a mistake, *une gross erreur,* what would her friend say? If she divulged the nature of the mistake, the girl tribe would call a meeting to come up with a solution for her, and she was not ready for that.

"*Je suis très bien*, Roxy, *et tu*?"

The laugh on the other end of the line was infectious. "After these past months, I've learned enough French from you to know you're giving me the stock answer. But I'll let it pass. I have a favor to ask, and I wondered if you're free tomorrow to meet me at the place Mac bought. Mac wants your advice. Frankly, I want it too. I don't want my guy going off the deep end, putting in a vineyard where he has no business doing it."

Marguerite perked up at the thought. "Yes, of course, for friends, I always have time. A new vineyard, you say?"

"Yeah, he's thinking that the old Prescott ranch might be perfect for it. While I think he's going to end up spending way too much money on this project when we could live just as comfortably in my place, it keeps him happy. I'm willing to sacrifice having things my way to keep Mac happy."

Marguerite knew that it was more than this, so much more. Roxy, though she didn't want to admit it too often, was as crazy in love with Mac as he was with her. To think that their love hadn't died over the space of a decade and a half was amazing.

She tried to push away a stab of envy. "Tell me the time and give me directions. I will be happy to serve as your vineyard consultant."

Typing the information Roxy provided into her online calendar, they exchanged final pleasantries before hanging up. Marguerite rested her hand on the phone for a moment, letting the envy surface once more. Even Roxy. Even Tess.

The girl tribe had met their men, and while they remained committed to each other, the frequency of their time together faded with each new addition. They would not lose their connection, but it had changed. Assuring herself that she was fine on her own was a lie.

Her mind flashed to Deke, to the pleasant dinner companion and accomplished renaissance man and rugged rancher. Then her mind moved to the contorted cow in his truck bed, and her lighter thoughts turned black once more. The fall colors painting the vines outside faded as melancholy memories crowded in.

"Um, Ms. Marguerite?"

She started, wondering how long David had occupied the space that held Fernando's skinny body only a few minutes before. It had only been a few minutes, correct? How long had she been daydreaming?

"Yes, David, are you finished already?" Making a show of stacking papers on her desk and tapping them even, she looked up expectantly. When she settled on the confusion on the young man's face, she realized that her hope of good news was unrealistic.

"Yes, I finished. I checked everything three times, just to be sure. Most of the stuff is fine, and the balances agree to the inventory sheet."

When he didn't continue, staring down instead at the clipboard and shaking his head, she had to ask.

"You said most of it. Is something out of balance? Minor discrepancies can be expected."

David shook his head again, raising his eyes to meet hers. He blushed that fire engine red. Worry made unusual lines appear, turning parts of his face so white that his freckles stood out in bright relief. It wasn't his usual combination of visible feelings.

"It's not a little bit, ma'am."

Marguerite felt the spiral drop in the pit of her stomach. It was fear, pure and simple.

"How much is missing?"

David moved forward now, the clipboard extended and a finger pointing to a particular entry. When he was close enough for Marguerite to read the item, he stopped, seeming to wait for instructions.

She sat back in her chair, hoping for an expression of ease that she was nowhere near feeling. She'd seen enough to know the chemical that was shorted.

"You see, ma'am, it's this one, this herbicide. It's a highly concentrated one, isn't it? And we're missing a lot of it. Like, a whole container. That's enough to spray all of Witch Hill for the season, isn't it? I looked all over the shed and the other outbuildings for it. Fernando said he's sure the computer's wrong. But how could we be so far off?"

Chapter 21

"I appreciate you taking the time to visit today, Deke." Mac clapped a hand on his shoulder as he pumped the other of Deke's in a surprisingly hard grip. "As you can see, Powers and Geno are here comparing notes on the house. Or rather, what they've already begun to call the little shop of horrors."

Deke had noticed the Ashland Construction logo on the truck parked besides the house, along with another advertising Geno's carpentry business on its side. A Range Rover he assumed to be Mac's took up the only other free space by the main building, and he'd pulled around an old barn to find a place to park. The spot offered no view of the house or drive, but meadows on the other side of a well-maintained fence stretched to the edge of dense woods and the rise of a steep hillside. Now, with Mac almost pulling him along, they rounded the barn's corner, Mac still in animated explanation.

When they both turned towards the dilapidated house, Deke couldn't help the astounded laugh that squeezed out of him.

Beside him, Mac grinned sheepishly. "Yeah, I get it, okay? Hollywood dude buys ranch, only said ranch is falling down around his ears. It's a money pit, I recognize that. Hell, I'm not even sure how good the water is. But I don't know. I have a feeling about this place."

Deke eyed the structure and wondered what his new friend had gotten himself into now. Windows were broken, which meant any number of creatures had taken up residence inside. The porch sagged badly, and overgrowth from surrounding plants twined through holes and broken boards. In more than a couple of spots, light showed into rooms upstairs through holes in the roof. Even if the place was full of antique furniture dating back a hundred years or more, as was the story, much of it was probably in no condition to use.

"Man, I hope you've decided to spend that fortune I hear you're making on your last movie, because this is going to need it." Still, the need to make something usable and good out of what was falling apart was a sentiment he understood.

"Yeah, probably every last penny from that movie and a whole lot more by the time I'm through. The place hasn't been inhabited by humans in a couple of decades. I guess the former owners lived in a trailer, according to what I've been told. Luckily, you don't need to worry about the house."

On cue, Powers crawled carefully out of what remained of a front window. Following him, the dark hair of another man appeared, covered in cobwebs. As they each reached the ground, Deke recognized Geno's tall thin frame. The carpenter scrubbed at his hair, leaning over to rid himself of the cobwebs and their probable inhabitants, turning back to look at the house and shake his head in apparent disbelief. When Powers made a comment, both men laughed heartily. Turning back towards Mac and Deke, both waved before returning to their consultation of a multi-paged list on a clipboard in Geno's hand, something Powers seemed to match in a tablet held in his.

At his side, Mac said, "By the way, I hired Geno on your recommendation. It appears that in addition to being a master carpenter, he's a general contractor. If Powers tells me the bones of this place can be saved, I'm going to have Geno oversee all of the work on the house. And believe me, we're talking basics here, like indoor plumbing and electricity, neither of which the house has. The outbuildings, like this barn, are in much better shape than the house."

Their footsteps crunched on gravel in unison as they left the house to the experts and moved towards the barn. Deke eyed the imposing edifice, an A-frame with pitched side wings to accommodate stalls, and a hayloft above.

"That figures. Over the past few years, locals have been renting the land for grazing. I know, because the executor of the owners' estate sent me an invitation to rent some of it too. I declined." At the time, it had appeared to be a good idea on paper, a way to spread out his herds when grasses were light. But it was hard enough to keep up with the land he had, much less worry about animals on parcels half an hour away.

"Let me guess. They made necessary repairs to the barns to protect their livestock." Mac put a hand to the door, smiling at the rusty screech of it trying to open on old hinges. The dankness inside made them both sneeze, and instead of going inside, they headed for the fence in front of Deke's truck.

"Okay, maybe they didn't have time to fix everything. Maybe they only did what they needed for their animals." Mac sneezed again.

"Yeah, like fencing, and troughs for the wells." He hesitated, not wanting to offend Mac. Flatlanders who came to the mountains made many first-timer mistakes. He didn't think that Mac would buy a place that had no decent water supply. But it never hurt to ask.

"The first thing you need to do is check that your well is producing, you know that, don't you?" Worries about his own water supply ate a hole in his gut every time he considered it.

"I'm on that already. Had the pump guy out, and he said that the main well will provide plenty of water, as soon as he replaces the pump. Cha-ching. There are no holding tanks, so I need to add those. Cha-ching. And the whole system to get the water pressurized to send out needs to be replaced. Cha-cha-ching." Mac laughed ruefully. "At this rate, I'll be making movies until I'm in a wheelchair to pay for everything."

"But at least you're taking care of this old place, making it into something special again. If I remember my local history right, the original Prescott family raised horses. The cattle came later." He turned to look out over the acreage, imagining it as it had once been, verdant green in spring, tanned to pale gold in the summer, color dancing in trees in the fall and blanketed by a coat of snow in winter. It would be good to restore this to something that picturesque once again.

Mac crossed his arms, staring out over the pasture as Deke did. If he was truly concerned about making the vision of a new and revived Prescott ranch come true, Deke didn't see it in his face. Instead, he saw awe and reverence and wide-eyed magic.

"Yeah, about the cows. That's part of why I needed to have you come here and walk the land with me."

*****

Pulling her car to the shoulder of the drive a distance from the barn, Marguerite shut off the ignition and put her head back against the seat, powering the window down to capture the breezes. A truck belonging to Powers, Mac's SUV, and another truck she didn't recognize filled the area in front of the house. She was early and since no one was in sight, she decided to give herself a few minutes of peace before taking a look at the ranch that Roxy had decided would be named Mac's Folly.

Closing her eyes brought no respite, though. Every time she did, she flashed to the memory of that contorted animal in the back of Deke's truck. Sadness warred with humiliation followed by anger. How dare he think that she could be responsible for this?

She'd been over the spraying reports time and time again. Nothing was unusual, nor were the amounts they used deadly in any way. But she knew without any doubt that what began as run-off from the vineyards ended up on Deke's land. If she had any doubt before, the downpours during crush confirmed it. Deeply carved gullies and trenches cut through the vines, and all of them pointed directly to Three Rivers Ranch.

Responsibility weighed heavily on her. Ultimately, she was the one who signed the reports, and she was the one who determined what needed to be sprayed and when. While Fernando was the vineyard manager, he left the chemistry, as he put it, up to her.

"I didn't take any of those fancy classes in school like you did, Margie." He'd been puffing on a cigar, a rare one in her presence and far enough from the vines that he deemed it acceptable. "Besides, you'll be doing it all yourself soon enough. Best that I stay out of this."

And he had. That meant all of the blame, if there was any, fell on her shoulders.

Could she have confused the measurements, giving Fernando the wrong instructions about what to mix and how much to apply? Even if she knew that what was reflected in the logs was correct, that didn't mean she hadn't erred when she gave directions.

Anger warred with regret. Again, the contorted red and white cow appeared in her mind. *Merde*, but she needed to block that vision out. If she did not, it would give her nightmares for years. Could she be to blame?

Non, she refused to think that way. She didn't make those kinds of mistakes. Other kinds, the kinds that involved good-looking cowboys, were ones she could confess. But she never made mistakes when it came to her work.

The other self-doubts were real, though. She'd placed her trust in Deke, and he'd shown her the error in that. He had been all too eager to demonstrate what he thought she'd done to his land, and to his animals. He had to know what seeing an animal like that would do to her.

Guilt, in waves so deep and so dark. They shared this, a commitment to the land and its creatures and keeping things safe. A commitment to old ways and professions that dated back to before this continent was settled.

The rap of knuckles on the hood of her car startled her.

"What are you doing parked over here?" Roxy's face appeared in the side window, cheerful and smiling as she leaned over. "Everyone else is parked on the other side, by the house."

She forced back her thoughts and gave a half-hearted attempt to match Roxy's enthusiasm.

"Everyone? Who else is here?" She opened the door and stepped out into the shade of the old barn.

"Mac, and he's working with a team to fix up this old place. Wait until you see the house – it's a mess. I honestly don't see how he thinks any of it can be salvaged, but that's not my problem. I'm perfectly happy living in my apartment over the restaurant. I don't need a big fancy house."

Turning towards the pasture, Roxy gestured towards the expansive fields surrounding the buildings, linking her arm with Marguerite's to pull her towards the open spaces. When they reached the meadow's edge, she said, "Besides, this isn't my dream, it's Mac's. I have my empire."

"Yes, indeed you do, my friend. But isn't it better to be sharing it with someone you love, someone who loves you beyond anyone else?" Marguerite leaned against a fence that was sturdier than she expected.

Roxy turned towards her in surprise. "Do you hear yourself? There's so much yearning in your voice, I'd think you're jealous."

"Moi? Je ne suis pas jaloux!"

"Marguerite, sweetie, your French is showing, and we both know that this only happens when you're upset."

"*Je ne suis pas* – I am not – upset. It happens that the last few days have been very trying. Fernando will be retiring at the end of the year. David is still very young and inexperienced. I am beginning to realize how much of the weight of the work will be falling solely on my shoulders." She bit back the rest, unwilling to explain her guilt. When a sniff escaped, she wasn't sure who was more surprised, Roxy or her.

"Hey, what's going on? You never cry, other than a tear at Serena and Dane's wedding, but we all had waterworks there. And not even a sniffle when Gabby announced she's pregnant." Roxy frowned as she paused. "What gives?"

Marguerite shook her head as she drew in a gasping breath, desperate to regain her composure. Things added up, one problem on top of the next, until her dream of peace and home here in the foothills crumbled around her. But Roxy couldn't know, couldn't even be allowed to guess. If she did, the whole girl tribe would swoop in, the very last thing she needed.

"It is nothing, *m'amie*, I assure you. If I feel sorry about anything, it is that we have less time together, the girl tribe, because of all of these men hanging around us." She waved a hand in the general direction of the trucks by the house.

She stared at Roxy, daring her friend to contradict her. In fact, the biggest piece of her sorrow was Deke. She hadn't imagined she'd miss his enlightening conversations, or wish that she could wrap herself in his arms on rainy nights. He couldn't have been in her life long enough to fill it, not to the degree that she was missing his presence.

When a small smile played at the corner of Roxy's lips, Marguerite was about to burst into another tirade. But Roxy turned abruptly and walked behind the barn.

"Come on, let's change vantage points. I know that Mac's most interested in doing something with the land closest to the house first. You can get a better view of it from over here. What do you think? Could this be a prime vineyard or what?"

Matching her friend's action and leaning against the fence, she emptied her mind of her worries. Plenty of hours strung ahead of her when she could worry without causing any comment. Instead, she examined the lay of the land, the pitch of the sun, and the composition of the acreage spreading to the base of the steep hill.

"This would make a wonderful vineyard, Roxy. The soil is of decent quality, even with the rocks. But grapes, ah yes, they appreciate a little stress. They would be happy here." Kicking loose rock and dirt, she bent down to take a sample in her fingers, feeling for texture. A little spark of excitement shivered through her. Here was another opportunity to build something new, a tribute to her friend.

"I thought it might work," Roxy said smugly. "I do pay attention when you lecture us endlessly, you know."

"I do not – " but she cut herself off when she noted the teasing grin on her friend's face. "All right, maybe I do lecture – but just a little bit, and just so that all of you are better educated about the finer aspects of wine. *Il est de ma responsabilité, tu sais.*"

That, and she might have been responsible for so much more, so much horror and loss. Could she have been that careless? One moment of inattention and the chemicals could have become the poison Deke believed her capable of applying with deliberation. While it wasn't intentional, it did look like he was right. She was at fault.

"You're getting that look again."

"What look?" But she knew. The concern on Roxy's face told her that she'd better mask her expression and be diligent about keeping up the façade.

Voices built behind them, male voices. Roxy turned towards them first, and the softened smile confirmed what Marguerite suspected – Mac was coming towards them. Another deep voice belonging to Powers and a voice she didn't recognize were involved in an intense discussion refereed by Mac.

Turning on her heel to greet the men, hand outstretched to meet the newcomer, she came face to face with the only man she didn't want to see.

Chapter 22

"I don't understand what the problem is."

Her longer legs ate up the ground, rounding the barn to her car with Roxy close behind. She didn't want to discuss it. When she caught sight of Deke's face, his eyes hooded and none of his usual easygoing charm in evidence, it had been enough. She wasn't sure if she wanted to beg forgiveness or burst into tears and run.

She chose a modified version of the latter, determined not to give way to the tumultuous emotions racing through her.

"Marguerite, goddammit, stop and tell me what the hell's gotten into you."

She couldn't, not now, and maybe not ever. But she also knew from experience that Roxy wouldn't allow her to brush off the reaction.

Coming to an abrupt halt brought Roxy crashing into her back. When the two of them caught each other and righted themselves, she saw the concern and confusion on her friend's face.

What was the American saying? The best defense is a good offense? She could be offensive.

"C'est que l'homme. C'est un salaud. Je ne veux plus jamais le revoir dans ma vie."

"Hold on, hold on. I get that you aren't happy with one of the guys. But he's a salad? My French doesn't extend much past curse words, I'm afraid."

Roxy's attempt at humor almost broke her down again.

"He is *un imbecile*."

"Okay, that I can get. Who's an imbecile? I know it can't be Mac. Did Powers do something to hurt Tess? Because if he did, I'll - "

"*Non, non, non*. Not Powers."

"Geno?"

"I do not know this Geno." Honestly, she hadn't even notice him. All she saw was the censure on Deke's face. It had every right to be there.

Roxy tightened a hand on her arm, and she looked at it, not sure when it had arrived there. She glanced up to find a speculative gleam on her friend's face.

"Ah, so it's Deke who's the imbecile." The knowing tone was almost too much, as was the sympathy in the expression.

"Rox, what's going on? I thought we were going to have a meeting and get Deke's and Marguerite's opinions on the land. Now where are the two of you off to?"

She didn't bother looking at Mac, despite the frustration in his voice. Roxy hadn't turned either. When the hand on her arm loosened, she knew her friend was giving her a choice.

Run or stay?

*****

"I still don't get it. Why did this happen again?"

"I'm not sure. One minute she was calling him names, and the next, Mac was there and there really wasn't any explanation that I could offer."

"But clearly something's wrong. Marguerite never acts like this. She's always so controlled."

"I am sitting here, you know." She slapped a hand on the table for emphasis, but the noise did nothing to startle Roxy, DK or Tess. They all eyed her carefully, like they were afraid she might break down or explode at any moment.

Yes, this was all so uncharacteristic of her. She grimaced as she realized she was only providing fuel for their fire, the one that she felt singe her whenever she considered Deke's harsh look.

He thought she did this, and deliberately. And she could offer no defense.

"Marguerite, sweetie, do you need something? Some wine? Maybe some ice cream?"

She laughed at that, the noise foreign because it wasn't her usual sound. In fact, she was on the verge of crying, and if she did, there would be a full night's worth of explaining to do.

Hiccupping in the next cackle, she reached for the proffered wine glass and took a long drink. The fact that she didn't swirl, sniff and sip as was her norm probably wasn't lost on her friends. They exchanged cautious glances, then leaned forward.

"Why don't you tell us what the problem is?" Tess scooted closer on the couch and put a tentative arm around her shoulders. DK reached across the space between chair and couch and squeezed a knee, and Roxy grabbed the wine bottle and poured more into her glass.

She sniffed. There was nothing she could do about it. Her emotions were too near the surface. When the silence stretched for minutes, she squared her shoulders and read the troubled demeanors around her.

"I think I may have made a mistake, a grave error." Trying to give more volume to her voice, she continued when no one replied. "And if I made this mistake, Deke has every right to despise me. I despise myself."

When three voices disagreed and attempted to reassure her, she raised a hand.

"I cannot tell you why, not yet. First, I must investigate this further. Then, if I am at fault, I must rectify the situation. Once this is finished, I will tell you about it."

*****

"I don't get it. What's with the death ray stares between you and Marguerite? I thought that the two of you were getting along."

He twisted the beer bottle in his fingers, leaving identical watery rings in the wood at intervals. He could feel Mac's gaze on him. Luckily he had escaped the continued scrutiny of Powers and Geno when those two decided to remain at the old house.

"Deke, I don't know you well enough – yet – to dig. That's not going to stop me though. If I have to, I'll call Vince and get him to come over and ream you."

Regret, anger, self-disgust. All lined up as neatly as the wet bottle rings on the scarred wood. In his silence, he hoped that a story on the blaring TVs across the bar would capture Mac's attention. And he hoped to hell that Vince wasn't already on his way.

The shopworn Mallory's waitress came by and arched an eyebrow at their empty bottles, popping her gum as she avoided idle chit-chat. She'd come to know their habits over the past few months. Mac almost always had a second. Deke, rarely.

Deke raised his finger and twirled it, and she left with a slap of fresh napkins on the table. And Mac's eyes darted to the napkins before frowning even harder in Deke's direction.

What could he say? Where could he start? He didn't want to implicate Marguerite, at least not until she had a chance to say something for herself. And he suspected that even if he only described the nature of the problem, Mac would connect the dots. He was a Hollywood pretty face, but no dummy in the brains department.

Mac filled the conversational void. "You know, I was kind of surprised that Marguerite came back this afternoon. She looked like she was about to jump in her car and roar away. Roxy wasn't holding her back. It seems that she returned because she wanted to."

Deke nodded, deep in thought. The pounding ache in his head that started the moment he saw Marguerite was now louder than a stampede of cattle across open meadow. The hurt he saw in her face when she'd spun around and faced him, followed by regret and self-loathing, might have cut him more than it did her.

He didn't have any right to expose her to the calamity up close and personal. He still wasn't proud of what he'd done, driving over to her house with a truck bed full of grief.

"Yeah, she'd got a lot of class that way. Doesn't leave a fight, and doesn't back down, even when she's wrong."

"What's she wrong about?"

He hesitated once more. He needed to apologize to her. And he needed to give her a chance to apologize to him and come clean. The expression on her face, recoiling in guilt as she'd eyed the contorted animal, told him she now knew.

He was right about the chemicals. She had a problem. And there was no doubt in her mind now that something at the vineyard or the winery was the cause.

Their waitress returned with no more words than before, setting their drinks on the table with an audible clunk and whisking away the empties. Shaking his head, he slid the fresh cold beer into his hands, rolling it back and forth and allowing the condensation to pool under his hands. He couldn't get her out of his mind, sorry once more that he'd let his temper overrule his better judgment.

She'd had tears in those violet eyes at the Prescott Ranch, he would have bet his prize steer on it. When she returned to the group, Mac and Roxy with their heads bent in a heated exchange behind her, she'd straightened her shoulders and settled into a defiant stare. Nodding her head, she waited. He had nodded back. What else could he do? Her face dissolved slowly from waves of hurt to a mask of assumed indifference.

Mac and Roxy stopped their argument, Mac next to Deke and Roxy standing close by Marguerite. Roxy shot a look at her friend, but her gaze was locked on Deke's. And he only saw Mac's questioning glances in the periphery of his vision.

When no one said anything, Mac finally clapped his hands. Roxy jumped, intent as she was on Marguerite, and shot Mac a reproachful look. Deke ignored them both, and it appeared that Marguerite did too.

The woman did things to him, angered his easygoing energy, riled up his need to protect, and poked at his libido, all at the same time. What if they'd met under different circumstances? Without the pall of the poisonings between them, what could have happened instead?

Mac followed his clap with fast words. "So, what do the two of you think? Cattle ranch? Vineyard? Exotic animals? Exotic grapes? Orchards of heirloom fruits? Any ideas?"

Silence stretched yet again. He wouldn't be the first to blink. He suspected that neither would Marguerite, which left them at something of an impasse.

"Come on you two. I know you both have some ideas. Wait, is the land so bad that we can't do anything with it? Oh hell, Rox, you were right. I bought a dump. Is there a toxic waste site here that no one told me about?"

Mac's attempt at humor did little to lessen the tension, at least as far as Deke was concerned. Marguerite didn't twitch. Her haughty expression would have better belonged in a diplomatic court or staring down her minions on some age-old estate.

Roxy broke in. "Now Mac sweetie, I'm sure this is a wonderful piece of property." Her saccharin sweet voice was so unlike her, Deke almost smiled, knowing she was aiming to loosen the ropes of tension binding the whole situation. On the edge of the group, Powers watched, arms crossed and frowning, while Geno leaned up against the tailgate of his truck, the trace of a smile on his face saying more than words. He was enjoying the show.

Enough already. Nothing would be solved today, and nothing would be gained by continuing the standoff and expecting that one of them would give.

He opened his mouth, intent on his appraisal. "This would make great ranch land."

And was shocked when Marguerite's statement coincided with his. "A vineyard would be perfect here."

They glared at one another again, surprise now stronger than stubbornness. And each opened their mouths to argue.

"Hey, that's great – wonderful in fact. Look, we can do both. Rox, what do you say we leave the details for another day? I'm sure you and Marguerite have a lot you haven't had time to discuss." The pointed look he gave her wasn't lost on Deke, as he continued, "And I'm going to grab the guys here and head over to Mallory's, because there's a lot we need to discuss about the property."

"Deke? Hey man? You with me here?"

Startled, he looked up to find Mac eying him with wry amusement, the noise of Mallory's rushing back around him.

"Something on your mind, Deke? I promise you, I can keep secrets."

Chapter 23

"I can't believe October's nearly over, can you?"

Yes, she could believe it. Work wasn't lessening just because the grapes were in. There were daily measurements of the sugar and alcohol in each large bin of grape juice, and punch-downs of grapes, and pumping over juice in place of punch-downs in the steel tanks. Once the sugar in the juice had fed the yeast to turn into alcohol, barrels were filled with the fermenting end product and racked to continue the aging process.

In short, autumn was never a quiet time of year.

But she was glad she'd made time today for the girl tribe. It was a rare occasion, all six of them together without the men and boys who made up the ever-growing extended family. And they welcomed her without question or concern.

Marguerite shook her head. They should be concerned. How did she lose a container of one of the most noxious herbicides around? A controlled substance, no less. It made products that homeowners could buy look tame in comparison.

"Marguerite? Earth to Marguerite?"

She shook her head again, trying to rid herself of the concern, even if only for a few hours. Gabby sat on her right, blooming with the glow of pregnancy and happiness.

"I am sorry, Gabriela, I was lost in my own thoughts. What was it you wanted?"

Gabby laughed, giving her hand a squeeze.

"I was commenting that it's almost November. The year is flying by. Before you know it, it will be DK and

Vince's fairytale wedding. You're standing up for DK, right?"

That made Marguerite smile. As close as her friends were, they were also very different. Gabby and Rick took their boys to Lake Tahoe on a quick getaway vacation and came back married. Serena spent endless hours on minutiae for her Hawaiian destination wedding to Dane, worrying the details until she'd driven herself and everyone around her crazy, and in the end there wasn't a single hitch, not a one.

DK was as calm as could be, despite having her large family ready to descend like locusts for the event. She'd set out her expectations so clearly that all Marguerite had to do was place orders and agree to the wonderful maid of honor dress DK's artistic sense guaranteed was perfect for her.

Her friend hadn't even blinked or backed down when the mother of the bride called and insisted that the wedding needed to take place in a church and in Chicago, her birthplace. She was proud of DK for standing firm. She knew what it cost her, because DK got the call when she was sitting in the winery office.

To Gabby, she confirmed, "Yes, and it is my pleasure. Granted, I have not served as a maid of honor before, but I had assumed that it would be much more work than DK is allowing. The only thing she hasn't told me is who Vince asked to stand up as his best man."

Gabby's happy smile drooped a little as she looked around for the rest of the girl tribe. Tess's backyard had turned to fall brilliance, with the leaves on its fruit trees changing colors, the roses providing a last big blast of showy blooms, and perennial beds offering seed heads in intriguing shapes and sizes. Tess and Serena were examining the seeds on a large-leaved plant with an abundance of gestures and exclamations on Serena's part. DK and Roxy laughed from the kitchen, in charge of the finger food that comprised the menu. Gabby appeared to be stuck and looking for a way out.

"I'm sure she'll tell you, maybe tonight. The guys discussed it already, that I know, and Vince's made his decision. I guess I'm kind of surprised DK didn't mention it yet."

"Didn't mention what?" DK put a tray of aromatic appetizers on a side table laden with napkins and plates and turned back to the two. Roxy followed her out with another tray that shared space with the first, waving Tess and Serena in from the garden.

"Com'on, food's ready. And you don't want the hot stuff to get cold or the cold stuff to warm up."

In the mild fuss of women reaching for plates and food, she wasn't fooled. Gabby knew, and it didn't appear that Gabby thought it was such a great idea, whomever Vince had chosen. That gave her an inkling of who the best man would be.

As everyone settled, Marguerite walked from woman to woman offering red or white wine. The chatter continued with no particular topic at the top of the list, and she waited until she was seated herself with food and wine before taking advantage of a brief pause in the conversational flow.

"DK, you haven't told us. Who did Vince select to be his best man?"

She swore DK paled a little under her freckles, and Roxy's tighter glance between the two said that she too knew already. Tess and Serena were quiet, out of site beyond her peripheral vision, but she swore that the tension in the breezy gazebo notched up more than such an innocuous question would warrant.

"You know, it was Vince's choice. Yes, he did consult me, and at the time I thought it was a wonderful idea." DK stopped and put a thumbnail to her lips in consternation, then looked at what she was doing and returned her hand to clutch her half-empty plate.

Her stomach flipped once, and she set aside her full plate in favor of a larger sip of wine. It passed her lips untasted, even as she fought to be serene and plaster a non-judgmental expression on her face. She did want to disappoint DK or cause her any pain or remorse. She had enough of that herself for the whole girl tribe.

"Rip the bandage off, DK." Roxy took her own gulp of wine, setting the glass and plate aside and leaning forward.

DK bit her lip before answering. "I'm sorry. The timing on this is all wrong. I didn't intend to tell you on a fun evening like this." She looked around at the other women in apology. "Vince picked Deke to be his best man."

She forced herself not to flinch, taking a demure sip of wine this time and settling back deeper into the plush pillows as the wicker chair creaked slightly in the sudden hush. It seemed that even the birds and bugs understood that this moment called for silence.

Her friends waited, each displaying a different level of worry or concern. True, she could unleash her temper and ask why him, of all the men that Vince knew. Then her mind flashed back to the contorted beast, its red and white coat gleaming from the rain in the back of Deke's truck as its open eyes seemed to stare at her in accusation. It killed her temper before it had much of an opportunity to rise.

"I am glad that Vince has found such a good friend to represent him on this important day." Even to herself, her words sounded stilted and too formal. Her accent deepened with the emotion as her voice dropped to a whisper. "You honor me by choosing me for your special day. Thank you."

No one said anything, expressions of surprise replacing concern as one by one, the women regarded her thoughtfully. Only DK still looked worried.

"I'm still sorry, Marguerite. At the time, I thought it was a great idea. You and Deke seemed to be hitting it off, and I thought, what the hell, maybe they'll be another match around here." She bit off whatever she was going to say next and waved her hand as if to dismiss it. "Anyway, if you think that you can't do it now, I'll understand."

DK was making it so easy to back out, and she was tempted. No one would think the worse of her.

But she would think the worse of herself. Her own inattention had caused this problem. She had only herself to blame. The fact that Deke, and who knows how many others, blamed her too was only right. She was somehow at fault. She would not ruin DK's wedding with her own cowardice.

"Thank you, but I want to do this for you. Consider it my gift for you." She added a practiced smile. "Well, that, and the wonderful bridal shower I plan to throw for you. And the setting of the winery decked out to spotlight you gloriously on your special day." Adding an impish smirk that she hoped would fool everyone, she said, "And the racy and completely inappropriate bridal gift I've already chosen."

DK slumped in her chair and let out a long whoosh of air. Around her, the other women started talking again in low voices. Only Roxy still stared at her with a puzzled look, one that said sooner or later, she was going to demand Marguerite provide her with an explanation.

Chapter 24

The whir of machinery came through the open window, its few inches of screened space taking advantage of the mid-fall warmth. Soon it would be cold and rainy – at least he hoped so.

Deke slapped the file shut, grateful that he had found a day when no one and nothing on the land needed his outdoor attention. He was behind on paperwork and computer entries, given his twin distractions of thoughts of Marguerite coupled with the wolf pack's sudden need to babysit him at every turn.

Mac had finally let go of the bone at Mallory's when Powers and Geno appeared. Other than an odd look from Powers, Deke felt like he'd escaped relatively unscathed that evening, grateful that Mac's attention was diverted to how best to save as much of the crumbling ranch infrastructure as possible.

Spinning to his computer, his eyes ranged to the pasture in the distance, the one where his hand had discovered that cow in its death throes. There was nothing anyone could do at that point, and Deke was about to send the man for a rifle to put the animal out of its misery when it had taken the decision out of his hands. One final ragged breath, and it was gone.

And one impulsive decision to give in to temper, to show her exactly what she was doing to innocent animals, had proved to be disastrous too. He hadn't had a chance to apologize, and he though often about going over to the winery to find her and say – what?

He was sorry he'd exposed her to the end result of her carelessness, was that it? Something told him that she hadn't poisoned anything deliberately. The shock and anguish she exhibited didn't line up with someone who had patent disregard for the consequences of their actions.

The knock sounding on his door had him spin to face the opening. Something in the posture of the man filling its frame told Deke this wasn't going to be good news.

"Hey Carl, come in. I thought you were planning to clear the dead trees on the trail today."

The man lifted a bottle of water to his lips, his eyes still on Deke. When he finished his drink, he moved forward and dropped into the guest chair, slouching low.

"Yeah, I started on that. Then I got the weirdest call from my dad. Something about maybe needing to leave for his retirement earlier than he originally thought, and what did I think about that, and could I help him with some banking things. It went to voicemail because I was out of range, and maybe it was a good thing it did."

He took another swig of water, emptying the bottle. Crushing it and replacing the cap, he tossed it towards the trashcan in the corner and rimmed it. Both men stared as the bottle fell on top of the papers inside with barely a sound.

Deke broke the ensuing silence. "You know we recycle, right?"

Carl flashed up at him in sharp surprise, then got a rueful smile on his face. "Sorry man, yeah. I just have a lot on my mind." He sat forward, taking the ball cap off his head and scrubbing at his dark hair before replacing the hat and lifting his eyes to Deke. "I need some sage advice."

He wasn't sure how wise he felt these days.

"What kind of advice?"

The man shifted again, his agitation now more apparent. "My dad's still got this crazy idea about retiring to Vegas, though what the appeal is, I don't know. He never talked about it before that I can recall. In fact, I never thought he'd retire."

Deke leaned back and put an elbow on the chair's arm, propping his chin on his hand to wait for whatever came next.

Carl leaned back and looked out the window for a time before continuing in a quieter voice. "His health isn't good. He's got this cough that won't quit, and when I ask him if he's been to the doctor about it, he says that it will all go away once he's in Nevada, like that's the cure for everything. He's still smoking those smelly cigars too." He shook his head and brought his gaze back to meet Deke's.

"I'm really worried about him. When I ask him what he plans to use for money to fund his retirement, he cackles – there's no other way to describe it – and says that he's got it covered, oh boy, does he have it covered. And I'm almost quoting him on that."

"Maybe he's saved well over the years." Other than the cough, Deke wasn't sure he saw the problem yet.

Carl waved a dismissive hand. "Yeah, he's saved recently, but there were plenty of years when my brothers and sisters and I were younger and he didn't have anything to save. When he and Mom split up, he paid child support. It wasn't cheap. They never divorced, since it was against Mom's religion. But he had his own household, such as it was. That isn't cheap either." Carl paused to shake his head in disbelief. "No, he might have some money saved, but it definitely isn't enough, even with Social Security, to fund the kind of lifestyle he's talking about."

Deke was concerned now. This sounded nothing like the Fernando he'd come to know over the years, a careful and thoughtful person who wasn't prone to craziness.

"Is he planning on buying a mansion or something?"

Carl shook his head again, putting a hand to rub the back of his neck as tired worry crossed his features. "Not a mansion, but you should see the house he's planning to get. He showed it to me online, and it wasn't cheap. Said he could get it right now, and wanted to snap it up before anyone bought it out from under him. Then in his message, he said that he bought it, got the contract signed and everything. And that since the house was now his and he could move in any time, he thought he'd go by the end of this month."

Did Marguerite know this yet? Deke's first thought was that this would leave her in something of a bind. She relied on Fernando, just as he relied on his trusted long-term hands. Without him, she'd be responsible for even more work in the vineyard.

"How'd you respond to him?"

"I haven't yet. That's the great thing about a voicemail, you don't have to blurt something out right away. The thing is, I'd feel a whole lot better about this if I knew his health was okay, if I knew he was okay for money, and if I understood why he feels like he needs to go right away. That's not like him. He's always so responsible towards the people he works for. Because that's part of it, man." Carl paused and leaned forward.

"In the message, he told me not to say anything about this, because he planned to leave without telling anyone."

*****

He chewed the sandwich slowly, not tasting the filling his mother had selected for today's gourmet treat. She as on another kick to bring what she considered to be healthier food back into his diet, and this included throwing out all of the packaged meat products he bought at the grocery store. What she replaced them with he wasn't sure, and he didn't have the energy to ask right now. The flavors were bland and unvarying in his mouth.

"Isn't that tasty? And so good for you too." Emie stood in front of a cabinet with the door open, straightening his plates and glasses inside. She peeked out occasionally, nodding in approval when he picked up the second half and took a bite.

Deke paused with his mouth full and made a face at the sandwich as the absolute lack of any taste registered with him. Setting it down, he worked to chew and swallow around dryness and took a long drink from the water glass at his place. Then he stood and walked towards the trash, dumping the remainder in before opening the dishwasher to deposit the plate.

"Ma, thanks for lunch. I guess I wasn't as hungry as I thought."

She patted his cheek and he felt sheepish telling that fib.

"Oh, I know you didn't like it. That's okay I guess." She put her hands in her hips and looked up at him from her diminutive height. "You're a grown man, and you make your own choices now. You can't blame a mother for trying though." She smiled at him, her grin warm and wry. Then she turned back to the cabinets and went to work reorganizing the next one.

Her voice was muffled by the wood in the way when she said, "So I haven't seen that nice young woman around here in quite a while. Marguerite? What's going on with her?"

He froze. He wasn't sure he'd been able to think there was anything worse than his mother deciding to reorganize his kitchen and feed him her healthy food, but this was it. He didn't need her help in remembering every little thing he knew about his witch, either.

"Ah, she's just a friend, Ma."

His mother hummed inside the cabinet. He knew that hum, having heard it many a time over the years. She didn't believe him and she wasn't going to let him get away with brushing off the topic.

"Now Deke, you know I'm no teenage virgin here. I know why she was here in your house in the oh-dark-early hours of the morning. And I'm not judging. No, in fact, I'm applauding." She closed the cabinet door with a snap that made him stand up straighter. "So why haven't I seen more of her recently? She seemed like a very nice young woman."

Despite his own concerns about Marguerite's guilt, he didn't think it was right to badmouth her to his family. In fact, he still hadn't had that conversation with Jake, the one he kept meaning to bring up whenever they were together. If Marguerite wasn't involved in the poisoning, who was? Perhaps someone other than him needed to investigate.

Emie eyed him with open curiosity and a smile so wide that he wondered why her face didn't cramp up.

"We had something of a disagreement, that's all. It's not something that can be fixed easily."

She closed a surprisingly strong hand on his arm and dragged him towards the kitchen table. With a small shove, one that reminded him of every time she planned to grill him when he was a child, she pushed him back in his chair and dropped herself into the one next to it. Then she took his hands in hers and gave a squeeze.

"Now why don't you tell me all about it? Royan said – "

"You discussed this was Uncle Royan?" Embarrassment wouldn't even cover his feelings about that. Appalled, even.

"Why yes, of course, Royan's worried about things around here. He said that you took that last dead cow over to the winery, to show her. Now why would you do a thing like that, exposing her to that sadness?"

He pulled his hands free and stood, almost knocking over the chair in his hurry to gather his thoughts before things went completely sideways. Trying to distract Emie, he blurted out the only thing that came to mind.

"When did you discuss this with Royan? You and he are very chummy all of a sudden. I didn't know you were tight with him."

Emie looked uncertain for a moment, glancing down at her hands instead of meeting his eyes. When she looked back up, there was a trace of defiance in her face.

"Of course I'm chummy with the man. I've known him longer than I've known you, I'll remind you. And I'm old but not dead. Royan and I are – dating." She bit her lip right after uttering the last word.

He wasn't sure what to worry about now, his mother on the prowl to lean everything she could about his own situation, or his mother on the prowl with his uncle. The last idea bordered on gross.

"Ah, don't you find Royan to be a little – odd?" There was no more polite way to term it, as he remembered the dirty coveralls, poor hygiene and chew that he spat everywhere.

"Now honey, he's just lonely. Debby's been gone all these years, and he's had no one to take care of him. And no reason to take care of himself, if we're being honest. His girls don't give a damn about him. The only one who seems to check on him is you." Her face softened as she watched him.

He felt dirty in more ways than one right now. He'd been courting Royan's attention more for a chance to bid on his land than anything in the last year. And while he loved the old man, he hadn't been exactly open and welcoming for holidays and such. Uncle Royan didn't make for a nice party atmosphere.

He didn't know how to respond to Emie.

She shifted and stood to cross the room, stopping when she was next to him. She patted his cheek and her eyes twinkled.

"You are a good boy. I know you need his land to add to your legacy. I understand this. Royan does too, you know." Her voice softened to a whisper. "But neither one of us wants to you go it alone, son. You deserve a woman beside you, someone who'll treat you with respect and treasure you. That's what I had with your father, believe it or not, gruff old coot that he was. That's what Royan had with Debby. And that's what we both want for you."

Chapter 25

The laptop hummed under her fingers, and Marguerite paused in her typing to stretch and gather her next thoughts. She had been trying to recreate ever step in the vineyard processes that had anything to do with the missing herbicide. Her calendar, the logs for the vineyard, purchasing records – all were strewn across her desk. She'd been working on this on and off for the last three days, and she wasn't any closer to an answer.

Fernando had been little help. Much to her annoyance, she had a hard time tracking him down. It seemed that he was never where anyone remembered seeing him last. It took her a full day to catch up with him.

When she finally found him drawing wine from a steel tank and measuring its alcohol, she questioned him about what events and activities he remembered. He'd been short on words or explanations. In fact, he didn't even meet her eyes for the first few minutes, and when she called him on it, he surprised her.

"I'm just not feeling up to long discussions today, okay Margie?" He coughed violently and suddenly appeared older than she'd seen him looking recently.

"Would you like to sit down?" She grabbed a folding chair from the nearby stack and opened it, placing it within reach of the older man. He waved it away and turned to leave the tank room.

"Fernando, are you all right?" She couldn't keep the concern out of her voice, and when he stopped but didn't turn around, she started to worry in earnest.

"Nah, I'm fine. Just a little autumn chill in my bones."

Autumn chill? They were in the middle of a fall heat wave and he wore a shirt with the sleeves rolled up and no jacket.

"*Vraiment?* Then why are you not dressed more appropriately?"

He waved a dismissive hand over his shoulder, starting once more for the door leading to the vineyards. "I'm fine, no worries. You just go back to whatever you were doing and leave me alone."

The bite to his final words stopped her from following him. He had sounded almost angry, and she had no reason why.

The screen on her laptop flipped from the document she'd been typing to the screensaver. Its words, *'Vin pour les ages',* wine for the ages, twirled slowly in the center of the screen. The darkness around it reflected her face, the worry of her thoughts obvious in the lines of her frown. The room behind her fell into deeper contrast, all expect for a brighter spot where none should be. Perhaps her screen had become dirty? She rubbed her fingers across the screen, but the image remained.

It was more of a cloud of light than a specific shadow. It lit the corner of her office, hiding the file cabinet and part of the photo on her back wall. The form appeared to be a woman, an older woman, and it was holding out an arm with a finger pointing. And it looked angry.

Marguerite jumped up from the chair and spun around. She planned to give whomever was playing tricks on her a piece of her mind. The winery was no place for *ces escapades*, not when work needed to be done.

But there was no one there.

Her heart raced, and she felt the adrenalin pump fast in her veins. The scare made her palms damp and she wiped them quickly on her jeans. This was a figment of her imagination, she was sure of it. Examining the corner of the room, she saw nothing that could have been reflected this image to her computer. In fact, the room was dark for the most part, since evening had long since fallen around her.

Slowing her breathing, she started to feel silly. Here she was, a grown woman, jumping at shapes that were all in her mind. She was concentrating too hard on this problem. She felt responsible, and it was doing strange things to her thinking and her vision. There was nothing to be scared of.

But when she turned back to the slowly spinning words on her laptop, she cringed. Because there, in the corner of her office, the image was reflected once more. And now it was as clear as her own face. It was the witch, and she looked furious as she raised her accusatory finger and shook it in rebuke, shouting something that thankfully couldn't be heard.

*****

Never had she been so grateful to see the lights of her porch guiding the way up the steps to the security of her home. When she'd slammed the laptop shut and spun to probe the darkness again, something urged her to grab her things. She'd locked the office door with shaking fingers, grateful for the lights of the tasting room and the patio outside to lead her way. She fumbled and dropped the car keys twice before she got the right one in the ignition and turned it. When the car fired immediately, she almost put her forehead on the steering wheel and wept in gratitude.

She drove home on autopilot, her mind trying to process what she didn't believe, that the ghost of the witch had taken up residence in her office and was pointing her finger directly at Marguerite. Not that she could understand what the ghost shouted in her direction, but she had a fair idea of why it was angry.

She had poisoned the land. Not intentionally, but that didn't matter in the end. And the witch was determined to protect it.

Marguerite sprinted for the steps and was proud of herself for only bobbling the front door key once before getting it in the lock and turned. The lights burst on when she slammed her hand on the wall switches inside, hitting every one of them within reach, just as she slammed the front door shut and locked it. Then she leaned back against it and let her eyes range slowly over the open space, willing every shadow into the light and every dark corner revealed.

There was nothing here. Nothing and no one had followed her home. She was safe here. She was alone. The ragged breath she pulled in and pushed out did not calm her as it usually did.

She treasured her freedom, her independence. At the moment, though, being alone did not seem to be such an appealing idea. It would be nice to hear another human voice. It would be even better to have a warm piece of skin to hang on to.

Before she could consciously resist it, her mind snapped to Deke. It wasn't just any human she wanted. It was him. When had this happened? Her attraction to him was inexplicable. She had no reason to rely on him for anything.

Taking another cleansing breath, she shook her head and focused on the path to her kitchen and the bottle of wine that she'd opened last night, a wonderful Zinfandel from a neighboring winery that was almost as good as her own. A glass of wine, perhaps something light to eat, and an early shower and bed would sustain her. Things would feel better in the morning and her mind would be clearer. Tomorrow, she would consider what she could do to make amends.

Her boots echoed hollowly on the wood floor, the sound cut off abruptly when she crossed the rug, resuming when she was on wood again. Lights burned brightly, and she considered continuing on to her bedroom and bathroom and turning on those immediately. Darkness did not seem to be her friend tonight, and the occasional animal scurrying outside added to her jumpiness. Detouring for the mp3 player and speakers on the bookshelf, she selected an instrumental piece and raised the volume high to drown out any outdoor sounds.

By the time she had a wineglass in hand, filled it, and took a longer than usual first sip, she had almost convinced herself that she was, in fact, being foolish. There were no such things as ghosts. There was no witch, merely a legend about a child who had probably died in the woods not long after her unfortunate parents. Whatever she thought she saw in her office was the result of too much worry and long hours.

Thinking that some cheese would be a good idea to fill her empty stomach, she turned towards the refrigerator and stopped with her hand outstretched for the door handle.

The witch had aged now, an old crone with a bent form visible even in the kitchen's bright lights. Her hair rose around her head as if she had her fingers in a light socket, static seeming to jump between the ends. Her eyes were crazed, wildly accusing, and her hands were both raised, fingers pointing at Marguerite.

Blinking did not make the image go away. In fact, it seemed to take on a solid form, one that could be touched and felt. Marguerite pulled back her outstretched hand and tucked it across her body to attempt to stop its shaking. She couldn't swallow, couldn't speak, and couldn't draw her eyes away from the creature. Of its own volition, her hand reached out again to test what her head told her couldn't be there.

That's when she heard it, the voice rasping and cold as the middle of winter. A chill ran through her bones when she registered the words.

"Vous détruisez ma terre!"

'You are destroying my land.'

She couldn't make sense of the vision any more than she could absorb the hatred in the words. Marguerite dropped the wineglass, slipped on the spilled red on the floor as she tried to get her feet moving, and ran for the front door.

*****

It wasn't that late. He'd convinced himself that what he wanted to do warranted an evening social call. Not that they'd been all that social recently, but he hoped that might change.

He wanted to apologize. Pure and simple, that was it. And if it meant that they could talk out their problem and find an equitable solution, perhaps he could do something about the need he felt to wrap his arms around her and feel those lush lips under his again.

It looked like all the lights were on in her cabin when he rounded the curve in her driveway, and he frowned. This wasn't something he intended to discuss with her if she had company. But hers was the only car parked by the place, and he pulled in next to it and shut off the engine.

When he expected the silence of the rural night to rush into the void, he was surprised to hear music, very loud jazz the almost hid the racket of tree frogs chirping. Through the window, he thought he caught sight of Marguerite, wineglass in hand, dancing or some such thing in the kitchen.

Clearly she was trying to have a relaxing evening, alone and without company. He hated to ruin her few hours of leisure. He doubted she had much more of it than he did, and he knew how precious he considered his tranquility.

It was best to get this over with, though. Waiting another day didn't seem right. He wasn't sure she knew about Fernando's intention to disappear into the night. He was sorry he'd brought his anger to her door. And he definitely wanted to see if there was anything left of their mutual attraction.

He eased out of the truck, the lights from the porch and the house doing a more than adequate job of shining a path to her front door. What if she unleashed her anger on him again? No, he couldn't allow that. He would be his most charming, his most convincing, and he would change her opinion of him.

His boot hit the bottom step before he could talk himself out of doing this.

A piercing shriek stopped him midstride, his foot raised and partway to the second tread. Before his mind could process what he heard and send a message to his feet to move, the front door flew open and Marguerite streaked out, a hand over her mouth and red covering the front of her shirt and jeans.

She tumbled down the stairs and ran straight into him. He doubt she saw him, because she cried out again when his arms came around her and he could hear panic in her tone. He couldn't stop their fall, the slow motion of impending disaster only giving him time to thank the gods that he was only one step up the flight to the porch.

The path came up quickly under him, and air left him in a wheeze when he landed, given resonance by the words he wanted to ask her. What happened? Of course, it came out as an unrecognizable grunt as she landed on top of him. Points of gravel made themselves known along the bones in his back, and his mind processed the pain in a fog. His arms tightened, holding her closely as her attempts to free herself lessened.

They lay on the path for minutes, how long a time he couldn't count as he caught his breath. With each inhale, he drew in the spicy fragrance that he associated with her. Each exhale dropped her body back completely on his, the pressure an exquisite form of torture. He'd been right all along. She was the perfect armful.

He registered the sound of her panting in his ear right before she put both hands on his chest and shoved herself upright. Straddling him now, she pushed the curtain of curls back over her head and exposed her face to the murkier light reflecting from the ground around them.

Her eyes were huge in her face, the terror clear. She glanced around, eyes darting quickly, and the rapid clenching of her hands matched the jerky movements of her gaze. And she was babbling.

"La sorcière est ici. Elle est dans la cuisine. Elle est en colère. Je ne le fais pas."

Her rapid words drifted over him and he struggled to make sense of it. Something about the witch. The witch cooking dinner? No, that wasn't it.

She glanced back up the stairs and a full body shiver moved through her and into him. Whatever had terrified her was bigger than her famed control.

His breathing returned to what would have to pass for normal. There was no way his body wasn't going to react to full on contact from this gorgeous woman, one he'd thought about for months and had enjoyed only once. It was that once that he couldn't forget.

Gradually, she stopped babbling, her words ending in a hiccup as she drew in three big breaths and exhaled them just as hard. That pressed her down on him further, a sensation he wasn't going to complain about.

She focused on him now, the fright in her gaze slowly replaced by bewilderment. No doubt her eyes were hiding any violet color now, and he wondered if she could tell what her position was doing to him. Like it or not, whether the situation was appropriate or not, some parts of him were enjoying this unexpected pleasure of her sitting on him like he was the finest show horse around.

"Deke." The stutter of that single syllable, her tone astonished, made him smile. He didn't even fight it.

"If you didn't want me to come knocking on your front door, Princess, all you had to do was say so, you know." His gruff drawl had little to do with intention. It seemed his voice was as effected as the rest of him by her close presence.

"Deke," she said again, with more puzzlement this time. Then she seemed to realize that she was sitting on him. If she recognized that he had developed a hard-on, leaving no doubt about how he felt about holding her, he couldn't say.

She almost jumped sideways in her haste to get off him, landing on one knee and quickly scrambling to her feet as she stared down at him. Hair hid her face from the light, so he had no idea what she was thinking. With her body gone, he took stock of the sharp pinches and aches already erupting along his back. A couple of spots were particularly painful, the sting telling him that a rock or two had drawn blood.

Still, he didn't want to move, not yet. Not when he could watch her body, even if he couldn't read her eyes. Not when the tightness in his jeans would be a dead giveaway that he wasn't as cool about this as he let his words indicate. So he lay there and waited.

Her breathing slowed to a more normal pattern and she pushed the waves of hair back and twisted them at her neck with an unconscious gesture. Her face was as cool and distant as her voice when she finally spoke.

"Deke, what are you doing here?"

*****

At the witch's words, she'd thought of nothing other than escape. The old crone would destroy her, she was sure of it. When the grasping claws of old hands reached for her, her mind froze as she did the only thing possible. She fled.

The impact that thwarted her flight knocked the breath out of her, but it did nothing to stop the torrent of panicked words flowing through her brain. The witch would get her, and she had to race away. But strong arms anchored her, foiling her attempts to get up. Slowly, reason seeped back into her system, and with it, the knowledge that she was being restrained by something that wasn't ghostly. In fact, it was undoubtedly and completely human and very male.

Powerful thighs supported her weight easily, while the muscled chest under her hands was a surprising cushion for her own softness. She felt safe here. Instinct had her hands traveling to the belt on a narrow waist.

Mon dieu but she was a mess. All she could think about now was how arousing this was, laying on top of a man who held her like she was something precious. His open shirt collar was mere inches from her face, and she had the sudden urge to place her lips there to find the pulse point she was sure would be beating a rapid staccato rhythm in time with her own.

It took a moment for her to look up into his face, and when she did, she quickly pushed herself upright. Had she conjured him, the only man who had been on her mind these past days and weeks? That was worse, or better, depending. He sparked every nerve ending to life, heating her blood to boiling when she'd been chilled to ice moments before.

He wasn't immune to her, of that she was certain. His breathing was labored, and she was sure it had nothing to do with what happened moments ago. No, his eyes were burning in the light cast down the steps from her open front door, and she could see the deep blue reflecting her own heated thoughts. His body shifted under hers, and she felt the hard ridge of arousal.

When she said his name, he smiled. It was that easy-going smile that made it seem like he had all the time in the world and no cares. What he said next made her blink. Princess, he called her Princess. Did he believe that she had deliberately thrown herself at him? Jumping off him cost her a knee that was possibly skinned under her jeans, but it was a small price to pay.

Getting to her feet cost her more, both in energy and loss. She wanted nothing more than to stretch out on top of him again, bring his face to hers, and get lost in the sea blue of his eyes and his lazy smile.

Pulling herself together was an effort, but there was no way she would let him see how he affected her. It was inappropriate. It was lethal – he was lethal.

Knotting her hair into some semblance of its usual order, she schooled her face into its polite mask and asked the obvious question.

"Deke, what are you doing here?"

He frowned up at her without responding, rolling to his side and rising to his feet, only pausing once with what appeared to be a grimace. When his back came into view, she saw the damage their fall had inflicted.

"You are bleeding."

He looked over his shoulder as if trying to see his back, then his eyes moved up to hers.

"It's a small price to pay to help a lady in distress."

His tone made her tremble inside, the sensation of sinking quickly replaced by heat. But she would not let him know how much he affected her.

"I am not in distress."

He turned to her fully then, making a point to look at her hands clenched in front of her. Despite her ability to control her face, her hands were trembling. She broke them apart and shoved them into the back pockets of her jeans. Then she realized that he was staring at her breasts, and she brought her arms back around to cross over them. She wanted to look anywhere but at him.

"What happened to you?" The sharp harshness in his tone made her eyes snap back to him, but he was looking her up and down, worry lines appearing on his forehead. His hair hung loose. She hadn't noticed that before, probably because he had been flat on his back at the base of her steps. Her fingers itched to smooth it away from his face, and she tightened her fists to keep the shaking from returning, but for a different reason now.

The rolled up sleeves of his well-loved pale denim shirt made the sinewy structure of his forearms appear even more powerful. Those arms were rock solid, to that she could attest. It was funny that when they'd had their brief thing before, she hadn't allowed herself time to appreciate his many fine physical qualities in detail. With effort, she dropped her arms and rolled her neck to release her tension.

"It is not important."

Willing herself to relax, she planted her feet wider. She waved her hands as if to shoo him away, and he quickly mirrored her posture, set his feet apart like he was planning to stay for a while, and crossed his arms on his chest.

His shirt pulled tighter with his movement, and her fingers tingled with the memory of what that chest felt like only minutes before. When he winced, she thought about the cuts on his back, the ones that were deep enough to bleed. He had broken her fall. Without him, she might have broken her neck.

It was the least she could do, the polite thing to do. Her *maman* would be appalled if she sent him away without proper thanks.

She cleared her throat and licked her lips, knowing that there was no way she could keep the husky tone or heightened accent out of her voice. "Come inside. Let me see to those cuts."

Chapter 26

"Are you all right?"

He couldn't keep his concern for her out of his voice as he stepped into the house. The front of her clothes were covered with something. At first outside he was afraid it was blood, but here in the better light he could see that it was too thin, too purple. Wine?

She shrugged without committing to anything and walked across the living room to the bookshelves. Something she did silenced the loud music he'd forgotten was playing. It must have been playing the whole time they'd been outside, but it faded into the background when he was hip to hip with her. When she didn't turn around immediately, he let his eyes wander the rooms to keep from crossing to her and spinning her around again.

A throw rug in the living room lay bunched to one side. His eyes followed that path to an orange and an apple that led a trail to the kitchen. They were joined there on the floor by a banana, the overturned fruit bowl tipped on the corner of the island gracing the kitchen's center. And around to one side, he saw the purple of more wine on the floor, with shards of glass sparkling in the overhead light among the liquid.

"What happened to you?" He would keep asking until she answered him. The icy Princess who never appeared ruffled was more than a little disheveled now.

He meant to soften the gruff worry in his voice, but it was impossible. Focusing on her, he found she wasn't paying any attention to him. Instead, she was standing a few feet away, scanning the open space. Glancing around the kitchen and great room, her eyes grew apprehensive and her shoulders hunching as if she expected an attack.

He couldn't help it. He closed the distance between them and grabbed her hands, shaking them a little to get her attention. When her eyes met his, he tried to smile reassuringly.

"Tell me what happened, Marguerite. Let me help you."

She was shaking her head in denial before he finished his words, and she tried to pull away from him. The rug tripped her and she would have fallen backwards if he hadn't pulled her into his arms.

That was the only reason he did it. It wasn't that he wanted to press those rich curves more closely against his body, or that he wanted to see the bright violet sparkle of surprise in her eyes as she stared at him. And her lips, her luscious lips, were only a breath away.

He was lying to himself. There were a hundred reasons why he wanted her in his arms, and that was only the beginning.

Her gasp was only a vague sound he registered when he lowered his head. He couldn't help himself, and ground his lips against hers in frustration and possession. Because she did possess him, there was no doubt about that. If she branded him and stuck him in a pen, she wouldn't own him any more completely.

Her lips softened against his, and he eased back enough to return the sensation. His tongue traced the line seaming her closed lips, and by some miracle, she opened for him. It felt like that first blessing of rain in the fall or the flush of the rich grasses in the spring, deep and rich and welcomed.

She tasted of wine, spicy and delicate, and of herself, rich and intoxicating. When her tongue came out to mate with his, he felt her tremble. Her fingers curled into his shirt, and she pressed herself closer to him. Since she didn't appear to be running away, he released the tight band of his arms across her back and ran his hands lightly down her spine, finally cradling her hips.

This is what he wanted, what he hoped they could become if the damned water issue hadn't come to light. The thought of that made him pause. He hadn't apologized. They hadn't cleared anything up. Things were still poisoned between them.

Lost as he was, in her and in his own concerns, he missed the cue. She withdrew, not pulling away from him completely, but leaning back enough so that she could stare into his eyes.

"This is wrong." A deep breath that pressed her chest to his followed her words.

He waited a moment, trying to convince his body and desire to cool. But neither his body nor his desire paid attention. They focused one hundred percent on the woman in his arms.

Closing his eyes only made her scent stronger, and with heightened senses, he inhaled the wine she wore on her clothes and heard the stirring of creatures outside in the night. Somewhere, something in the cabin ticked occasionally. Her breasts pressed against him again.

"I know." The statement was pulled out of him reluctantly. When she began to step back, he let her.

He crossed his arms to kept himself from reaching out for her again. The tightening of his shirt reminded him of the cuts on his back as the denim rubbed open wounds. Bruises that undoubtedly already showed made themselves known.

"You are hurt. I meant to clean your cuts."

He looked up to find her regarding him with emotions he had a hard time identifying. She spun around, pulled a chair away from the dining table, and turned it towards him.

"Sit here. I will get some antiseptic and bandages."
She turned away and stopped, glancing to the side but not
right at him. "If you remove your shirt, I can tend to you."

Her voice had dropped half an octave. He gulped
against the sudden image of her, running her hands around
his waist and loosening the old denim, then undoing the
buttons one by one as she explored the skin below. Then
she would push the shirt off his shoulders and – and what?

Shaking his head did nothing to eliminate the picture
this painted in his head, and his jeans. His body was on
high alert around this woman, this witch in her own right.

Making fast work of the buttons when she
disappeared down the hall, he yanked the shirt free of his
belt and jeans and turned it around to look at the damage.
Nothing torn, but four significant bloody patches matched
the aches he felt increasing on his back. He flexed his
muscles, attempting to ease the pain. Anything for a
princess in distress. He glanced again at the wine and
glass shards on the kitchen floor as he straddled the chair.

*****

She watched him from the dark hallway, unable to
look away from his broad back. From here, she could see
the scratches with blood already dried around them. Deep
blue-purple bruises marked his spine and crisscrossed his
toned shoulders. It must be very painful. When he
stretched, her eyes followed the tensing and release of
each tendon and muscle. Then he dropped into the chair
backwards, his chin resting on his clasped hands on the
chair's back, appearing to examine the wine pooled on her
kitchen floor.

Mère de Dieu but he was a fine specimen of a man.
She let her gaze wander lower, to his buttocks covered in
taunt denim, and peaking out to one side, a toned thigh
pulled equally hard at the fabric.

And yet, despite the strength that he wore like it was his given nature, he had been surprisingly gentle when his arms were wrapped around her. Surprised or not, when she landed on him outside, he did his best to protect her. That was what he did, protect things. His land. People. Even the stories of his family's past.

He sighed and shifted in the chair. She couldn't delay any longer. She was the one who had insisted that she attend to his wounds, correct? There was no one to blame but herself, yet again.

Her boots hit the wood floor and he glanced over his shoulder at her, then back at the kitchen floor.

"What happened, Marguerite? Tell me, and let me help you."

Her throat tightened at his gentle tone, the same one she expected he used with difficult livestock or an upset horse. The yearning she felt to confess all, the missing herbicide and her vision of a ghost, was almost overwhelming. Foolish woman. She knew that nothing she could say or do would make things right between them. Nothing could wipe away her shame, and because of that, she had to put a good face on things.

"Nothing happened. I was clumsy and I spilled some wine, and I broke a glass in the process." She set the bottle of antiseptic and cotton balls on the table in front of him, placing the plastic medical kit next to it with a louder snap than necessary.

When he didn't respond, she peeked over to see if he was buying her story. His frown told her she'd failed.

"And that was why you came barreling out your front door like the devil himself was after you?"

There was no response she could think of for that. Her confidence slipped and she scanned around for the ghost of the old crone. But all she saw was her perfectly normal kitchen.

Embarrassment had her bristling. She had been seeing things, sure, but she was not about to explain herself to this – cowboy. Who was he to think he had the right to question what she did in her own home? And what was he doing here in the middle of the night anyway?

"Why are you here, Deke?"

She didn't bother to keep the sharpness out of her tone, deepening his frown. Even the thin line of his lips was attractive, though. It would be so easy to run her finger along that seam, coaxing his tongue to come out and play. Gasping on the thought and the spear of heat running through her body, she swung away from him.

His hand gripped her arm, the move so fast she doubted a rattler could have struck faster. It wasn't a bruising grip, but it left her with no doubt that he was frustrated with her. It was habit that made her try to pull away, and he half-stood from the chair, as if he would follow her but wouldn't let go.

"I came to apologize. Damn it, Marguerite, let me do that at least."

"Apologize?" It stopped her struggles and her thoughts.

He looked down at his hand on her arm and pulled it away like he'd grabbed hot fire. Then he dropped back into the chair and ran that same hand through his hair, messing it up further. Her fingers itched to follow his path, though whether it was to arrange it or tangle it further, she wasn't sure.

"I shouldn't have done what I did the other day. I shouldn't have brought that ugliness into your life. It isn't your fault."

She knew exactly what he referred to. The memory of the dead cow danced across her vision. Then she locked on his final words.

"What do you mean, it isn't my fault?" He was forgiving her?

He stood from the chair and paced into the living room, and the vantage point reminded her that there was a reason he was exhibiting so much skin in her home.

"I'm sure that you didn't do anything intentional to cause it. Something in the run-off did cause it though, I'm sure of that. But I don't think you were responsible."

Her gut clenched with his words. Little did he know, and if he did, would he still be so forgiving?

"Sit, please. I need to clean those cuts." There was little she could do to control the lowering tone in her voice. Her emotions were all on the surface. First the witch, then their fall, and now his forgiveness. The fact that all she seemed to be able to see was his broad back, scarred now because of her, distracted her from any other thoughts. Busying her hands with the antiseptic and cotton balls to avoid continuing to stare, she jumped when calloused hands closed on her upper arms and squeezed.

"Do you forgive me?" His voice had dropped an octave, if that was possible, and the warmth and contrition in it lit fires inside her in places that had long been dark and cold. She refused to meet his eyes.

"Yes, Deke, I forgive you." She inhaled with more energy than her body needed, and with the air came his woodsy scent. Her body hadn't forgotten it. In fact, it might always remember him.

"The hell with it." He bit off the words in her ear, and she gasped for another breath when he spun her around. His eyes were shining that brilliant blue, and they were the last things she saw before he crushed his lips down on hers.

*****

He hadn't intended to kiss her. He really hadn't. All he planned to do tonight was apologize and see if they could salvage anything that resembled a friendly relationship.

But her fear was palpable when she landed on him, the terror coming off her in waves. Her precious control, something she seemed to pride herself on above all else, had shattered over some event, and he wasn't leaving until he understood what had frightened her. He wanted to protect her.

Those big violet eyes did him in every time. Her glossy voice, the French accent thickening as it dropped, stirred him like no other woman's. The memory of her soft shape lying on top of him, molding to him as if her body was made for him and him alone, made the blood rush even faster in his veins.

If he lacked finesse, so be it. There was a time for coaxing, a time for slow. And there was a time to act.

She tasted better than wine, better than the most exotic meal, better than sin. The gasp she'd uttered right before he swooped in left her lips parted for him, and he took advantage of it, diving his tongue in for an even deeper taste. It took her only a moment to respond, her tongue tangling with his as she tilted her head.

His hands loosened to skim up her arms, tracing her shapely shoulders through the thin material of her blouse. Each fine bone left an impression on him, leaving him sure he could draw her shape by memory alone. When he tangled his fingers in her thick hair, he anchored her mouth to his and decided that apology or not, taking things too far was a damned fine idea.

He couldn't get enough of her. If he'd finished off a bottle of tequila all by himself, he wouldn't have been as intoxicated. His hand slipped to her cheek, caressing her soft skin. His fingertips had never felt anything this silken, this supple, this enticing. She made a small mewing sound and tilted into his hand, giving a deep sigh and leaning into him as she did so.

Suddenly he needed to feel her closer, wanting her body pressed up to his and yielding in all the right places. His hand slipped from her nape down her back, following each dip in her spine, until it rested against her lower back. Then he stepped forward and tightened his embrace.

She broke off the kiss so fast, his head couldn't process it. He blinked down at her, not understanding. Her hands were trapped between their bodies, and she flattened her palms on his chest. They seemed to move in a quick caress before she froze, her eyes wide as she stared up at him. Then she pushed, not hard, but he got the message.

His hand at her back dropped to his side, but the one on her cheek had a mind of its own and stayed there, his fingers caressing. Even as she stepped away from him, leaving coldness where there had been so much warmth seconds ago, her head tilted further and her hand came up to cover his. She ran her fingertips over his hand once, then dropped it and turned away.

"I did not expect that." Her voice was hoarse, and there was a hint of something he couldn't identify in it. Was that tears?

"I wasn't wrong, Marguerite." His feet refused to move to follow her as she crossed the kitchen, her back still to him.

He waited. She stopped, flexing her shoulders and leaning her head back for a moment. Her rich hair cascaded all the way to the globes of her butt, and he fantasized about combing his fingers through it, coming to rest on those perfectly rounded curves.

She turned, her eyelids dropped to half-mast. Whatever she was thinking was hidden from him. Shaking her head, she gave a small sad smile.

"No, it was not wrong."

He wanted to cover the distance between them and pick up where they left off, but her sudden straightening, shoulders back and chin up, stopped him. She seemed to come to some sort of decision.

"Sit down. I have yet to clean those cuts. I would not want you to get an infection because of me, on top of everything else."

Chapter 27

Why must he stare at her like he was parched with thirst and she was the only source of water around? His eyes were hungry. She tried to hide her glance down his body, and it pleased her to see that he seemed to be as aroused as she was by their kisses. His jeans strained at the front, the denim only partially hiding an enticing outline.

She wanted to forget about all of it. The cow – but she deserved it. His apology – not necessary. Her own apology would take more courage.

Even across the room, she could see the blazing color of his eyes. The longer they stood, neither one of them moving or speaking, the more that color faded. He shifted his jeans almost imperceptibly. Then he sat down in the chair as he'd been before, backwards with his arms crossed.

"I am sorry that I hurt you." She moved forward with her words. This was not the apology she needed to provide, but it was all she could start with.

"I've had much worse, believe me." His voice was distant, slicing into her emotions. It helped her to busy her hands opening the brown bottle of antiseptic. Cotton balls went flying in every direction when she tried to pry off one, and she realized she was shaking.

Relying on a deep breath to steady herself, she schooled her voice to be as noncommittal as his. "Tell me about some of these injuries."

He sat silent for a moment. She liked that about him. He gathered his thoughts, of this she was certain. It was the same thing he did when he started a story, or when he pondered his response to a question. He did not feel the need to rush in to speak for the sake of saying foolishness.

She doused the cotton with the liquid and bit her lip as she took in the cuts. There were four of them, one at his right shoulder, two close together on the center of his back, and one at the base of his spine right about the belt on his jeans. Just to the right of the central cuts, a dent at his ribcage ruined the perfect symmetry of his back.

"You can probably see one right off." There was a note of self-deprecating humor in his voice now. "Or at least, that's what I'm told. I don't have eyes in the back of my head."

"You are dented." She matched his tone, but she couldn't help running her fingers over the spot. It looked like it had hurt when it happened.

He sucked in a sharp breath, and she pulled her fingers away. Perhaps it still hurt him. Then he gave a weak chuckle.

"That's one way to put it."

"What happened?" She pressed the cotton to the highest cut, swabbing away the dried blood.

"I was stupid. Turned my back on an angry steer. Got kicked. Broke two ribs, and there was little the doctors could do to stabilize them completely because of where they are. They healed with time, but not completely straight. Ergo, a dent."

His humor at this was real, but she was appalled.

"How did you not become more seriously injured? Broken ribs must be taken seriously. The doctors should have done more. This is not something one should laugh about." She heard the indignity on his behalf in her voice, and willed herself to tone it down.

Moving to the central cuts, she moistened fresh cotton and dabbed again. Nothing seemed to be oozing despite her ministrations. At least she would not have him bleeding to death on her conscious too.

Her fingers slipped again, and this time she let the cotton ball drop to the floor. His skin was smooth under her fingers, like caressing fine satin, warm and seductive. A single vertebra separated the two cuts, marred now by a bruise with dark blue outlining the purple. She pressed it, and she heard him inhale.

"I am sorry. I am hurting you." She bent to retrieve the cotton from the floor, flustered now. Her hand shook as she reached for the discolored ball of white, and her vision blurred. Her eyes filled with tears, and she dropped a knee to the floor to steady herself.

What the hell was wrong with her? Her feelings for him were – overwhelming. His attraction was undeniable. That brief touch alone triggered heat that moved through her body at the speed of a runaway barrel rolling down a steep hill. To think that she had caused him this pain along with the rest of it was too much.

"Marguerite." His voice seemed to choke on her name. She looked up at him, taking in the turbulent gray-blue of his eyes, the same color of the Atlantic tossing the shores off the Brittany coast in a winter's storm.

His eyes searched her face, darting from feature to feature. There was no puzzlement. In fact, he radiated a calm that spread to her. He reached out a hand, caressing her cheek until the skin tingled. In fact, it tingled all over her body. She craved having that same caress move over every cell.

A smile lit up his face, the one that turned up one corner of his mouth higher than the other. On another man, it would have been a smirk. On Deke, it was endearing. Her own lips turned up in shaky response.

Then he leaned down. Was he moving so slowly, or was she seeing it in slow motion? It didn't matter. What mattered was the end result.

When his lips moved softly over hers, she thought perhaps he was trying not to frighten her. She parted her lips, tracing the shape of his mouth with her tongue. His hand skimmed her jaw and moved to the nape of her neck and he squeezed lightly, bringing her up on her knees to meet him more fully.

What more could she do? She had to kiss him back. Arching her neck, she pressed into him, his thigh blocking her progress. Putting a steadying hand on the firm muscle, she felt his body jerk in response. If she moved her hand a little bit upward –

How he managed to get off the chair so fast, she wasn't sure. One minute, her palm was straying to engaging territory, and the next, he'd hauled both of them to their feet, his hands on her shoulders and pulling her closer. Dimly, she heard the sound of the chair hitting the wood floor, but she did not care. Her hands moved to meet his chest, the sprinkling of fine hairs curled and coarse in a line that she longed to follow from those circling his flat nipples to disappear into the waist of his jeans. His kisses were more enflaming than the finest of wines, and her palms trailed lower to feel his muscles of his abdomen contract involuntarily under her touch.

He grabbed her hands, breaking off the kiss and stopping her travels. Deep blue stared into her eyes again, a question there waiting for her to answer.

He was giving her the decision to make. There was no contest. She was long past thinking this through. Words weren't necessary as she stepped back and held on to his hands, pulling him down the unlit hallway.

*****

His heart raced at a stampede's pace, one he was sure she could hear as she pulled the drape across the window. It blocked out what little light there was, and in the darkness he heard the rustle of clothes.

"Stop." He hadn't intended to sound so commanding, but it did the trick. She stilled on the opposite side of the bed.

Fumbling on the bedside table, he found a lamp, his fingers tracing upwards impatiently to find the switch. When soft light filled the corners of the room, his eyes snapped back to where she stood.

She'd unbuttoned her shirt, the sides hanging open and the whisper of black lace showing in between. Her arms hung at her sides, and her face looked away from him towards the foot of the bed.

"I want to see you." He waited for a sign that she agreed, but there was none. "I want to undress you, and I want you to do the same for me."

This time she looked up, her eyes slightly glassy as if deep emotions swayed her. He was sure his looked the same, glazed with the lust that he didn't want to fight any longer.

Kicking off his boots, he knelt on the bed and crawled to the middle. After a moment, she smiled and did the same. Straightening, he pulled her up with him so that they were torso to torso. He could barely contain his need to rip off every barrier between them so that he could feel every sigh, every quiver, and every silky inch of her.

His hands weren't quite steady when he pushed the shirt off her shoulders and tossed it behind her. He dropped his gaze to watch his fingers trace the curves of her breasts, following the lacy edges of the black bra as it dipped and swirled around her form. His last movement ended in front, fingering the clasp and looking up into her eyes for permission.

She smiled wider now, the desire on her face making him harder in anticipation.

"If you need me to stop, you'd better say the words right now."

She grinned and didn't even pause. "I do not want you to stop." Her emphasis wasn't lost on him, and it was his turn to grin.

He flicked the clasp and the bra fell free, allowing her breasts to tumble into his hands. With a silent apology for the calluses, he palmed them gently and ran fingers around the dark nipples, already hard and tempting his mouth.

What could he say? He needed to follow this temptation more than he needed to breathe. Lowering his head, he took one succulent tip between his lips and he tugged. Her moan wrapped around him as tightly as any rope. Her hands tangled in his hair and she held him there for long minutes. When he loosened his hold to ravish the other luscious side, she sounded a whimper of protest before another low moan shook through her.

How long they stayed this way, he lost track. All he knew was that she was the most breath-taking woman he'd ever enjoyed, and he wanted the dark hours, when they didn't argue or work at odds to one another, to last for eons.

Her hands roamed over him, and he felt the tug of her fingers in his hair pulling him away from his worship. Straightening, he found her lids barely open, the trance-like daze on her face making him feel strong and humble at the same time. She pulled him forward for a long, overpowering kiss that scattered any thoughts he might have. All he could do is feel, enjoying this lush woman as she slowly took him to a place where nothing mattered but this.

*****

Par tout ce qui est saint, who knew that the man could kiss like this. How would she have known that he could find the perfect pressure of hands and mouth to pleasure her, and she was still half-dressed? She wanted to be pressed against the full length of him skin to skin, making him crazy until he drove into her as wildly as she wanted to surround him.

Her hands crept down his taunt abdomen, enjoying the shiver of his muscles as she traced the path of ginger hair lower. When her fingers closed on his belt buckle, he made a sound of protest and grabbed them. Still kissing her gently, he squeezed her hands, then pushed them aside to get to the button on her jeans.

First or second, it didn't matter to her. If both of them weren't completely naked soon, she would scream in frustration. But he kept her occupied. His mouth roamed from lips to earlobe, tugging it between his teeth, and the sensation ran through her body and settled at the apex of her thighs. Then he nipped her neck below her ear, and she shook with his touch.

"Permettez-moi." The droll sound of the French words on his lips made her smile, changing to a gasp as his fingers slid inside her jeans, following the descent of the zipper. The intrusion felt wicked and welcomed at the same time. When his fingers traced the lace, he chuckled. Then he pushed the jeans from her hips, effectively trapping her on her knees.

Leaning back, his eyes followed the trail his hands had a moment ago, and he grinned. *"Mademoiselle Devereaux,* if this is your go-to-work attire, I can't wait to see what you wear for a night on the town."

She giggled. She couldn't seem to help herself, the sound so foreign to her own ears she might have been speaking Chinese. Then he slipped those wicked fingers inside the elastic of her panties, pushed them down to join her jeans, and rolled her to her side.

"I think we can get rid of the rest of this pretty fast, don't you?" Without a pause, he yanked off her panties, jeans and socks in one tug. Then he stretched out next to her, propping his head in his hand as he gazed down at her.

"You are really something, you know that?" The murmur of his words was barely a whisper as he traced fingers down her centerline. When he reached the one place she really wanted him to linger, he moved back up again instead. This time, he circled her breasts. His expression was absorbed and thoughtful.

She cleared her throat, wishing she could find appropriate words to give him in return. For once, though, her communication skills failed her. He still wore his jeans, and yet their positions didn't feel uncomfortable. In fact, she felt sheltered by the intimacy.

"You are still dressed." She blushed at stating the obvious.

He got that lazy grin she was coming to love, and settled on his back next to her, his arms behind his head. "Think you can do something about that?"

She propped herself up next to him, mirroring his earlier position and attempting his lazy grin in return. Her fingers were itching to learn his body, much as he'd been trailing over hers. The belt was a puzzle, though, and she would need both hands. Sitting up would be too intimate, so she got to her knees and leaned over him, intent on trying to open the offending metal. When his fingers traced her nipples lightly, she hissed at him.

"If you want to be naked, you must let me concentrate. Why will this damned belt not open? *Merde!*"

His hands covered hers and he laughed, the sound bouncing off the walls and coming back to her in waves of heat. He made short work of the buckle, then put his arms back behind his head. "It's all yours."

She licked her lips, then moved the tab of the zipper and pulled it down as slowly as he'd done hers. When she glanced up at him, he was watching her gravely.

This was silly. It's not as if they had not had each other's bodies before. They'd had a night of sex. But somehow, this was different. Something had changed between them, and she wasn't sure what it was.

Black briefs made an appearance under the zipper, and the bulge was unmistakable and impressive. But she knew that already. Her breathing was coming faster now, more excited than she had been as a child on Christmas morning.

Crawling down the bed, she stood at the foot and grabbed the cuff of his jeans legs, pulling. He obligingly lifted his hips and helped her. Then she yanked at socks, and finally, she put on her best sinful smile and crawled up the bed again, locking her fingers on either side of his waist in his briefs.

"Want help with that?" The casual interest in his tone contrasted with the brilliant colors kaleidoscoping in his eyes. He was as eager as she was.

Chapter 28

Dusty rose painted the sky outside. It was what – about six in the morning? He should go, but the witch nestled against him made it difficult to move.

He could shift her aside, but he found he didn't want to. What he really wanted to do was weave his hand into her long hair as it was draped across his belly, pull her face up for a tender kiss, and do everything they'd done to each other all night long all over again.

Her face was peaceful in sleep, the only time he'd ever seen her without a conscious guarded expression. Well, there was last night too, and the night a couple of months ago. Every time she came, the sated glow she had was kind of like this. That is, until her mind started worrying something and took off at a gallop faster than any horse he'd ever ridden.

And she snored, as she was doing now, a happy snore. It was easy to sleep with, more like a purr. It calmed him when he hadn't even known he needed it.

Did they have a chance?

Marguerite shifted in his arms, lying on top of him. He smiled. Last night, when she'd cheerfully yanked at his briefs and sent them flying across the room, she'd conveniently tumbled back into his arms, landing on him like she had at the bottom of the steps. Only this time, the cushion of the bed caught them, and he caught her, wrapping his arms around her and pressing her against his erection. The leg that wasn't caught between her opening thighs wrapped around a leg in possession. She laughed outright, a triumphant sound, before her lips covered his in a scorching kiss.

And that was just the first time. When she wrapped her soft hand around his hard length, running her fingers up and down experimentally, he thought he'd lose it like a pimply-faced high schooler. Then her lips followed, and he was gone in the pleasure of the moment.

Not that he'd shied away from his own tortures. Lips tracing the line his fingers had before, closing on her center, pumping into her with his fingers as she chanted his name. The woman liked to talk during sex, and he'd have to study his French to translate everything she said. When she exploded under his mouth, though, he understood perfectly.

This last time an hour before was lit by moonlight. He'd doused the bedside light and opened the drapes as the almost-full moon followed its arc across the night sky. Marguerite bathed in sensual pleasure and moonlight was a sight he wanted to see again and again. Her hands linked with his as he rose above her, her eyes linked with his as they both came, was more religion than sex.

Maybe it was more like making love.

His body jerked at the thought. This was all because he'd come over to apologize and ended up with an armful of frightened woman instead. He frowned. They'd never discussed what scared her last night.

She stirred against him, her eyes opening slowly and blinking at him. The violet was muted now, paled in the darkness. Then she smiled and stretched, making sure to press enough of herself against him that his body stirred.

Glancing out the window, her smile faded. She looked back at him, and a flash of uncertainty crossed her features before she pulled in her emotions and hid behind her mask. That damned mask again. He could feel the tension roll through her.

"Good morning." She tried to roll away from him, but he tightened his arms and pulled her face up to his. He wanted one more kiss before she put distance between them.

The kiss was languid, tender where last night had been urgent, with none of the victorious undertones that had colored their couplings during the night. His body roused to full alert, and with regret, he pulled away from her and put on his own fixed smile.

"Good morning, Princess."

Confusion flooded her eyes at his words. Her chin raised perceptibly and she pushed off his chest. This time, he let her go. Her backside moving towards the bathroom door made him wish he had a different kind of job, the kind where getting up at dawn to tend animals wasn't a spoiler for another tumble.

The door slammed shut, and he sighed. They seemed to be back to where they were before. Whatever they'd shared during the night didn't seem to change her opinion of him in the light of the coming day.

He got up and sorted through the clothes on the floor, then scanned the room for his missing briefs. No sign of them anywhere. It wasn't the first time he'd gone commando, but he didn't think she'd appreciate finding them one day.

The door heaved open again as he fastened his belt. His shirt was still downstairs. She wasn't looking at him, intent on tying her robe. Then she began gathering up her clothes and tossing them on a chair. She looked anywhere but at him or the bed as she turned her back.

This distance was not going to happen again. If he had to shake sense into her, he would. When he put firm hands on her shoulders and pulled her back against him, she stopped absolutely still.

"Marguerite, where have you gone?"

She spun in his hands then, examining his face. "What do you mean?"

"After everything we shared last night, you're shutting me out. I want to know why."

Her expression was defiant, and she opened her mouth. Then it slammed shut as hard as her bathroom door and she seemed to wilt in his arms.

"We have to talk." Her words were quiet.

The sudden chilled breeze glide across his skin had nothing to do with his lack of a shirt.

*****

"Come. I will make us coffee." When she tried to pull her hands away, he wouldn't let her. Instead, he tucked her against his side, draped an arm snuggly over her shoulders, and marched them through her bedroom door.

In the advancing daylight, the kitchen was an even worse disaster than it had seemed the previous night. A sticky mess marked the boundary of dried red wine. Would it leave a permanent stain in the hardwood floor? The chair Deke had upended lay across her tangled throw rug. All of the lights blazed into the early dawn. By rote, she turned them off as they passed switches.

He let go of her after a squeeze and reached down for the chair, setting it back on its feet. Then he flattened the rug and looked at her questioningly.

"It was there." She pointed out the spot in the path of her race to the safety of the front door last night.

She kept moving to the kitchen, stepping around the wine and shattered glass to reach the espresso machine. The cabinet above held coffee beans and mugs. She hoped this type of coffee would be satisfactory for him. He might not like fancier coffee. He probably boiled something in an old metal pot until it turned into sludge. Isn't that what cowboys did?

When she shut the cabinet door, she jumped. He was standing next to her, holding an apple, an orange and a banana, grinning as she scowled at him.

"Why did you scare me like that?" Her voice gave an aggravating squeak at the end of her question and it pissed her off. Why was she always off-step with this man?

"It wasn't my intention to scare you. I was right behind you. Where did you think I was going?" He shrugged into his shirt as he teased her, and she felt vaguely disappointed when his broad chest with its intriguing ginger hairs disappeared from her view.

If she threw the jar of coffee at him, would he catch it, or would he jump aside? She was tempted to see how it would turn out. But that would accomplish nothing. At the very least, she needed to explain what she had learned about the herbicide and make her apologies. Filling the machine's reservoir with water at the sink gave her a moment to gather herself for the effort.

"So, what happened here last night?"

His voice came from the floor, and she spun around, sloshing water, to find him on his hands and knees, retrieving glass chunks and splinters from the dried wine stain.

"Be careful – you will hurt yourself on that glass. I've already done enough damage to your body."

He stood, one hand filled with pieces, and stalked towards her. Damn, but he was in her personal space, standing so close that she could see each color blend in his eyes. A corner of his mouth quirked in that engaging way, and he waited before saying anything until her gaze dropped to his mouth.

"Is that what you call it? I can think of plenty of other more pleasurable labels for what we did with each other, Princess."

Le bâtard ce moquiat d'elle. Laughing out loud, mind you. He was acting like a peacock, strutting around with pride over getting her to bed. Why she would show him, the rascal, she would –

Then he leaned in and kissed her, and her mind emptied. Anger faded into bliss. His lips insisted, and hers responded.

Then he stepped back and reached around her to open lower cabinets. Finding the trash can on the second try, he dumped in the glass, washed his hands at the sink, and turned back to her as he wiped them in a towel.

"Yup, that was some damage all right."

He was such a tease. She kind of liked it, and that surprised her. She had always thought men who teased did it because they didn't appreciate the woman who was the object of their pranks. But this didn't feel like that. This made her feel – special.

Folding the towel and replacing it on the rack, he placed his hands on the counter's edge behind him and leaned back as if he had all the time in the world.

"Now, when are you going to tell me what happened?"

That ruined her buzz. She bit her lip, turning back to the espresso maker. He didn't speak while she made their coffee, handing him his mug first as she finished making her own. When she turned back, he was still standing in almost the same position, the mug held out to hers now.

"Cheers."

She clunked her mug with his and waited for him to take a taste.

"It is probably not the way you like it. But this is all I have. I like strong espresso in the morning, and sometimes decaffeinated espresso in the evening. Sometimes I make it iced as well."

Hell, she was babbling. This is what this man reduced her to. She couldn't control her emotions or her actions, she forgot normal conversational skills, and her life was on edge.

"You probably boil your coffee, which is not the best way to make it. In fact, I took a course on – "

She jumped and nearly spilled the hot brew over her hand when his fingers came over her mouth. It was probably a good thing, since she was making no sense.

"I like espresso. In fact, I have the same brand of machine, though mine is probably a little older than yours by the look of it." He took a sip before continuing. "And I never drink mine iced."

He regarded her solemnly over the rim of his mug as he took another drink. "Tastes good. Now, when I remove my hand, you're going to tell me what scared you so badly last night. And I'm going to help you solve whatever that problem is."

She couldn't stop herself. Her eyes darted for the corner of the kitchen where the witch had appeared. A shaft of sunlight lit the offending spot. When his eyes followed hers, he frowned. Then he dropped his hand, put it on her elbow, and led her over to the dining table. He put his mug on the table without a sound, then held out a chair for her.

She didn't want to. He was being much too high-handed and demanding. But she sat anyway. It helped her knees not to quiver at the thought of the old crone's pointing fingers.

Putting another chair opposite hers, he sat down and leaned forward, wrapping his large hands around hers as she clutched her mug. "Whatever it is, we can deal with it together. So tell me."

The sincerity in his eyes was real. There was no judgment or pity. He was taking her seriously. She hoped that he would continue to do so when she explained what she saw.

Chapter 29

She didn't wanted to tell him, he was clear on that. When he wrapped her hands in his, they were cold as a glacier despite the hot coffee mug they gripped. Wide eyes stared up into his before darting to the corner of the kitchen.

He kissed her lightly then, aiming for chaste encouragement.

"Marguerite, whatever it is, don't worry. There's nothing that could be that bad."

When she bit her lip with eyes that widened even more, he almost dragged her back to bed. But that wouldn't get him any answers.

"I, I, ah, I thought I saw the witch."

Her words ran together so fast that he had to struggle to understand them as her accent deepened.

"First she was at the winery. Then she was here. Except she was different each time."

He found his voice with effort, making a point to keep his hold on her hands.

"Different how?"

"The first time, she was my age. Then each time I saw her, she was older. Last night," she glanced at the corner again and shuddered, "she was very old."

He wasn't sure what to say. "Maybe it was a trick of the light?"

"*Non*, I am sure. The face and dress were very real. Last night," she faltered, and he ran a thumb over her knuckles to comfort her, "last night she was yelling. I could not hear the words, but I could see her anger."

An angry witch was never a good thing.

"You do not believe me." Her voice held defeat with none of the fire he had come to expect of her.

"I believe you when you say you saw something."

She shook her head sadly, pulling her robe snugly around her curves.

How could he explain what he was thinking?

The choice was made for him when his cell phone rang. He shrugged it off, expecting it to beep with a voicemail. Marguerite shifted, pulling at her hands. How could he unravel this in a way that made sense?

The phone rang again, its sound now more urgent. She shook her head, and he knew she was giving him permission to answer. But he didn't want to let her go, not with so much hanging between them. Disappointment painted her usual vibrancy a dull hue.

He shifted both of her hands to one of his and unclipping the phone from his belt, glancing at the display. He thought about ignoring it, but the read out said it was Carl. It wasn't a call he could blow off.

"Yes Carl, what do you need?"

"Boss, we need you down at the main barn right away. It's important." His voice sounded strained, and there were murmurs of tense words in the background.

"Can it wait?"

"No, Boss, I don't think it can." It wasn't like Carl to manifest a problem where there was none.

He assured him he'd be there shortly as he rose and drained the coffee in quick succession. Letting go of Marguerite was harder.

Truth was, he didn't want to let her go. He wanted to comfort her. She probably thought she might be a little crazy for thinking she was seeing a ghost.

She walked him out to the truck without further comment, pulling her robe around her as tightly as her grim lips. He reached inside the cab for the spare shirt he always kept on hand, stripping off the bloodied evidence of their hard landing. She put out her hand for it.

"I will get out the stains for you. It is the least I can do."

No emotion was discernible in her level gaze, but her accent was thick. He thought he saw a trace of resignation. Maybe she thought he was leaving because he didn't believe her.

But the problem was, he did.

*****

Deke's body hummed with satisfaction, but it held a distant second place to his mind, hurling along in overdrive from Marguerite's confession.

She thought she saw a ghost, namely, the witch of Witch Hill. Not once, but multiple times now. And seeing the witch in crone mode meant bad things were about to happen.

And he'd assured her he could help with her problem, whatever it was. What had he been thinking? The answer to that was easy – he hadn't been, still a little bit high on great sex and a closeness that he hadn't felt to any other woman.

At least she told him.

Carl and a few of the hands were standing with a man Deke didn't recognize when he pulled up to the barn. If they noticed that he was coming from the direction of the main road instead of his house, no one commented on it. Carl raised his eyebrows but focused instead on whatever the visitor was saying.

Everyone was silent when he walked up. When no one moved to introduce the stranger, Deke moved forward with a hand outstretched.

"Deke Kermarrec, owner of Three Rivers. How can I help you?"

The man put out his hand, the distress in his eyes clear. "Mr. Kermarrec, I'm Tom Matteson from the National Organic Program of the US Department of Agriculture. I'm a certifying agent." He shifted from foot to foot, looking around at their audience. "Is there someplace where we can talk in private?"

Ice filled his belly as he stared at the man. An unannounced visit from the USDA was never good. He waved a hand towards the old farmhouse and began walking in that direction, with Matteson and Carl falling into step with him. Behind them, he heard a ripple of conversation from the hands as they dispersed slowly back to their work.

Deke led them to the old ranch office on the first floor. If he was lucky, his mother wasn't up yet and wouldn't also join their parade.

"Deke? Is that you? What's going on?"

Emie appeared from the kitchen, giving him a once-over with her pat on the cheek. "Do you men need some coffee?"

"That would be great, Ma, thanks." He was grateful that for once, she wasn't asking any questions, though they were brimming to overflowing in her eyes. He was sure he would be in for a grilling once the coast was clear.

Shutting the door behind them, he motioned the others to chairs opposite the desk before taking his own seat behind it. Leaning forward, he noticed that the agent wasn't looking around the room or at him, but at papers in a folder in his lap.

"What can I do for you, Mr. Matteson?"

"Please, call me Tom." He pulled out two pages stapled together and passed them across the desk. Carl leaned in to see what was on the pages as Deke picked them up to read.

"As you can see, Mr. Kermarrec, the USDA was informed by the University of California at Davis about your incidents of inappropriate herbicide use."

Deke stayed forward in his chair, his attention on the words on the page even as he listened to the man speak. It could have been Chinese on the page for all he recognized as his mind got stuck on the conversation.

"Based on the levels of herbicide in the water and grass samples you sent in for testing, that use has exceeded the guidelines for application. The test performed on the dead animals you submitted for necropsy indicated that they had ingested high levels of this herbicide. And this violates your certification as an organic beef production facility."

"But we don't use herbicides here." Carl looked almost angry as he spoke. "Three Rivers prides itself on its use of only organic, sustainable and biodynamic practices." When his gaze swung back to Deke, that anger had grown. "Boss, you've got to tell him what you've found, and you've got to make them stop."

Matteson's expression was now openly curious as he looked between them. Deke felt the pit of his stomach tighten and his body tense further. This wasn't the way he wanted to make his problem public.

Taking a deep breath, he settled back in his chair and looked out the window. From this vantage point, he could see Witch Hill, the base of the vineyard faded to its fall hues and dropping leaves. It wasn't due to herbicide now. But in the spring or early summer, when the grasses and weeds were growing? He was positive plenty of it was used.

Sitting forward again, he clasped his hands on the offending pages and regarded the agent carefully.

"Tom, everything that Carl said is true. If you check your records, you'll find that no one on the ranch is certified to apply this herbicide. We don't use it, and don't store any on the property. But we're having something of a situation with one of our neighbors."

The man across from him shook his head sadly, the sympathy on his face making Deke wish he'd dealt with this as soon as he'd become aware of it. Maybe it wouldn't now be so dire.

"Mr. Kermarrec, I'm sorry. It doesn't matter how it got in your water or on your land. What matters is that this part of your ranch is claimed as certified organic land, along with the livestock you're raising there. Until this is cleared up and you've been recertified in that area, you can't claim that your affected livestock is organic."

The tick-tock of his great-grandfather's old clock on the wall was the only sound in the room. With it, Deke could feel his heartbeat slow. It wasn't calm he was feeling. Evidently the witch had a good reason to be hanging around in her old crone mode these days. There was nothing he could do at the moment but ride out the storm.

"It's Deke, please, particularly since I have a feeling we're going to be working together for a while."

A knock on the door was followed swiftly by his mother entering with a tray in her hands. With a bright smile on her face, she put the tray on a side table and turned to the men.

"Now, how does everyone want their coffee?"

*****

"What do you mean you lose organic certification?"

Deke kept his eyes turned towards Witch Hill as his mother dropped into the chair the USDA agent had used a short time before. He'd had words of encouragement to follow his proclamation, but that wasn't the difficult part. The hardest part was figuring out what to do next.

Confront Marguerite? He had hoped they could work out a solution between the two of them, but that never seemed to be happening. Bringing the Dawsons in as the owners seemed to be an escalation, and if that happened, there was little hope of salvaging whatever they might have had as a couple.

He didn't want to have this discussion with his mother, but he figured that she'd bug him until she had the full story. She already had bits and pieces of it, and Emileen Preston Kermarrec with only part of a story was never a good thing. She'd make up what she didn't know to fill in the blanks.

Keeping his feet on the desk and his eyes outside, Deke waited for his mother to take a break in her ramblings. "Ma, there's a problem. You heard part of it from Royan, and now you'll hear the rest of it. We believe that there is significant run-off of this herbicide from Witch Hill Winery, and that's what's poisoning the well and being taken up by the surrounding pasture area. Cattle that were grazing there were poisoned by the concentrated levels. I've shared this information with Marguerite, and she hasn't denied that they use the chemical."

"Marguerite, as in the winemaker? I knew you two were friends, but – "

He didn't miss the sly smile in her voice on those words, and his boots thunked to the ground as he spun to her.

"We're friends, yes. Though after this, I doubt it will be close friends."

"Oh, so you are close?" This time a smile lit up her face. She clapped her hands twice and jumped up from the chair, coming around the desk to him.

This was definitely not the reaction he expected. When she dropped a kiss on his head and hugged him, she stopped and sniffed. Then she sniffed again and turned his chair so that she was looking into his eyes.

"Where were you last night?"

"What?" This conversation was now officially completely out of his control.

"I asked you where you were, and don't try to lie to me, Edouard Kermarrec the Third, because you know I can see right through you." She crossed her arms and regarded him thoughtfully. Yeah, she always could tell a fib a mile away.

When she smiled suddenly and kissed his head again, he didn't know what to make of it.

"You were with her, weren't you?"

"Ma, I was at home, in my own bed, and – "

"No you weren't, and I know it. Royan and I saw you leave here about eight o'clock, and we didn't see you come back. And we were up very late."

He saw his opening and he dove for it like a fox for its hole. "You and Royan? What were the two of you doing together up so late?"

His offensive backfired on him when she tapped her foot and shook a finger in his face.

"Don't change the subject, young man. What I do, with or without your uncle, is none of your business. I'm a grown woman. But you smell like perfume and if I'm not mistaken, sex. And I want to know who she is, because I have eyes in my head and ears to hear with and I think I know a few things."

Like he said, a little knowledge in Emie's mind was a very dangerous thing.

It was suddenly all too much. The feelings he had for his own violet-eyed witch, the old crone appearing to her, and now the USDA on his doorstep. He put his head in his hands and rubbed his forehead until the skin seemed to burn. Then he felt his mother pet his head again like he was a child.

"Now Deke, I know you always want to protect everyone and take on the world all by yourself, not bothering anyone else. But you have family and friends to help you. So now tell me everything, and we'll figure out what to do."

Chapter 30

"Yes, thank you. If you could come out before the end of next week, I would appreciate it."

Marguerite barely heard the assurances of the man on the other end of the phone. Pooled wine and hardwood floors were not a good pairing, and despite scrubbing and soaking after Deke left this morning, the stain of spilled red wine remained evident.

She wanted to repair the damage immediately, because she suspected that soon, she would need to explain to the Dawsons about the missing chemical. She would have to report it to the state, as required by their application license. Fines were steep. She doubted that she'd have a job for much longer after that.

And what about Three Rivers? Deke hadn't said anything further about the test results he'd shared with her, but she doubted he would stay quiet for much longer either.

She felt the prick of tears and shook them away, straightening the papers on her desk and listening to the vague sounds of David and Fernando out in the tank room. Thankfully, the tasting room was quiet today, and she had time to collect her thoughts and harvest what good she could out of the situation.

And that kept bringing her back to Deke. She had never connected to a man as well or as easily as she had with him. The more time they spent together, the closer she felt to him. It had been the best sex of her life, *phénoménal*, his appetites matching hers at every turn. And the more she considered how much they would need to overcome to be together, the less chance she thought they had.

It was too bad that now he would undoubtedly turn away. He didn't believe her about the witch and he probably thought *qu'elle était folle*, and more than a little bit crazy at that. And he blamed her for the poisonings on his ranch, something that she was guilty of even if she had no prior knowledge of it.

Now she would lose it all. Her job – poof. Her friends would be gone when she told them what had happened, and she would be forced to move away to find work and would lose track of them even if they did not disown her.

And the man. She would lose Deke. That hurt most of all.

The bell rang marking someone opening the tasting room door, and she ran a hand over her hair to make sure she hadn't worried it out of place.

"I will be right with you." Standing, she turned to her mirror and pulled out her lipstick. Battle dress always helped her maintain composure.

"Oh, there you are. I hope you don't mind that I showed myself in."

Marguerite spun around, lipstick only partially applied. The petite woman in the doorway was smiling. Her jeans were casual and the sandals on her feet bore well-worn frayed marks. Bright blue toenail polish matched the top she wore, a tie-dyed filmy blouse that blew gently around her.

"Ah, hello. If you will wait in the tasting room, Mrs. Kermarrec, I'll only be a moment." She didn't know what to make of this guest.

"Oh, we don't need to stand on formalities. You'll call me Emie, that's all there is to it. I wanted to come and chat with you, dear, since Deke's told me so much about you."

Marguerite felt her face freeze into her standard welcoming smile, even as her insides churned in turmoil. Deke would not have discussed their – whatever it was they had — with his mother, would he? She would no sooner discuss the particulars of any relationship with her own mother if the world were ending.

Her silence didn't seem to bother the older woman a bit as she advanced into the room and came around the desk to wrap her arms around Marguerite in a friendly hug. She sniffed, hopefully not a sign of tears or a cold. She hugged harder and sniffed again. Then she patted a hand on Marguerite's back and stepped away from her, smiling so wide that it was a wonder her face didn't split.

"So, tell me all about it. About you and Deke, I mean. I'm not trying to pry, sweetie, but I'm just so thrilled that my eldest has finally found a woman that turns his head as much as his father turned mine."

Her world shifted to another dimension. Could it get any stranger than this? Deke's mother wanting to have a *cœur à cœur* about Marguerite's relationship with her son?

If they even still had a relationship.

"I am sorry, Mrs. Kermarrec, but I don't know what you're talking about."

*****

"Can't wait to get started on this, man. I did more research than I have on any article in about a year, and it's all good stuff. Much more than I can squeeze into the word count, I'll tell you that. I'm thinking there's a series in this, at the very least."

Deke stared at Vince across the shiny tabletop at Gold, and he almost smiled. Vince's enthusiasm could be contagious, just like his biting comments could cut you in two. Luckily, Deke hadn't been on the receiving end of any of those, at least not yet. Mac had, and it looked painful.

"Anyway, my plan is to interview you, and then I'm going to talk to Marguerite. I want to learn more about the witch appearing at the winery, which would make sense since it's built on her old stomping grounds."

"Don't talk to Marguerite about this." He heard the threat in his tone and tried to dial it back with a smile. Vince didn't appear to be slowed down or fooled, though, when his eyes narrowed in examination, fork of food halfway to his mouth.

"Of course I'm going to talk to her. Who better? Some of the vineyard workers have claimed to see the witch in the vines and around the inside of the winery too. I'm sure Marguerite has stories."

Yes, she had stories, but Deke was damned if he was going to allow Vince to bother her about them. It was bad enough that she was terrified already. More talk about the witch wasn't going to help.

"Vince, I'm serious. Leave Marguerite out of this. She has a lot on her mind right now."

The sly smile he got in return made him wish he'd chosen more distant and objective wording.

"Oh, and how would you know how much she has on her mind, pray tell? Oh wait, could it be because you and the luscious winemaker have a thing going on?" His fingers stayed in the air in a pantomime of quotation marks.

"We don't have anything going on. We talk because our properties are next to each other, and we share concerns about the environment." Okay, that wasn't completely true. He had the concerns and he shared them with her. To date, that was as far as that particular discussion had gone.

"Yeah, I heard about the crappy news you got from the USDA. What's that about, anyway?"

Deke took a sip of coffee and picked at his lunch, the sandwich no longer interesting. In fact, the only thing he wanted was to find Marguerite and have it out with her, once and for all. Ma's words echoed back to him.

'You have to clear the air between you, son. If you care about her, you have to get things out in the open and

fix them. Only then will you be able to figure out if there is a relationship left to salvage.'

He'd never told his mother about the sightings of the witch. In fact, he only let his mother know that they had problems and secrets, and that things weren't looking so hot.

Across the table, Vince snorted and dove back into his plate of pasta, evidently willing to wait until Deke felt like talking. He had a lot of pasta to work through, and it looked like he might be a while.

While he chewed and swallowed, he regarded Deke steadily. "Ok, so I get that you don't want to talk about that. As I understand it, it's a disaster. So tell me about you and Marguerite. How much frostbite have you gotten from the Ice Princess?"

Deke almost choked on the small bite of sandwich he was attempting to swallow. If he wasn't absolutely sure Vince was trying hard to get a rise out of him, he would have jumped across the table and pounded him.

Instead, he swallowed carefully, wiped his mouth with the napkin, and folded it to the side of his plate. He couldn't meet Vince's eyes, not without letting some of the built-up anger and frustration show on his face. Then he rose and put a hand in his pocket to pull out some bills for his share.

Vince rose as well, eying him like he was a mountain lion about to spring. "Look, I get it, okay? I'm prying. I have no right. I just wanted to see how deep things were. From what I can see, that's pretty frickin' deep, my friend."

Deke still wanted to slug him.

"Sit down, finish your sandwich, and we'll talk about the article, I promise. I know how hard it is when you fall, buddy, I really do. I crawled into a bottle for way-too long when I realized I had feelings for DK. Worst days of my life, and that's saying something. Took a big wake-up call to crawl back out again, and by then, I'd nearly lost her. Take a lesson from my shit and don't make the same mistakes. Don't wait and think you have all the time in the world."

Vince sat down again after delivering his soliloquy, picked up his fork, and headed back into the pasta for another round.

What the hell? He thought he knew the man, and then this pops out. Yeah, there had been stories about how Vince left DK right before Thanksgiving a year ago, and about how their shared agent put them in a room together after telling Vince in no uncertain words not to screw things up. But below the bluster, Deke could see the pain still evident in the man's eyes.

He sat down, leaning back and pushing away his plate. He hadn't been that hungry to start with, and he wasn't hungry at all now. Vince kept shoveling food in, working his way through what must have been a pound of pasta. The amount of food he could consume was in stark contrast to his tall thin frame. When he finished the last bite, he too leaned back, pushed the plate to the edge of the table, and patted his belly.

"DK keeps me honest at home, lots of fruits and vegetables and a balanced diet and all that shit. Sometimes, though, a man just needs to pig out on some pasta. Don't tell DK. She'll put me on a short leash."

And he smiled. The smile said it all. If he never ate pasta again in his life, he wouldn't care, as long as he had the woman he loved.

That was how it was supposed to be.

Vince made a show of pulling his tablet into the space he'd emptied of his plate, dropped reading glasses on his nose, and consulted his notes. "So, the witch. What's her real story? I know your family had a role in taking care of her generations ago. Care to tell me how?"

Deke shifted and let his eyes range over the people in the restaurant. Flynn's Crossing was still a small town, and he knew many of them on sight and by name. Being here his whole life meant he'd seen a lot of comings and goings.

He cleared his throat, thinking how he'd missed out on Marguerite coming to town. He'd heard about her, of course. And with their shared friends, he'd had plenty of opportunity to get to know her earlier. But he'd waited.

Maybe he'd waited too long.

He couldn't do anything about it this minute. He needed to promise himself that he'd clear the air between them before too much more time went by. Focusing in on Vince again, he laid his hands flat on the table and nodded his head once in agreement.

"Seven generations back, my ancestors settled Three Rivers. My great-grandfather so many times removed got on his horse and rode west as far as he could in a day. Then he piled a monument of stones, marking his corner. He did the same things the next days, turning north and then east. By the time he was closing the southern boundary, he was at the base of what is now Witch Hill."

"So he filed his claim then?"

Deke nodded, thinking of the stories he'd heard about how much competition there was for the land back then.

"He filed his claim. He built a nice log cabin for his second wife and their growing family. He cleared land, planted crops, raised animals. And then one day in town, he heard the story about the little girl on the top of that mountain next door."

Vince leaned forward, and Deke couldn't help himself, he slipped into story-teller mode.

"You see, some of the ladies of the town wanted to rescue the girl, thinking they'd try to find someone to adopt her. But no one could catch her. She knew the woods so well by then that she just disappeared. And no one had claimed the mountain, since it was rocky in some parts and heavily wooded and steep in others, not good for anything that people could think of."

"And what happened then?" Vince sat forward, looking as eager as a child. It made Deke smile and lean forward as well.

"Well, Great-Grandfather got back on his horse, rode to the southeastern corner of his land, and rode south for a day, around the bottom of the mountain. He marked that spot, rode west, marked that, and circled on back to the homestead. Next day, he rode into town and claimed Witch Hill."

The next part of the story was always harder, no matter how many times Deke told it. Vince's fingers were poised above the tablet's keyboard.

"He was worried about the little girl. He'd heard about her family being killed by some nasty prospectors, then tracked again by Indians who were forced off their own land and were taking their due wherever they could. Her mama was killed with a baby on the way too. The girl was the only one in the family to survive. She took to the woods, and while people saw her from time to time, it was only when she let herself be seen. Folks figured she'd become an animal, torn clothes and wild hair and grunts instead of words. But Great-Grandpa felt sorry for her."

Vince raised a finger to pause the story, and signaling the waitress over, he asked for dessert and more coffee. When Deke waved away the offer of pie, he ordered a big piece a la mode for himself and motioned Deke to continue.

If the man was going on a food bender, he'd gladly provide the entertainment while he waited for his friend to burst.

"His wife was none too pleased, as you can imagine. He'd claimed land that had no purpose and therefore no value as far as anyone was concerned. He had a growing family to support, and yet he wanted to help this wild animal of a child. But despite the unrest at home, he was determined. He found her den in the opening of a cave, her bed a nest of branches. There was water close by, but most of the area was open and without good shelter. Winter was coming, so every day that he could, he climbed the mountain and worked on a single room log cabin for the little girl."

"Is it still standing today?"

Deke shook his head. "As the current day story goes, the cabin that Fernando the vineyard manager lives in is that cabin, but it's in the wrong place. That cabin came later, though for who or why, I don't know."

"If we could find the footprint for the girl's cabin, it would be something to photograph for the layout. Plus, it would prove the story."

Deke shook his head. "When we were kids, Jake and I crawled all over the mountain looking for it. We found the entrance to the cave, though as soon as we mentioned it, Dad covered it with boulders so we wouldn't get trapped inside. We found the spring. But we never found any evidence of the cabin."

Vince looked disappointed as he forked big pieces of apple pie into his mouth, the ice cream barely hanging on for the ride.

"Anyway, Great-Grandpa tried to win the girl's trust. When she came close to him while he was working, he tried to talk to her. He tried many times. But she always ran away. Finally, the cabin was finished, and he left her food and supplies now and then, even clothes. After a long time, she would sit silently at the edge of the clearing and watch him when he made his deliveries, but he never could convince her to come down off the mountain."

"So what happened to her? How did she survive up there?"

"No one really knows. She lived the rest of her life on the mountain. According to the stories, Great-Grandpa's firstborn son was entrusted with leaving supplies for the girl, by then grown into a woman. Then his firstborn son after him took over responsibilities. By then, the girl had grown into a very old woman, and the people of the time dubbed her the witch, based on her cackling noises and her weird ways."

They were both silent for a few minutes, Vince running the fork back and forth on his plate to pick up every crumb. What kind of diet did DK have this guy on, anyway? Soon he would pick the plate up and lick it.

"It's kind of sad, really." Vince continued to polish the plate as he spoke. "She was only a kid, and she never stood a chance." He set down his fork and looked up at Deke, his eyes sad. "It was nice, what your great-grandfathers did for her."

Deke nodded, lost in his contemplation of the current resurrection of the witch. "Yeah, it was. Now if she would only stay gone, we'd be at peace."

"Stay gone? What do you mean, stay gone? Is there more to this, man? Because if there is, I expect to hear about it for my story."

Chapter 31

"Marguerite, thank you for coming my dear."

She stood patiently for the kisses on the cheek, happy that her boss seemed to be in a friendly mood. When the invitation arrived for a meeting at the owners' house, she didn't know what to expect.

Waving her into the living room, Davinia disappeared into the kitchen. In the expanse of the living room, her husband Marcus stood and walked to Marguerite. He towered over her, both in height and in breadth. He probably towered over almost everyone on the planet. The legacy of his fierce football background endured in his muscled frame. And yet she'd heard that when he was in the emergency room working with a small child, he was the gentlest of teddy bears.

"Marguerite, sit down, sit down. We really appreciate you coming over in the middle of the workweek. We know how busy November can be in the winery."

"It is fine, Marcus. I am never too busy for you and Davinia." Though how much longer they would care remained to be seen.

"We're waiting on one more person, actually, the person who is the reason we needed to get together in the middle of the week. He said it couldn't wait."

She froze. There was nothing in Marcus's genial tone to indicate this was ominous, but the shiver ran through her even so.

Davinia bustled in, a bottle of wine in one hand and a carafe with what smelled like coffee in the other. Setting them down on a side table already carrying glasses and mugs, she turned with her trademark smile and walked to her husband.

"I have coffee and wine, since I don't know what Deke will want to drink. That's who is coming over, Marguerite, our neighbor Deke Kermarrec."

This was her only opportunity to share what she knew. If she waited until Deke told his story, it would make her look a thousand times worse.

"Davinia, Marcus, I have something I would like to explain to you before Mr. Kermarrec arrives. You see, about three months ago – "

When a brusque knock on the door interrupted her, it was all she could do not to swear out loud. Damn the man for having the worst timing in the world. Or damn her for not using an earlier opportunity to come clean.

Marcus rose and made his lumbering way to the door, throwing it open and putting out a hand to an unseen guest to shake. When he backed up, Deke made his appearance around the expanse of the open front door.

He met her eyes first, and she shivered. Missing was his usual easy-going smile. He wasn't frowning at her, exactly, but he did not look happy to see her. But he must have known she would be here.

Davinia stepped between them, effectively blocking their eye contact, and Marguerite dragged in breath, unsure what to do next. She could not leave, on this she was clear. She couldn't hide. She had her pride.

But she was at fault.

"Marguerite." She had missed his passage across the room, and he loomed over her with his body blocking their exchange from the Dawsons. She couldn't bring herself to meet his eyes again.

"Deke." Her voice pitched low from the constriction in her throat that she didn't seem to be able to control. When he didn't move and said nothing more, she finally looked up.

She expected anger, or perhaps vindication or victory. Instead, she saw sadness and regret. At this distance, his eyes were an intense blue-green, turbulent and stormy. As he continued to stare at her, the colors muted and his expression turned resigned.

"What can I pour for you? Marguerite, wine? Deke, wine, or perhaps coffee or something else? I wasn't sure what you'd prefer." Davinia's voice interrupted their stare, and Marguerite was grateful that their consummate hostess was too busy to see the tension that grew the longer they stayed in the same small space.

Deke turned and agreed to a glass of wine, much to Marguerite's surprise. When he smiled his trademark lazy drawl, she blinked. Gone was the hard man that stood in front of her moments before. As he chatted with both Dawsons about the return of his mother, she used the time to practice her breathing. It was not calming her as it should today. In fact, if anything, she was becoming more agitated as time passed.

Marcus handed her a glass of wine and she grasped it tightly. Where was her poise? Where were her topics of idle chitchat? As the conversation flowed around her, she took a small sip of wine, but today, it tasted like vinegar to her.

At what price had she created this wine?

Deke's friendly answers to question about Three Rivers finally petered out the small talk, much to Marguerite's relief. Now would be the time. He would explain why he was here, he would accuse her, and all would be over.

"Davinia, thanks for being willing to pull together this meeting of the four of us so quickly." He sat forward, and for the first time, she noticed the folders he had in his hands. None were particularly thick, but there were four of them, and as he handed two across the room to Davinia and Marcus, he only paused briefly. By the time he'd turned to her and handed her a folder, his mouth was open to continue.

She had only seconds, if that. If she was able to speak first, perhaps she could explain how this was *une erreur*, a simple mistake that she would rectify. His accusations would undoubtedly ruin her.

"You must know – "

"This is information – "

She looked at Deke, his words riding over hers. He frowned. Did he just shake his head to tell her no?

"Deke, please do go ahead." Davinia looked at her oddly. Of course she would. Marguerite had never been anything but unfailingly polite and charming. Her boss would have no reason to understand her current panic.

Deke leaned forward in his chair, his folder already open to the first piece of paper as he began to speak. Resigned, she leaned back and took a longer than usual pull of wine before setting the glass on the table. It would be best if no one saw her hands shake.

"I wanted us to meet today to come up with a plan for a problem that is affecting both our properties. Marguerite and I have been discussing this, and I believe that the best way to craft a solution will be for us to work jointly as landowners." He held up the first page in the folder, and she opened hers slowly to follow along.

The first page was the report from the USDA, citing the herbicide contaminates on Three Rivers. Following that was a letter retracting the ranch's organic status for those affected areas. She looked at them without seeing the words. She waited while Davinia and Marcus read through the documents, their faces becoming serious as frowns grew with their comprehension.

Deke didn't even glance at her, and she couldn't blame him. What did she expect to see in his eyes anyway?

"This is terrible news, Deke. To find this kind of poison on your property must be a shock to you."

Marcus nodded at his wife's words. "Have you had the toxicology verified yourself? These reports could be wrong, you know."

Deke nodded his head and stated that he had, in fact, suspected that there might be a problem. As he related the deaths of animals grazing in that pasture, and the subsequent testing at the vet school, she felt her heart turn to ice. She was surprised it could still pound. But it did, as the dull rhythm in her ears attested to. It would be better to rise, now, make her apologies, and leave to pack as soon as possible.

"What is the cause of this chemical?" Davinia's question was aimed at Deke, but she gave Marguerite a strange look. Her apprehension must be showing. She tried to empty her face of expression while she unknotted her fingers in her lap.

"That's just it, we're not completely sure. Marguerite and I couldn't come up with any obvious answers."

Her heart stopped for the space of three seconds. He wasn't accusing her, as he had every right to do. He wasn't blaming her in front of the winery's owners. In fact, he let her off the hook for any culpability.

Why would he do this?

"Pourquoi voudriez-vous faire cela?"

The question burst out of her before she could stop it. Davinia and Marcus snapped their attention to her, startled. She knew they didn't speak French, something they'd laughed about in the past. Now it seemed like a blessing, as long as Deke understood.

"Je le fais parce que je crois que nous pouvons arranger les choses." His words were smooth and without hesitation.

He believed they could work things out. Did he mean between the ranch and the winery? Or did he mean between the two of them?

She sat silent, staring into a face that was now blank of any obvious expression, but with eyes churning gray and green.

"I'm sorry, I don't understand." Davinia's statement seemed to be directed towards both of them as her gaze switched between the two of the sharply.

"I'm sorry, it's a habit that Marguerite and I have fallen into. She gives me an opportunity to practice my rusty French." He broke their shared link to focus again on Davinia and Marcus as he flipped to the third page in the folder. "Here is more information about the specific type of herbicide, about its uses and its toxic effects."

This time the couple across from them waited longer before they read the sheet, obviously expecting more. When Deke said nothing, their eyes dropped to the page.

She felt his eyes on her, and she turned. There was a question in his, and she knew what he was asking. Did she want to say it, or should he? When she broke his gaze and picked up her wineglass instead, she thought she heard him sigh.

"Marguerite, do we use this herbicide at the winery?" The question was delivered by Marcus in a tone that meant business.

She swallowed and hoped that the vague but noncommittal expression she hoped to set on her features had worked. "Yes, we do, Marcus."

"I didn't realize we used anything that was so toxic." Davinia's tone conveyed her dismay, and Marguerite winced.

"It is an industry standard. During the months when the grasses and weeds compete for nutrients and water the vines require, it is the most effective way of controlling them."

Marcus shook his head, his finger running down the information on the page. "This chemical could have severe physical consequences for anyone coming into contact with it. I think we need to discuss what other means we can use to contain unwanted growth. Perhaps we can hire an expert in sustainable practices to advise us before the next growing season. Maybe someone like Deke, if he's open to it."

He glanced at the other man, waiting for an indication of agreement. Deke nodded his head, then turned to her. This time, his gaze was stern, like he was prompting her for something.

She knew what he wanted. Now was the time to agree as well. He didn't need to know that she was missing a full container of this same concentrated herbicide. Diluted, it would treat the whole vineyard for seasons to come.

She could tell young David that she'd found the container. That would mean she could keep the situation to herself. It wasn't the most ethical thing to do, and it made her feel sick to even consider it. But if she told the truth and exposed her knowledge, her job was gone.

The man, she suspected, would be gone for her no matter what. She would never be able to have a relationship with someone she lied to.

Chapter 32

She should have apologized. She knew she was guilty, and while he said nothing about it in public, Deke knew it too – just not the extent of it. And yet, she'd allowed him to remain neutral in his discussion with Davinia and Marcus. Never once did he lay the blame at her feet.

He had paused frequently during the discussion, staring at her and waiting. If he looked disappointed when she said nothing, it was his problem, not hers. If he seemed resolved to maintain their distance when he gazed at her before he left, that was on him too. Her missed call signal indicated that he'd called frequently in the time since, but only once did he leave her a message.

"Marguerite, I'd like to talk. I'm sorry things got so convoluted. I miss you."

His voice on the message was ragged and frayed, deep with emotion. He'd left it in the early hours of the morning, when the night was darkest. She knew, because she'd spent those same hours gazing at her bedroom ceiling. While he'd called since then, he hadn't left a single word. She couldn't bring herself to erase the lone voicemail.

She stared at the red wine stain in the wood floor. The man she'd hired to replace the flooring said it would take a few weeks to find matching material. Then he would call and set up a time to do the work. In the mean time, she had a daily reminder of her own stupidity.

And of the witch. She would not return, would she? The kitchen corner remained empty, but that brought no peace. The haven of safety that had once been her home had now been invaded, both by the ghost and by her own pathetic thoughts.

Stupide, imbécile, bête. There were too many reasons to name. For not apologizing when she knew the probable reason for the poisoning. For knowing the extent of the problem and not revealing it. For letting herself get caught up in feelings for a man who both accused her and aroused her.

To David, she had lied outright when he asked what they were going to do about the missing container of herbicide.

"Oh, I located it. Didn't I mention it to you? It wasn't stored with the rest. We put it in another storage area because we would not need it until next year." The young man looked confused, but only replied that this was good news, right?

She took another sip of her wine and paced the distance to her living room. She hadn't said anything to Deke about the container, not when the discussion at the Dawsons had ended and he walked her to her car with no words exchanged between them. When she shut her door, he remained standing with his hands on his hips, watching her. Looking up at him, she couldn't read anything into his expression.

Dropping down into the sofa, she set her wineglass on the side table with unsteady hands. She examined them as they shook in front of her eyes. The fact was, this situation was more complicated than anything she'd ever faced, and considerably more *tragique* as well.

Pounding on her front door startled her and she sank further into her seat. The witch would not knock, would she?

"Marguerite, open up this damn door."

"We know you're in there. Open up, sweetie."

She breathed in a huge sigh when she recognized the voices of Roxy and DK outside. Still, she was paralyzed, unable to move from the sofa or call out in acknowledgement.

"Her car's here. Check the door." Roxy's authoritative voice rang out over whatever anyone else said outside, and the door handle jiggled.

She had locked it. Why, she was not sure. She never locked it before now, always feeling safe.

"Locked. Do you know where she hides the key?" Sounds of pottery being shifted on her porch finally convinced her limbs to move, and she rose and made her unsteady way to the door, flipping the lock and swinging it open part way.

"Finally. What the hell were you doing in there anyway? And why is the door locked?" Roxy burst in, bags in hand, followed by DK, similarly laden with packages. Tess brought up the rear and held out a huge bouquet of flowers.

"From the garden. We heard you needed cheering up, and we're here with cheering up supplies."

Roxy started pulling things out of the bags she'd dumped on the kitchen counter. "Chocolate and vanilla ice cream. Caramel sauce, which I remember is your favorite."

DK added her bundles to the melee and said, "Boxes of tissues, just in case, and butter cookies, also your favorite."

Tess rummaged in a lower cabinet and reappeared with a large vase. "And flowers, to remind you that there is beauty in the world."

She stared in disbelief at the growing mound of items on the counter top. This kind of activity wasn't unusual when one of the girl tribe was hurting. In fact, she had herself participated in more than one of these so-called interventions.

"But why are you here?"

"We told you, sweetie, we heard you needed cheering up. Now sit down over there, we'll open some wine and you can tell us all about it." DK took her unresisting arm and led her over to the couch, setting her gently in the same spot she'd just vacated and taking away her almost-empty wineglass.

"Hey, what happened to the floor in here, Marguerite? Did you spill some wine?"

Roxy's words were delivered in a normal tone, without accusation or judgment, but she couldn't help it.

She burst into tears.

*****

"Mac has a way of getting stories all screwed up." Roxy delivered the pronouncement fondly. "But I'm glad, for once, that he was gossiping."

It took her a while to sort it out, why her friends were here. Mac talked to Deke, who nearly bit his head off. Since the only thing the men knew how to do to be supportive was to head for the bar and a game of pool or darts, that's what the wolf pack did. And given enough tequila, Deke had said that he and Marguerite had broken up, not that they were ever together, damn it. And then he said nothing more.

While some of the nuances were lost between the wolf pack and their girl tribe other halves, enough was said to make the women think that she needed them.

Marguerite pushed the ice cream around in its bowl, the caramel sauce adding to the melting mess. It had the consistency of soup, not that she cared.

"I am sorry that you came all the way out here for nothing." She looked around at her friends, trying to smile.

"From what you said, it's not nothing. You and Deke had a relationship until you had a disagreement and it didn't work out. You feel responsible, so you feel terrible."

Tess set her own bowl aside and leaned forward. "Are you sure you don't want to be the bigger person and apologize?"

That set her off. She never apologized. Even when she should.

Shaking her head, she took a spoonful of the syrupy mess and used it as an excuse not to answer. But no one filled the silence that followed.

They all watched her with differing amounts of sympathy, empathy and support. She'd been there for each of them in one form or another. And now they were here for her. But it was hard to admit that they were correct. She should apologize, and for more than she'd told them.

"I never apologize. It is a sign of weakness."

Her friends blinked and exchanged puzzled glances.

"But Marguerite, I can recall specific instances where you've urged each of us to apologize." Tess's words were followed by heads shaking in agreement from DK and Roxy.

"That is for you. For me, *non*. Besides, he is as much to blame for the way things were left as I was. He should apologize as well."

She realized she sounded like a child having a tantrum, but it seemed she could not help it. Leaning back in a position that she hoped they would take as nonchalance, she tried on another smile.

No one smiled back. DK frowned. Tess worried the edge of a shawl. And Roxy looked – well, she wasn't sure what that expression was on her face but there might be a string of swear words to follow.

"Are you listening to yourself, Marguerite? I mean, really listening?" And Roxy continued on with an impressive string of curses that included French, Spanish and something that Marguerite thought was Russian.

The strain of holding on to so many stories, of keeping so many lies, was getting to her. She couldn't help herself when she giggled, a noise that made Roxy stop and the others gaze on in horror. The giggles soon became hiccups, and that led to tears again. DK passed the tissues box and Tess patted her back.

"I don't know where you get these stupid ideas in your head, but it has to stop, okay? Apologizing is a sign of strength, because it lets the other person know that while you recognize you're wrong, you still want to maintain the relationship with them." Roxy shook her head. "Always be ready to apologize, sweetie. Unless you want to end up alone in your life."

Chapter 33

The sun was barely up, and she'd beaten its rise by a couple of hours. Driving always soothed her, allowing her to think in ways that sitting still would not allow. Her snappy little car ate up the miles as she tried to empty her mind of every emotion.

Her friends had been adamant. Apologize if she wanted her relationship with Deke to go anywhere. Otherwise, there was no hope. She was wrong, so was he. It didn't matter who blinked first.

Except in her book, it did.

What if she said she was sorry, and he did not respond in kind? What if he laughed? What if he was angry?

What if she told him the truth, the full truth, and he did not forgive her but publicized her error instead?

Perhaps it was too early to go to work, but at least there, she felt she was on solid ground. There, she knew what she was doing. Relationships? Not so much.

She circled over a freeway ramp and headed back towards Flynn's Crossing, the rising sun in her eyes. Even with her doubts, she trusted Deke, with her heart and with her body.

His lovemaking had been warm and thoughtful. Coming together with him was like being burned by the heat of the sun. She had never found that before. And she would undoubtedly lose it if she did not take the first step.

When the exit came up, she took it automatically. Even this early, the town was bustling with activity. Farmers and ranchers, commuters and parents, children on their way to school. Everyone seemed to have a purpose, a place to be and someone who expected them.

Could she have that? It would be a risk. She loved to take risks, but not with her heart. She held herself apart from others so that she could always step away when she needed to.

Princess. He called her Princess.

"Why do you have this nickname for me?"

He'd smiled at her slightly pissed off question.

"Because you carry yourself like royalty, as if the rest of us poor peons are merely subjects here for your amusement and service."

There had been no malice in his eyes when he said it. In fact, his eyes had shown bright blue, the same color they glittered when he was inside her, or when he was forcing her to climb that tall hill to release. He would never let her fall.

Except now, perhaps he had.

A short beep from the car behind her brought her eyes forward once more, automatically putting her foot on the gas when she noticed the green light.

What did losing Deke mean to her, after all? It wasn't as if they were ever truly together. Their relationship was never that – a relationship. It was more like two rocks grazing each other as they fell down a hillside.

At the stop sign, she picked up her phone and scrolled to Deke's message. His face came up on the screen, and she stared at it. Like she'd done often in the past days, she played the message again.

'Marguerite, I'd like to talk. I'm sorry things got so convoluted. I miss you.'

A friendly horn behind her startled her into driving once more. She should call him and apologize. But would he understand? What if she told him everything? Her mind traveled over the same ground countless times, but she never came up with a different answer.

He would never forgive her.

"Ms. Marguerite? Are you okay?"

She jerked, oblivious to the fact that she'd parked in her usual spot under the big oak tree next to the barrel room's entrance. How long she'd been sitting there, staring into vine-filled space, she had no clue. David bent to peer in her open window, the question hanging in the air between them. Snapping eyes forward, she noticed Fernando leaning against the doorjamb, hands in his pockets while he worried yet another lollipop stick in his teeth. His face held more curiosity than concern.

Jamming the door open with so much force that David almost tumbled on to the gravel, she replied, "I am fine, David, simply fine. I have much on my mind this morning, that is all." She gathered her purse and briefcase quickly, her hand only hesitating when she reached for that ominous cell phone. When her fingers closed around it, she shoved it as deeply into her purse as she could before straightening.

"I have some calls to make, so I will be in my office, gentlemen. I do not wish to be disturbed for a time. I will find you once I am ready to discuss plans for moving the barrels today."

And she sailed past them both, barely hearing Fernando's humph of disbelief as the metal door to the dark interior crashed into the rock used as a doorstop.

Cool air washed over her skin when she finally slowed, her eyes adjusting to the lack of light. She hadn't even noticed that she was sweating until a chilly wave made the hairs on her arms stand up. Sucking in a breath, she found no comfort in the astringency of aging wine and rougher tang of old wood, scents so familiar that they should bring her ease. The phone, silent in the bottom of her purse, was like a ticking time bomb, louder than her heels on the concrete.

"Marguerite, do you have a few minutes? I'd like to go over the winter events to make sure we're in agreement about which wines we'd like to feature."

She bit back a rebuff, knowing that Davinia would sense her agitation and want to discover the cause. The bomb ticked louder, but she stopped and put a smile on her face before turning as the older woman intercepted her.

"Yes, of course. But may I have a moment to drop these things in my office? I'll be right with you."

Marguerite turned back towards her office before Davinia had a chance to agree, and she entered her lair with more speed than grace. The briefcase landed on her desk chair, the purse crinkling the stacks of papers on her desk and sending some sideways as she clawed inside the big bag. Why she decided to have a huge bag she wasn't sure, since she rarely filled it. And now, when she wanted to wrap her fingers around the phone and dial his number, praying he'd answer before she lost her nerve, she couldn't find it.

"Are you all right, my dear?"

Her head snapped up to find Davinia standing in her open doorway, a sheaf of papers in her hand. The older woman was curious, examining Marguerite's face like it was a business problem she intended to unravel. She crossed her arms, the papers wrinkling into her elbow's bend as she filled the opening. For a petite woman, she could take up significant space when she chose to.

Marguerite shook her head, her facial muscles refusing to pull into the polite smile she knew needed to be there. Without it, she was vulnerable, unmasked, with her emotions bare for the world to see.

"You aren't all right, I can see that."

She spun to move the purse to the credenza, ready to set any of Davinia's concerns at ease, when she caught her own reflection in the glass covering the photo of grapes on her back wall. Her eyes were more than a little wild, cavernous over the tense line of her mouth. She'd obviously run her hands through her hair more than a few times, since it was pulled in every direction except its usual neat curls. And as she pushed her hand into her purse again, searching desperately for that phone, she realized she was shaking.

Taking another cleansing breath, she turned back to her employer again. "Davinia, I'm sorry. There is something I need to attend to. I should not be long, but if you would not mind?"

She let the question trail off. Davinia frowned at her, but there was no anger in her expression. When she spoke, her frustration was clear.

"Marguerite, I think of you as another of my daughters. I worry about you, just like I do about them. I won't pry into your secrets, but you've been off-kilter and on edge for weeks now. Fernando said you're biting people's heads off. Mind you, he's not going around you and complaining," she held up a hand to stop the question Marguerite already felt forming on her lips," but he's worried about you. So I'll ask you once again, is there something I need to know, or to do?"

The premonition jarred through her again with Davinia's words. First Deke, his too-perceptive gaze tracking her movements with more stealth and determination than one of his herding dogs. Then the girl tribe's pointed questions. And now her employer, the one who would have every right to fire her.

Turning back to the framed photo, she made an effort to quiet the tremors in her hands. Pushing her curls back into alignment was easier than organizing the confusion of her thoughts. The candle she kept on the file cabinet in the corner reached its fragrance out to her, and she steadied another breath on its lavender aroma. In the distance, she heard the men raising their voices as the forklift clanged to life.

Spinning fast enough to make Davinia blink, Marguerite straightened the upset piles of papers on her desk.

"I am sorry. It is my fault. I have been distracted, and I am allowing it to show in my work. That is not appropriate. You have my sincere apology for that, and I will express the same to the workers and beg their patience. It has been a trying time in recent months."

Davinia's eyes narrowed almost imperceptibly in her dark face, though her expression remained concerned. Marguerite felt the gaze search over her features, looking for the cracks in her armor. There were many, and undoubtedly the older woman saw them all. What she chose to do about them was another story. "I'm not sure what's wrong, but know that I'm here to help. I regard us as more than employer and employee, I hope you understand that. Whatever is really bothering you, my dear, I hope you'll decide that you can confide in me."

And for the second time in less than a day, Marguerite burst into tears.

*****

"Well who the hell do you think she was going to call? Honestly, for a smart woman, you're really stupid sometimes."

Marguerite wanted to protest, yell, bitch. The hands resting on her shoulders gave a squeeze and another set pushed tissues in front of her and shoved a water glass closer on the desktop with only barely concealed frustration.

"Now what the fuck – pardon my French – is wrong with you now? Your intervention didn't even last twenty-four hours."

She couldn't help it. She laughed, the sound almost hysterical through her tears. DK shushed from behind her while Roxy towered in front of her, looking much taller than her short frame. This was the master chef, the commander of kitchens full of minions. And she wanted answers.

Marguerite swallowed back the sudden new round of pain. It was too much, all too much. And she nearly blurted out the whole ugly story.

"Ah, come on now. I didn't mean it. God, you're going to make me cry too now. Stop with the waterworks already." Roxy pushed the whole box of tissues into Marguerite's nose as DK tsk-tsked.

"What Roxy means, sweetie, is that we're worried about you. When Davinia called to say that you were very upset, she stressed the very part. And now we can see it for ourselves. But what we don't know is why. You seemed to be okay when we left you last night." DK gave a last shoulder squeeze before she shuffled around the chair to sit next to Roxy on the edge of the desk.

She pulled in a deep breath and blew it out slowly. Tying the tissue into a knot in her fingers, she finally looked up.

"I have a long story to tell you."

Chapter 34

His gut churned every time he thought about her. Her phone silence was deafening.

Why wasn't she willing to talk with him? At the Dawsons, he expected her to apologize, or at least to admit to her part in this fiasco. But she'd had no comments as he'd laid out the situation. Afterwards, and even when she had agreed to work with him to find the source of the problem and eliminate it, she'd said nothing more. He'd said all he knew to say in his message to her. It had been almost a week, and still no word.

What did she expect from him now?

He looped the wire in his gloved hands and walked towards the next fencepost. The hands had moved the cattle from the contaminated grazing area, emptied the water tank, and turned off the pump to the poisoned well. In another couple of hours, he'd have the area cordoned off. Only once it was secure would he feel like he had the time to pursue the elusive Ice Princess and see why she'd been ignoring him.

"Boss? I need to go check on Pop."

He looked up at Carl, taking in the fidgeting feet and the worry on the other man's face.

"Is he still sick?"

"He's never confessed to being sick in the first place, exactly. But he's also not going to a doctor for that cough. It's been months now. I'm ready to rope him and take him myself."

Deke's mood lightened at the picture this formed in his mind. It didn't last long, considering that he knew where

Fernando would be. And that led him right back to the woman occupying so much territory in his mind. He had to get things settled between them or he'd end up with an ulcer.

"It's the middle of the day. I'm betting you can find him at the winery and subdue him without too much fuss." He eyed the footage between him and the last few fence posts, then glanced up at the sky. By noon, they could be finished if they worked together. He could feel the expected rain hanging as a threat in the air. It matched his mood perfectly.

"Tell you what. If you give me a hand with this wire, we can get it done in half the time. I need to visit the winery anyway and talk to Marguerite. I can follow you over once we're done and help you convince Fernando to let you take him to the doctor. Hell, I can help you tie him up and throw him in your truck. Then I can take care of my business."

"Sounds like a solid plan. I wasn't overly fond of trying to convince the old man by myself." Relief made his words sound almost joyful.

Carl pulled leather gloves out of his back pocket and leaned down for a roll of wire. Walking to the next post, he began the painstaking job of tying on the wire, his twists no less skilled than Deke's. Satisfied that no direction would be necessary, Deke walked over to the quadrunner and pulled a bottle of water from the cooler in the back.

"Deke, is all this bad temper on your part because of the contamination?"

The question wasn't surprising, considering that was all the hands talked about in the past few days. He'd heard the rumblings, the dismay over the issue and various suggestions on how best to get the winery to cooperate. Then they'd give him a wide berth when he strode through a pasture or by the barn. He was sure his face gave away every raging thought he'd had about the lack of melting on the part of the Ice Princess.

Turning back to the fence line, he waited a stretch to calm his thoughts. Draining the water bottle, he hefted it into the back of the quad where it settled with a rattle of peeved plastic. He pulled his coat closer to block out a sudden draft of cold air, as chilly as her regard for him that evening a few nights back, and looked up the hill towards the winery.

"The Dawsons are more than willing to work with us. They're now interested in embracing sustainable practices for the vineyards. I think that's a huge step in the right direction."

Carl didn't reply. He unrolled a section of wire, twisted it in place, and pulled it taunt. The frown on his face was more pronounced than Deke had seen in a while.

"Have you heard something different from your dad?"

Carl shook his head almost immediately. "No, though I have to tell you, he acts weird whenever I've tried to talk to him about it. It's no secret that you've lost more animals than usual this year. When I've asked him about the chemicals he's had to use, he clams up. Doesn't want to talk about it and changes the subject as fast as he can."

Deke's frown darkened along with his thoughts. "Do you think he's hiding something?"

"I'm not sure what's happening. He used to be an open book, but lately, not so much. All he's willing to talk about at any length is how much he's looking forward to setting himself up in Las Vegas. It's like he can't wait to leave, but at least he seems to feel guilty about it."

He'd meant to tell Marguerite about Fernando's accelerated plans. She deserved to know. Maybe she already did. Besides, it gave him the perfect opening to discuss other business with her, like the unfinished business between them.

The flash of sadness and regret in her eyes as they parted at the Dawsons burned like an open wound. Did she regret their time together? Or did she only regret getting caught for her part in this mess?

He could still feel her soft skin under his fingers. That very memory made his body tighten and sped up his heart. But it was her mind, her entertaining grasp of a wide range of subjects almost as eclectic as his, that captured him as well. No, there were too many facets to the Princess for him to name, and once and for all, they were going to figure out if they had a chance for a future together. He hoped that the regret she felt was primarily because they weren't together now.

*****

"Excuse me, Ms. Marguerite, but I was wondering if you had the keys to the forklift."

David stood in her doorway, his face a picture of consternation.

"No, I do not have them, David. And please, will you finally call me Marguerite?"

He smiled at that, his freckles showing up more, if that was possible, as he blushed.

"Sure Ms. Mar – I mean, Marguerite. Thank you, really, thank you." He advanced into the room with a hand outstretched, and she had to laugh at his clear joy. Shaking hands with him involved an exaggerated pump of her arm to the shoulder.

Then he frowned again. "I wonder where the keys are."

"Have you asked Fernando?"

Now he looked frustrated, and for once, she could see the experienced adult under the guise of the fledgling winemaker.

"That's just it. I can't find him. He came in for a few minutes this morning, and then he disappeared. No one seems to know where he is."

All right. She had been hiding out in her office. In fact, she had been hiding out as much as possible.

Yes, she was scared and uncertain and this seemed the best way to cope with the feelings. But not to the exclusion of monitoring her employees. That would not do.

She rose and grabbed her coat off the back of her chair, waving David out the office door. "I'll find him. In the mean time, I'll show you where we keep the back-up keys. It is important for you to know this no matter what."

As she led the way through the tasting room and out to the tank area, she finished the thought in her head. If the Dawsons ever found out she'd lost a container of herbicide, she'd be out of a job and David would be running the place. He damn well better know where everything was.

"I doubt they'd fire you for that, Marguerite. I mean, really? People lose things all the time. A container of herbicide is hardly the crown jewels." DK's assurance a week ago still played in her mind.

"And tell us again – why didn't you say anything to Deke about this? I mean, I get why you still didn't tell the Dawsons, though I don't agree with it. But Deke? He's crazy about you, and I'm sure he'll understand that some kind of accident occurred." Roxy's matter-of-fact statement only made her gut clench more tightly.

"I am not sure it was an accident. What if I gave the wrong instructions? What if I was the one who caused his well to be poisoned? Even if I didn't mean to do so, the fact is, somehow too much herbicide was applied on Witch Hill, and in the runoff from the rain, it ended up on Three Rivers."

She'd said nothing about seeing the effects of that chemical on the animals. That contorted red and white cow face might be with her until the day she died.

"And why do you think he is crazy about me? He has done nothing to reach out to me, other than the one message. He wants nothing to do with me."

Roxy shook her head vehemently. "No, you have that wrong. According to Mac, who was with Deke and Jake and some of the other guys the other day Deke tried to drink out his troubles, he's like an angry bull stung by a bee and unable to pull the stinger out." When Marguerite had looked at Roxy with a confused expression, she shrugged. "Those weren't my words, they were Mac's. I have the meaning right even if the analogy isn't too slick."

"He is angry because his organic certification is being cancelled."

Now it was DK's turn to shake her head in disagreement. "Not according to Vince. He talks to Deke about every other day, and he said he's come to terms with it, is making changes to avoid using that piece of land until it's cleared as organic once more, and is moving on. While he doesn't particularly like what's happened, the fact that he knows the cause and has a plan to work on it with you seems to be enough for him."

Deke, happy only knowing that sustainability would be practiced here in the future? Marcus had directed her on this already, and Davinia went so far as to say that she was relieved they would be protecting the land for future generations. They said they were looking forward to hearing her plans on implementing these ideas as soon as possible.

No, he was up to something. He was probably plotting her humiliation by any means possible. Work was the only solution to her heartache.

Marching through the barrel room, she rounded the last stack to the far unused corner. "David, here is the lockbox with the extra keys, combinations, and other monitoring information." She rattled off the combination code, which the young man promptly entered into his smartphone. "You open it, so that you're sure you have it right."

He stepped around her, twirled the combination, and opened the box on the first try. Turning a triumphant smile back to Marguerite, he said, "No problem. My phone is with me all the time, so I'll never forget it. And I back it up to my computer at home, so it's safe." He spun back to scan the interior of the box. "Everything's labeled, that's great. And here is exactly what I need."

As he pulled the extra forklift keys out and took a few steps away, she stopped him.

"David? Shouldn't you relock something?"

He blushed and grinned sheepishly, shaking his head. "Okay, I got a little excited."

She smiled back at him. It was hard not to, since his constant good humor was infectious.

"Promise me something, David."

"Yes ma'am?"

She tried not to flinch at his formality. "Promise me you will never lose your youthful enthusiasm and turn into a cynical person like me."

Young eyes whirled to her in surprise. "But you're not cynical. You laugh a lot. You tease us all. You make this a fun place to work." He shook his head.

Wishing she'd kept her thoughts to herself now, she inhaled the rich aromas of wines aging in their barrels. Every once in a while, wood would creek, or the cooling system for the tank room would fire up. It was usually a peaceful place that brought her great joy. But not today.

As they re-emerged into the tasting room and stood near her office door, David looked uncharacteristically serious. "My grandmother, she used to have a saying for everything. I mean, everything. And she used to say that if you were in a bad mood, it was because you were carrying extra baggage on the inside. Drop that baggage, and it lightens your load." He blushed again. "You probably think that's silly."

Lighten her load. Yes, she was carrying many extra bags these days. And she had no idea where she could drop them.

"I think it's very perceptive of you to know what I needed to hear. And your grandmother was a very wise woman."

Chapter 35

The parking apron next to the winery's back door was crowded as Deke pulled his truck to a stop next to Carl's.

"I don't see Pop's car." Carl scanned the parking area, then turned his attention to another group of vehicles near the edge of the vineyard. "He must not be here."

"He might have gotten a ride with someone, or be working on another part of the property. It would be unusual for him to miss a day of work, right?"

Deke fell into step beside the younger man as a red-headed worker exited the winery door. Seeing them, he smiled.

"Hey Carl. How are you?" Shaking hands, he turned to Deke. "Mr. Kermarrec, sorry to hear about your troubles."

That was the thing about a rural community. Everyone knew your business.

"I was looking for Pop. Do you know where he is?" Carl stared around the open area again like he hoped his father would materialize.

David shook his head. "I don't know where he is. He was here this morning first thing, then he left. He didn't say where he was going. Sorry."

Deke was already walking for the door. "Maybe Marguerite knows."

Behind him, David said, "No, she didn't know he'd left at all."

"What the hell is that old man up to? He never misses work." Carl pushed a hand through his hair when Deke paused to look between the two men.

"He seems to be gone a lot recently, and he's distracted, almost as much as Marguerite."

Hearing she was distracted was a good sign. Maybe that meant she was as worked up over everything that had happened between them – and what wasn't happening – as he was.

Before he could comment, a rumble of engine noise sounded around the curve on the winery driveway, and a dusty old truck pulled into view. It wheezed to a halt behind Deke's, and the door opened. He knew who the occupant would be, but he couldn't help himself.

"Uncle Royan? What the hell are you doing here?"

The old man glanced around the assembled faces as if searching for someone, then frowned and shook his head. He seemed ready to spit on the ground and thought the better of it.

"I was looking for Fernando. Any of you see him?"

"That's who we're all looking for, evidently." Deke retraced his steps to join the small circle. "No one seems to know where he is."

Royan took off his hat and scrubbed at his hair. He seemed to be cleaner these days, undoubtedly his mother's influence. His clothes were freshly washed and his hair didn't need a cut as badly as it had a few weeks ago.

"Damn, I don't get it. Fernando called me up, all excited, and wanted to meet for coffee this morning in town. Said he had something to show me, something important." He noticed Carl's frown. "I hate to tell you, son, but he never showed up."

*****

She'd heard the unfamiliar truck outside, but thought nothing of it. Different vehicles appeared here all the time.

It might be a delivery or a worker checking in. But the rise of excited male voices was more than unusual.

This gave her a welcomed excuse to get out of her office, and with that, perhaps out of her own head. Ever since David had shared his grandmother's wisdom, that was all she could think about.

Baggage. Her guilt. Keeping secrets. David was able to teach her something after all. She must remember to tell him that.

She pulled on her jacket as she headed for the doorway and the beckoning late fall light outside. The tang of dried leaves overcame the aroma of wine, the closer she got to the door. One voice was raised in concerned questions, a voice she did not recognize.

As she broached the door, David was responding. "I don't know what's going on with him, honestly. He's been acting crabby and out of sorts, then the next day it's like he's cackling with glee over something. I asked him a couple of times, and he told me to mind my own business."

She stopped outside the door and took in the scene. David stood with two men she didn't recognize, one older and one younger.

Then the men shifted, and there he stood. Deke, bundled in a thick jacket and wearing worn jeans and heavy boots. His head was bare, and in the filtered autumn light, his loose hair shone in a gold that matched the leaves turning on the vines. It was a little longer than she remembered it, and her fingers twitched to burrow into it and nest.

Then their eyes met, and she froze. He could do this to her, pin her with his eyes alone. He looked equally startled, though he must have expected that she was here. This was her winery, after all.

She forced her feet to move and was proud of herself for not stumbling on the gravel. The men had stopped talking, but she had a hard time concentrating on anyone other than Deke. His eyes lured her closer.

Baggage. She must remember that she still had baggage to carry.

"Gentlemen, can I help you with something?"

Deliberately turning away from the man who held her enthralled, she faced the old man standing next to him. "Marguerite Devereaux. I am the winemaker here."

The old man grinned and turned a sly expression to Deke before he stepped forward with a hand outstretched.

"Why you're three times as pretty as Emie said you were. She'd kick my ass if I didn't mention how tickled she was to have such a nice long visit with you the other day. And I can see why Deke's so smitten."

*****

He could feel himself turning red, and while he wanted to glower at his uncle, he couldn't seem to turn away.

His Princess looked even more ravishing today, bundled into a coat that she probably reserved for working in the vines on cold days, worn as it was. Her jeans had well-washed wine stains on them, and her boots bore similar discolorations. As the wind picked up her hair, she grabbed it automatically and wound it into that informal knot she liked to do at the base of her neck.

It was her eyes that clutched at his heart, though. She'd been the epitome of poise, able to deal with whatever the issue was, until she saw him. He watched the change occur. One minute, she was the Ice Princess, ready to deal with her court. The next, she was frightened and ready to flee as a rabbit running from a predator.

"Mr. Kermarrec, it is a pleasure to meet you. And yes, please tell Emie that I too enjoyed our time together." When she glanced back at Deke, he saw none of the fear in her eyes. She'd shut down the gates to her kingdom. Damned if he was going to let her get away with it.

"I guess I'd better head down to his cabin. He's not answering his cell phone and he doesn't have a land line. I hope he didn't fall or something."

"He was here until about 9:30, if that helps you out at all," David responded.

"And he was supposed to meet me at 10:30. What's the old coot up to now?"

Royan walked away with Carl, and they got in their respective trucks and pulled away. David jingled the keys in his hand in Marguerite's direction and she nodded without comment. Then she turned as if she was going to walk away from him.

Damn that nonsense too.

He caught up with her, putting a hand around her upper arm and pulling her closer.

"We need to talk."

She stopped walking and looked pointedly at his hand. Anger flashed in her eyes right before she shrugged, clearly making an effort to quell the emotion. He had to admire her spirit and her assurance. He doubted he could turn off his feelings that quickly no matter what the situation.

"I am still doing my research on the practices that Witch Hill will implement for sustainability." She looked down again at his hand and attempted to shake it off.

"I'm not here about vineyard management and you know it." He couldn't keep the anger out of his voice. She brought out the extreme in him in any category.

"We have nothing to discuss, you and I." The coldness in her voice could freeze the planet.

"I disagree." He started them walking again, heading for the winery door. When she resisted, he added, "Do you want to have this out where everyone can see us and anyone can overhear? Or would the privacy of your office be a safer bet?"

She glared at him but started to walk again, her boots crunching the gravel, then stamping across the concrete floor of the tank room.

Hell if she didn't turn him on even when he was furious with her. And she was equally livid with him, based on her thunderous expression.

When they entered her office, he dropped her arm. If she wanted to leave, she'd have to go through him. He was ready to fight her if necessary when she pulled her purse out of a desk drawer and slammed it shut.

She pounded around the desk, her rage evident in every step. When she stepped up to him and stood almost pressing her chest against him, he fought the urge to close the distance. But mashing her luscious softness into him wasn't going to accomplish anything.

"I will drive home. You may follow me. We will have our discussion there."

Her eyes dared him to argue.

Chapter 36

She drove with studied control over the few miles around the mountain to her cabin. Speed limits were obeyed to the number. She turned on the signal for each turn, and made a show of checking traffic in both directions multiple times.

She was seething. Worse than that, she anticipated that Deke enjoyed baiting her. The longer she drove, the stormier she felt. And the skies looked like they echoed her emotions, drawing tense dark clouds across the horizon and making the afternoon light seem like dusk.

Pulling into her usual parking spot, she put the car in park with great deliberation. Next to her, Deke parked and opened his door, closing it again with a distinct thwack that carried as much angry force as she felt. She checked her face in the mirror, smoothing back hair that had been upended by the wind. Satisfied that she could put on a good show, she reached for her purse.

He wrenched open her car door as her hands closed around the handle, and that was all it took to set her off.

"What the hell do you think you're doing?" She surged out of the car with the words, barely missing an opportunity to barrel into him.

"I'm opening your car door to help you out. What the hell do you think I'm doing?"

Good, he was as angry as she was. She was spoiling for a good fight.

"Do not touch my car. Do not touch my home. Do not touch me." She stepped forward as she slammed the door shut, and he didn't back down, leaving her so close that she could see the myriad shades of color swirling in his eyes. Those eyes would be the death of her yet.

When he stepped closer, so close that they were almost nose to nose, he reached around her and put a hand on her car. Palm flat, he left it there, his eyes daring her to do something about it.

He gave her that lazy grin, exaggerated in the slow way it lifted the corners of his lips. She couldn't help but focus on those lips at the moment. His free hand came up just as slowly and reached out, cupping her cheek.

Her hand came up without any conscious prompting before he could react, and she slapped his left cheek with a crack, leaving an immediate mark. Her other hand was halfway to his face when he grabbed her wrist and yanked her into him.

When his mouth came down on hers, it was furious, the heat boiling off him and into her like a lightning bolt. Clamping her lips shut, she fought the invasion of his tongue, but it was a losing battle. She wanted him too much. If the only way they could be together was to fight, so be it. *Apporter la bataille.*

He broke away as soon as her tongue fenced with his. She watched his rapid breathing cloud the cold air around them, feeling the heavy pounding of his heart in his chest as he pressed against her breasts. The resonance left her aching.

"So this is what it takes to get the Ice Princess to melt." His statement made her focus on his face once more.

His lips pressed together in a thin line, none of the drawling humor apparent now. Skin pulled taut over his cheekbones and tense lines feathered around the corners of his eyes. *Glacé* transformed to dangerous agitation, until she was no longer sure what colors were mixing.

He forced her hands to her sides, retaining the hold on her wrists as he walked her back to press against the side of her car. His eyes didn't leave her face, and for the life of her, she couldn't read his mood now. There was no smile or gentleness in his expression, but the anger and bad humor seemed to be gone as well. He looked, for lack of anything else she could think of, puzzled and resigned.

"You melt me without any effort, Princess, and damned if I know what I want to do about it."

And he forced her hand to where their bodies almost met, to his crotch and the hardness confined in his jeans. When her eyes widened and her fingers closed instinctively, all he breathed was, "Yeah."

*****

Damn the woman for taunting him, for making him want her even when his brain told him it wasn't wise. They would never come to terms on this. Together they were as lethal as flint striking a rock and a thousand times more combustible. It was a damn good thing rainy season had started, or the whole mountainside might go up in the conflagration.

Her fingers traced the length of him, and he watched her eyelids droop and her lips part as if she was mesmerized. He too was caught in the spell, the almost tender stroking adding more blood until he was sure his zipper marked him for life.

They had to stop this. He was stupid to follow her home for a discussion. But this wasn't a discussion. This was an argument, and he couldn't even remember why they were fighting.

He shifted back, immediately feeling the cold wind come between overheated bodies and chill him. In front of him, she blinked, shaking her head a little as her glazed eyes refocused. Satisfied that he could move without falling over his feet, he took another step back, giving her space to decide what she wanted to do.

He watched her stare up at her front door, whatever passion she had been feeling dissipated and thoughtfulness replacing the lost look she'd worn only moments before. With choppy movements, she turned back to the car, opened the driver's door, and reached inside, returning with her keys. Then she selected one and held it out to him.

"This opens the front door." Her voice was low, so quiet that at first he believed it was a whisper of the wind. But it was hers, and the words and her melancholy expression made him pause before saying anything. "Go inside. I will follow you."

She sounded like she was as excited as if she faced a firing squad. Her hand stayed outstretched, the key in her fingers, until he reached out and took it, momentarily wrapping her hand in his in the process. She didn't pull away. When he waited, she shrugged and kept her hand in place. A small sad smile tugged the corner of her mouth up on one side, and he felt his own lips answer. Then he took the key and wrapped an arm around her shoulders to guide them up the front steps and across the porch.

When he stepped up to the door, she hesitated two steps behind him.

"I want you to know, Deke, that I didn't intend any of this to become *si fou*."

He turned the key in the lock without looking at her. When he pushed the door open, he waited to see what she would do next. When she said nothing and didn't move, he felt compelled to respond.

"So crazy? I don't know how we could have avoided it, Princess. It seems to be the violent effect we have on each other."

She brushed past him, dropping her purse on a chair and pointing at a dish on the entry table where he deposited the keys. Arching her back to shrug out of the coat gave him an opportunity to admire her form. That alone was enough to make his body tighten again.

Running her fingers through her hair, she let it cascade down her back. He doubted it was a conscious action, more likely something she did many times a day to straighten it. He'd seen her instinctive movements a thousand times now, and still they churned him up. His hands itched to replace hers, letting the silky lengths sift until there were no curls left.

"Why do you call me Ice Princess?" She turned as she asked the question.

He opened his mouth to answer and realized that no matter what he said, it would sound bad. Instead, he took off his coat and threw it to join hers. Then he stepped forward and wrapped his arms around her once more.

"You're not the Ice Princess now. In fact, it's so hot in here that you probably won't have to heat this place for a month."

His attempt at humor brought another of those sad smiles to her face. There was no trace of defiance now. She watched him, seeming to memorize his face as her eyes traveled over his features. He let his own gaze wander in turn. The most beautiful woman he ever imagined was wrapped in his arms, and if he wasn't careful, he'd be down those porch steps so fast that a stampede would look like a stroll in the park in comparison.

"I am sorry, Deke. So sorry."

"Sorry for what?"

She tried to push out of his arms, but he held on tighter. She sighed, bringing her trapped hands to his chest and setting her open palms over his heart. He wondered if she could tell how that small gesture made it beat ten times faster.

"Sorry for all of the trouble you've suffered. I should have listened to you. I should have paid attention sooner. Instead, *je vous ignoré.*"

"You ignored me – how? I seem to remember more than once being nose to nose with you. I doubt we ever ignored each other."

"You are deliberately misunderstanding me. That is no matter. I am tired of fighting you, of fighting myself." She looked up at him then, her eyes restive and the lines around them pinched in concern. "I want you, and I would like us to go to bed."

It was the sexiest thing he'd heard in months, maybe years. But she didn't seem particularly thrilled with the idea. In fact, he would say that her heart wasn't in it. That chilled whatever ardor her words caused.

He stepped back, and her arms dropped to her sides, her body seeming to shrink a few inches in defeat. He didn't want her to think he didn't desire her, but this was a two-way street. If she didn't want it too, what was the point?

Fighting the need to grab her and drag her down the hallway, he stepped back and turned to the living room, crossing the open space and dropping into her couch.

"Your mouth says words that your body isn't backing, Marguerite." She shut her eyes and remained where she was standing. Hurt cascaded through him. Defeat didn't suit his Princess.

"Why don't you come over here, sit next to me, and we can discuss whatever's on your busy mind." He patted the couch. "Come on."

Chapter 37

Did he even speculate what was on her mind? She couldn't bring herself to explain it. The apology she intended to offer him was stuck on her tongue like a thin dry wafer, and there seemed to be nothing she could do to free it.

If she could not tell him, perhaps she could show him. He'd stepped away, but she could still see the bulge of hard flesh in his jeans. He desired her.

And *dieu* but she wanted him. Perhaps tomorrow everything would *aller à la merde*, but for the moment, a crazed appetite coursed through her veins.

He patted the couch again, smiling encouragingly, and she returned the smile. It was time to act on her instincts. Striding across the room with purpose, she knelt on the couch at his side, straddled him, and took his shocked face in her hands.

"*Je vous veux,*" she whispered, leaning down until her lips barely met his.

"I want you too." His voice rumbled, the rough gravel in his tone adding impulsiveness to her actions. She licked his lips, playing with the corners of his mouth, and was gratified when he sucked in breath and his hands tightened on her back.

"*Me prendre au lit, s'il tu plaît.*"

He leaned back, his eyes examining her face with studious interest.

"I'll take you to bed on one condition."

"What is that?" Searing heat filled her at the intensity in his gaze. It started at the tips of her fingers and toes and coursed through her, settling in her core. Restless and impatient now, she was ready to command him to move.

"You promise me that tomorrow, you'll tell me what's bothering you."

It was the one promise she couldn't make to him, but he would never know that.

She nodded, and he waited like he expected more.

"I promise." She gave him the words.

He almost toppled them both to the floor then, moving so fast that she was reminded of the rattlesnakes on their first walk in the vineyard. He caught her up while she was still in flight, setting her on feet made unsteady by the magnitude of power in his eyes as he stared at her. Then he crushed her to him, and she lifted her face to capture his kiss.

God, the man could turn a simple kiss into a song. A passionate kiss like this became a symphony. When he was inside her, it would be like all the angels singing.

Breaking their embrace, he took a single step away from her, reaching for the hem of her turtleneck. His stare was compelling, the heat smoldering there dark and consuming, matching her own. She wanted to feel his hands on her, caressing skin already hot from suggestions in his eyes tracing her curves. When he yanked the shirt over her head and heaved it into a corner, his eyes glittered.

Then he traced a single fingertip down her centerline until it reached the waistband of her jeans. Curling his other hand around her neck, he pulled her in for a hard kiss that lasted too short a time. When his fingers came back to close on the clasp of her bra, he pulled away far enough to look in her eyes once more.

"I hope you're not fond of this lace." Then his fingers wrenched the material and the bra fell open, the clasp still hooked together. She couldn't help herself. She moaned in reaction.

"Your turn." His words were rough when he broke away from her, his arms open at his sides in welcome and the tightness in his voice sending shivers of anticipation down her spine.

Her hands shook as she reached for the buttons on his shirt, releasing one to see the thermal shirt underneath.

"I hope you do not care about this shirt." Her fingers grabbed the two sides and tore through the buttons. She pushed it down his shoulders and dropped it, then reached for the edge of the thermal and jerked it upwards. His grunt of approval made her smile. Then his chest was bare and she ran her nails down his skin, watching goose bumps rise in their wake.

There was nothing she wanted more than to jump him, pin him to her bed, and ride him until darkness covered them both. She was tempted. A string of passionate kisses up the hallway. It would take very little to knock him to his back and less yet to rid him of his jeans and boots. Then, it would simply be a matter of –

She never saw it coming, intent on her own thoughts. He picked her up and swung her over his shoulder, turning towards the couch. When he tossed her to its spongy surface, she bounced once before settling. And before she settled, he was lying on top of her, his face inches from hers and a hand cupped possessively over her core.

"This has gone on too long. We're going to settle things once and for all, Princess. Either you want me as much as I want you and we stop playing games, or you tell me to go, right now."

The compelling light in his eyes held her captive. His hand probed and his touch wasn't gentle, bringing her right to the edge of an orgasm with their jeans still between them. She watched his face, seeing neither triumph nor censure. It was lust, pure and simple, and a rainbow of emotions cascading from the light in his eyes.

If she sent him away now, he would know she was lying. He could feel the way her body tensed and stretched, burning for the release that only he could give. Her hips raised and pressed into his palm. For the briefest second, she considered sending him out the door because if he stayed, her heart was lost.

*****

He pulled the sheet out of her fingers. She probably wasn't even aware that she was pleating the material back and forth into a fan, or that she clutched it to her breasts. He wanted to see her, all of her.

"Where is this going Deke?" She reached for the comforter, and he pulled it out of reach.

He smiled when she gave an exasperated sigh and settled into the pillows more deeply. They'd finally made it to the bed, though not until after a round of sweaty, powerful lovemaking that left him lightheaded and seeing stars. When she'd reached for the belt of his jeans instead of answering his threat, he nearly shouted with joy. When she wrapped her fingers around his length and squeezed the most perfect exquisite pressure, he couldn't help himself.

Burying himself inside her in one long stroke had them both gasping. He couldn't move, not right away. His fingers clenched with hers, arms outstretched overhead on the back of the sofa, and he lowered his forehead to rest next to her head. She turned to watch him, the violet in her eyes completely hidden by her dilated pupils. She shifted impatiently underneath him and he grinned.

He moved, withdrawing slowly, and she hissed at him. Then he buried deeply again, this time taking his leisure in the stroke. She wiggled impatiently and opened her mouth to protest, and he had to kiss her. That shut her up.

When he reached between them and caressed her core, she clenched around him and spasmed, chanting his name as they moved together, her eyes burning into his and her fingernails biting into the backs of his fingers on their joined hand. Then she came, and he knew there was never a more beautiful sight than Marguerite, ripe with passion as her lush body pulled him over the edge after her.

That was hours ago. As their skin chilled, he stood and leaned down to her.

"I can walk." She pushed his arms away. "You do not have to carry me."

Petulant, like she was now angry that she'd let him take her to paradise. It piqued him just enough to ignore her words. When he lifted her up and strode down the hallway, he was glad to see that the action left her speechless. He knew it wouldn't last long.

The next time was slower, more gentle, almost reverential. She'd ridden him, but it wasn't the mad dash to completion this time. His hands had closed on her lovely lush breasts and toyed with her nipples while she ran fingers becoming increasingly frantic down his chest and belly to where they were joined. This time, climax was a rushing waterfall ride over the edge, and a peaceful return to earth like a feather drifting in a light breeze.

He noticed the chill raise hairs on her arms and lifted the blanket next to him, inviting her to curl up against him. She waited, obviously expecting his answer to her question. His mind had been lost in her, in the lovemaking of the evening. If she was standing, her hands would be on her hips and she might be tapping her foot impatiently. Instead, she simply frowned at him.

"Come on, curl up here. I can see that you're cold, Princess. And I'll answer your question."

She looked suspicious, but she settled in against him, her curves fitting his side in all the right places. He wrapped an arm around her shoulders and pulled her in tighter. This is the way he wanted things to be for the rest of their lives.

The thought didn't surprise him. Isn't that why he'd stayed away in the beginning? Didn't he know, even seeing her across a room, that together, they would be different? When she recognized the heritage in the *glacé* of his eyes, he'd been the one enchanted.

"You have not yet answered me." She wound his chest hairs around her fingertip and tugged. "And you are not to use that name for me anymore."

He snuggled her closer. "I'm still going to call you Princess once in a while." She opened her mouth to argue and he put two fingers over her lips to silence her. "You're regal in everything you do, and you deserve the title."

Her eyes filled with confusion and she looked worried again. "I do not deserve it." Her voice was unusually small and her body shrank against his. "You do not know."

"So tell me, and we'll decide together." He kissed her temple and pushed wild strands of hair behind her ear. He tilted her face up to his. He wanted to see her eyes when he shared his heart.

"Marguerite, *je t'aime*."

He felt all of her movement stop, even the rise and fall of her breasts against his chest. Only her heartbeat was still clear, hard and speeding against his own.

"Deke, I am sorry."

It was hardly the response a man expected when he told a woman he loved her. But maybe he'd read things wrong. Maybe she didn't feel anything for him in return. Maybe it was sex to her.

When he tried to extricate himself from the bed, she closed strong hands on his arms and held him in place.

"I am saying this wrong." She pinned him to the bed with a desperate gaze, licking lips he longed to kiss once more, if this was going to be the last time.

"No, I understand. I spoke too soon, or I said too much." He pushed against her again, and this time she let him swing his feet over the side of the bed. The shock of her arms coming around him, her front pressed against his back, made him still.

"I am honored and amazed that you feel this for me. I truly am." Her words whispered in his ear, a choking quality to the tone and her French accent more pronounced. "You must believe me when I say this."

He closed his icy fingers over her warm skin, letting his eyes fall shut and picture instead her face in the throes of passion. When she laughed a real laugh. When she lectured him on some subject, any subject.

"Please, Deke, turn around."

He stayed in place, unwilling to look into her eyes as she let him down easy. His Princess was about to dismiss him.

When he didn't move, she unwrapped herself and crept around him on the bed, falling to her knees in front of him and resting fists on his thighs. He had to open his eyes then. Her presence alone compelled him to.

What he saw first baffled him, then staggered his senses. His heart thudded painfully fast in his chest, the gallop long past being under control. She was smiling up at him, a warm, giving, tender smile.

"Deke, *je t'aime aussi.*"

Chapter 38

The coffee was scalding hot and not as strong as she liked it, but she did not care. She doubted he noticed either. They simply sat side by side, smiling at each other.

She loved the way he looked at her, like she was the most precious thing in the world. She did not deserve it. And yet, she loathed the idea of breaking the spell.

His eyes moved away from hers to the corner of the kitchen, and his eyebrows arched in surprise.

"Well look, we have a visitor."

She turned to follow his gaze and gasped. In the corner, the same corner once occupied by the crone, was a young woman with flowing blonde hair and worn but serviceable clothes. Those marked the era, many decades ago.

She shuddered, wondering what the witch would say next. Had the vision read her mind, her uncertainty?

It was then that she realized Deke was not looking worried or threatened. In fact, he looked almost fond of the apparition.

"Why is she here?" She hated the waver in her voice, but after the last visit, she had very low expectations of this turning out well.

"I don't know. She appears when she wants to appear, and to whomever she wants to see her."

"You have seen her before?" She was more than a little irked. Why had he not told her?

"Oh yeah, quite a few times over the years, actually. Ma says that you can tell what kind of mood the witch is in by the age she appears to be. She's a young woman here, so she's not menacing." He leaned in and she found herself doing the same, examining the witch as closely as he did. "In fact, she looks worried about something."

The young woman's filmy face pinched in anxiety and she kept glancing over her shoulder. When she seemed to focus on them again, there was terror in her blue eyes. She raised a hand, the palm up and gesture one of entreaty. Then she looked over her shoulder again, shook her head as if in fear, and disappeared.

"That was interesting."

She couldn't help the sigh of relief escaping her. "I do not like her."

He shook his head and took a sip of coffee, reaching out with his other hand to grasp hers tightly. "You have nothing to fear from her. She must get lonely, wandering around in the netherworld all alone. When I was a kid, I kept hoping she'd find a playmate, a friend, or someone to take care of her. Ma insists that when there is finally peace on the mountain, she'll find a family, and we won't see her again."

He played with her fingers, turning her hand over to place a tender kiss in her palm.

"What were you saying, before we were interrupted? Everything you want to say to me is something I want to hear." And he reached forward to kiss her lightly before settling back on his stool.

She pushed away her misgivings. Sharing her heart cost her dearly. Being honest was even scarier.

She still kept a secret from the man she loved. If her heart was true, she needed to tell him now, before things went any further. It would hurt if he turned away from her, but better to know that now than wait.

"Why so pensive?" His words were soft, just as his fingers were, tracing her face. The scent of coffee hung in the air, the morning light barely picking out the streams of steam above their mugs any longer. Thankful that it was Saturday, she knew she didn't need to rush. But the sooner she cleared the air between them, the better she would feel.

"I have something to tell you, something you may not want to hear."

He frowned, shaking his head. "I want to hear anything you have to say, Princess. Don't look so worried. How bad could it be, based on everything we've already been through together?"

Little did he know.

"It's about the contamination. I think that it is more complicated than we originally thought." In fact, she knew it was.

She watched his fingers tighten on the mug. Gone was the tempestuous he-man, the patient lover, the tender partner. His face was now somber and she watched his walls cascade into place. No hint of the easy-going laugh or the teasing drawl now.

"How could it be more complicated?"

She opened her mouth, then shut it again. Confession was even harder than apology. If she did this, she might change everything between them.

Leaning forward on instinct, she pressed her lips to his. She felt his start of surprise at her rapid movement, a clash with her solemn words. When she pulled back, his eyes were watchful, the myriad colors swirling as wine would in a glass.

This time, she was resolute. "Deke, about the herbicide, you need to know – "

At that moment, a strident ringing sounded from the direction of the living room. She bit off her words. Saved by the bell? The idea made her instantly giddy.

Then another chirping sounded, this time from her purse on the floor by the front door. In tandem, the two sounds created a sense of urgency.

"What the hell?" Deke stood, his backside clad only in the briefs he'd pulled on to sit on the kitchen stool, and stalked across the living room to his jeans on the floor by the couch. She watched him for a moment, regret eating at her once more.

At some point, she would be forced to tell him.

Her phone stopped ringing on its own, just as he pulled his from a pocket. A beep sounded from hers indicating a voicemail, followed half a minute later by a beep on his.

"It's Carl. He covers things on the ranch on Saturday morning so that I get a day off. If he's calling, it's important." He punched buttons as he spoke, not looking at her.

Sighing, she slipped off the chair and drew her filmy robe more closely around her, suddenly cold. Fishing in her purse for the phone, she checked the list of incoming numbers, then felt her pulse quicken.

Holding it up to Deke, she said, "It's David. I have no idea why he would be calling me this early on a Saturday. Something must be wrong."

He wasn't listening to her, intent on the message playing back. Her news could wait. Perhaps it would earn her a few precious extra minutes with the man she had come to love.

Tapping into her own voicemail, she tried to concentrate on what the phone was saying and ignore the man now rapidly pulling on his jeans. Then the words in David's message started to register, and she headed for the bedroom at a run to dress.

*****

"I still think I should have taken my car."

"And do what with it? Any place that we need to look will require four wheel drive, which it doesn't have." He gripped the steering wheel tighter and took the turn to the ranch faster than the road encouraged. The woman next to him didn't even flinch.

Damn it, the timing couldn't have been worse. He sensed that whatever she had been about to tell him would be something he needed to hear. And based on her face, it hadn't been something he would like.

"Perhaps he took a trip to see friends, or a short vacation."

She was still trying to rationalize it. As he glanced over to argue with her, the third such discussion they'd had on the short drive over, she leaned forward and stared at the group milling around the old ranch house. His eyes snapped front again, and like her, he scanned the faces waiting for their arrival.

No Fernando.

Gravel spit as the truck slid to a halt, and Carl was at the driver's door before he'd had time to turn off the engine. David and Royan were on his heels.

"Still no word. We did some preliminary searching, but nothing. I don't know where the hell's he's gone to." Carl's words were a mixture of anger and worry. Deke couldn't blame him. If his father was lost and possibly in trouble, he'd be frantic too.

Marguerite came around from her side of the truck and put a hand on David's arm, causing all three men to turn to her at once. Any surprise they felt at the two of them arriving together at this hour was well hidden, except for the flash of a knowing glint in Royan's eyes when he glanced back to Deke. The old man shuttered the expression before he could call him on it.

"David, are you sure he said nothing to you, nothing to any of the other workers, about being gone, or taking a trip to see friends, or anything else?"

David shook his head before she finished her words. "No, I asked everyone twice. Like I said yesterday, he came to work, said he had something to take care of and would be back soon, and then, poof."

Royan stepped between the younger men and stood close to Deke, delivering his opinion in a stage whisper. "I think he's in trouble. He didn't show up for coffee with me, which was where I think he was going when he left here. He hasn't been back to his house. His beater of a car's still there. And then, like Carl told you in the message, there's this."

The old man pulled out a basic cell phone, the kind that did nothing but make and receive calls and collect voicemails. He pressed a couple of buttons and held it out to Deke. Marguerite pushed closer and put her head next to his to listen in on the message.

Nothing. No words. There was a faint trickle of running water, a grunt, and then the call ended. And the caller was listed as Fernando. The time was an hour earlier.

"Play it again." Marguerite sounded impatient as she made a move to grab the phone from his hands. When he eluded her grasp and re-cued the message, he put it on speaker so that the whole group could here.

No one spoke as the message clicked off. Deke could only think about the many hundreds of places that Fernando could have fallen. Or he could have taken off and this was just a butt-call from some cheesy motel where he was meeting a girlfriend. Somehow, that seemed out of character.

"We will have to find him." Marguerite's words forced his attention to her striding towards his truck.

"Where do you plan to search?" He felt great satisfaction to see her pull up short. Then she turned around, and the lines of worry grooved deeply at the corners of her eyes. She looked at him with all of the misery he was feeling.

"I do not know. I just know that we have to do something." She banged a fist on his truck hood and he winced. "Come on, we have to go."

Deke looked around at the group gathered in the ranch yard, a mixture of ranch hands, winery workers, and in the center, Carl wearing his worry like an ill-fitting suit and Royan looking grim.

"Does anyone have any idea where he might be? Has he said anything to anyone about where he was spending his free time? It might not be recent. He could be someplace that he's been exploring for a while."

The men shook their heads and conferred with each other in low voices.

"Pop's been up to something for a while, Deke, I know it. He's been weird and standoffish for months. And all this bullshit – pardon me, ma'am – about going to Vegas? He's never said word one about this before." Carl kicked at the rocks underfoot and sent and spray of gravel knocking into the truck's side panel.

He gave up wincing.

Royan added, "He was real excited about something he was going to show me yesterday. Wouldn't tell me what it was, just said that it was something he'd been searching out for years, and now he'd found it and he was going to prosper from it."

"Prosper? He said that word?" Deke hadn't know Fernando well, but that didn't seem like something the man would say.

"Yeah, prosper. Haven't a clue what he meant, though." Royan spat in the driveway, and behind them, a female voice rang out, "Royan Kermarrec, what did we discuss about that disgusting habit?"

Great, now his mother was involved as well.

Emie sailed into the middle of the men like a battleship, giving his uncle a firm glare. Then she looked around at the assembly, her gaze finally settling on Deke.

"Well don't just stand there, son. Like your girlfriend said, you have to go and find him."

Chapter 39

The quad bounced along the track to Fernando's cabin, taking an overland route from the ranch.

"I still do not understand why we have to go together." Marguerite clung to Deke's back like a leech, and if he wasn't so distracted by the missing man, he would have enjoyed the sensation. Her jacket was unbuttoned, and through his own coat, he could feel her breasts pressing against his back. Short hours ago, his face had been buried between their lushness, his hands caressing her as he buried himself deep inside her. Right after he told her he loved her. Right after she responded in kind.

"Deke, are you listening to me?"

He cursed silently. A perfect morning, interrupted by panic and possible tragedy. And there was whatever she had planned to say to him too. He chose to ignore that until they were somewhere private once more.

"Yes, I'm listening. We're on this thing together because you are supposed to be looking around for signs of Fernando while I keep us upright." He heard her huff of frustration and countered whatever she was going to say next. "It's faster than the truck on these hills."

She stayed quiet after that. He drove more slowly as the track turned into denser forest at the base of Witch Hill. Panning right to left and back, he caught Marguerite doing the same out of the corner of his eye. When they exhausted the track and stopped at Fernando's cabin, she was quick to jump off and head for the door before he'd even turned the key in the ignition.

"Maybe he has returned by now." She pushed the door open without knocking and called out to the old man, but there was only silence in return. When the door framed her again, she was zipping her jacket and stuck her hands in its pockets, scanning around the clearing.

"It is cold in there, colder than it would be if he had returned last night." She spun in a slow circle before pacing back to him. When she said nothing more, he put a hand on her arm and pulled her unresisting body in to his.

"We'll find him, don't worry. There are people rushing all over this mountain and the word's out in the surrounding towns too. If anyone's seen him, they'll let us know." He rubbed her back and felt her tension. "Come on, we have to keep searching."

But she stiffened in his arms and took a step back.

"Deke, wasn't there a sound of running water in the background of his call this morning?"

He shrugged. "Yes, but more like a trickle. At this time of year and as often as it's been raining, that's a sound from almost everywhere."

She frowned and half-turned back to the cabin. "But it is not a sound of summer."

"No, it's not. What are you getting at?" He waited while she took two steps towards the cabin, then pivoted and paused only a second before heading for a very narrow deer track on the opposite side of the clearing.

"He came from here." She pushed aside some low shrubs and tried to move between the undergrowth. The path wasn't even one person wide, but the ground looked well-trodden. And by more than deer.

"Who came from here and when?" He got off the quad and used his gloved hands to hold back the worst of the shrubs.

"Fernando. I came to see him at the end of the summer, and he wasn't in his cabin. He was supposed to be home. Then when I was about to leave, he came out of the woods here."

"Maybe he was hunting something, or maybe he was taking a walk."

She pushed impatiently at the branches clutching her hair, swearing loudly in French. He couldn't help himself. He smiled.

"No, you are not listening. He came out of here, and his legs were covered in mud."

Deke stopped and almost let a branch snap into the back of Marguerite's head.

"Mud? In summer? There's no water here."

She turned around and regarded him like he was the dumbest steer in the herd, and maybe he was. Then it occurred to him.

"There's no water here. But I know where there is some."

*****

She clung to his back as the quad rolled to the right with two wheels touching the ground. Then it bounced back down on all four and listed to the left. The force smacked her into his body once more. It was like running into a stonewall.

He had been silent since they left Fernando's cabin. She didn't want to bring up what she had been about to say while they searched. The glimpse of his stern face right before both their cell phones rang reminded her that perhaps, despite his stated feelings for her, he would be too angry to remain friends.

But she wanted to be much more than friends, an idea that once planted, had grown deep roots and taken hold of the earth with no intension of letting go. Loving him would be worth the risk of things going wrong later. And later might mean within the next few days.

"Do you see anything?" He had pitched his voice to be heard over the whine of the quad's engine as it climbed the side of Witch Hill, running over brush and plants. She tightened her arms around him and tried to concentrate on their task.

"No. Is it much further?"

He shook his head, and his hair, pulled loose from its tie by branches as they snapped past, blew free across her face. She longed to bury her nose in it and inhale his woodsy aroma. He was a mound of contradictions, soft and hard, protective and easy-going, dedicated worker and urbane renaissance man.

"There it is." He stopped the quad, but seemed in no hurry to get off the machine. When she didn't remove her arms, he leaned back into her and she thought it was one of the most comfortable things she'd ever felt. He sat that way, his ear pressed to her cheek, and didn't say a word.

"There are tracks in the mud."

She startled and looked in the direction he seemed to be staring.

"It rained two nights ago, and the water coming out of the cave would have wiped them out. They can only be a day or two old. Come on."

She released him, feeling the chill of the shadowing trees and lack of sunlight next to the rocks. It was too still here, as if the birds and animals had fled. The ground was muddy, with small rivulets of water running in trenches cut on either side of the path.

"You said that Fernando had mud on his pants that day in August. This is the only source of water in this direction at that time of the year. It's a year-round spring, one that feeds one of the rivers flowing into the ranch. Even in drought years, it never dries up." He stepped to the side of the footprints, motioning her to step where he did.

She matched her steps to his and examined the water running from the cave entrance ahead. "This is enough to give you water for the ranch?"

He shook his head. "No, this is just run-off. The real water source runs deeper, but it surfaces for a short distance inside the cave. This is where Jake and I used to play when we were kids, until our parents found out and blocked the entrance with a boulder." He stopped and glanced around. "I bet it was that one right there."

"But that is massive. How could someone move it out of the way?"

He shook his head again. "I don't know. But someone did, because this used to be inaccessible. And come to think of it, I don't remember there being any light from the inside before."

They'd reached the entrance, and the cave was densely dark for a distance before showing a faint glow to the right about forty feet inside. She took a deep breath, and the musty smell was overwhelming, a combination of mud and mold and animal remains. Underneath it all, though, was a faint scent of something manmade.

"Do you smell that?"

He inhaled deeply, sniffing as he did, and exhaled with a loud gush. Then he did it again.

"That's not mother earth we're smelling. That's some sort of chemical."

He took her hand, and she felt herself shiver, a whole-body shake that had nothing to do with the cave. The way he touched her, a light caress of his thumb across the back of her knuckles as his fingers locked with hers, made her want again.

Concentrate, woman. You have an old man to find.

"Don't be afraid. It's not a small cave and by the look of it, there's now light coming in from an opening in the ceiling. Probably a cave-in opened it up."

He smiled down at her, reassurance in his gaze. Then his eyes grew serious as he continued to stare.

"Marguerite, don't worry. Everything will be all right. And we'll be fine." He reached across the foot separating them as she stepped forward, needing the security of his arms around her. His mouth came down and he gave her the gentlest of kisses.

It would be heaven to stay here in this position and simply be with this man. He was sure they would be fine, but she was not so convinced.

When he lifted his head, he gave her another encouraging smile. "Let's figure out what's going on here."

They walked forward slowly, slipping every once in a while on the thick mud.

"I don't remember it being this muddy in the past. But maybe that hole in the ceiling is responsible." He waved towards a pile of rocks leading up to a large opening above. Through it, she could see sunlight streaming in. The angle of it now in mid-autumn was low, but in the summer, it would be direct, highlighting the mess of the cave floor below.

"What the hell?"

She ran into him when he stopped, and when he didn't comment further, she grew impatient. Pushing around him, she looked into the darkest area of the cave and saw what made him stop.

Containers, a number of them. The one that caught her eye first was familiar. It was a large white bucket with warning labels pasted on every visible side. Herbicide.

"Good, the labels are still on it. We can trace it and find out who it was sold to. Though based on the circumstances, I'd say it was Fernando."

She moved to his side as he knelt in the mud, taking a picture of the container's numbering with his cell phone. He panned around the mess of other bundles, plastics, and wrappers strewn around the floor, taking more pictures. He lifted something in his gloved hand, distaste on his face, and turned to show it to her. It was a stub of a cigar, and if she had been closer, she would bet she would smell the same brand that Fernando was fond of. When Deke stood, she remained in her crouch.

She didn't want to move closer to see if the lot number and identification code matched the ones ingrained in her brain. She saw them in her sleep. To find the container here meant only one thing.

Fernando had taken the missing herbicide.

"We can ask Jake to run the numbers through the state database and see who purchased this crap. Based on the label, I believe it's the same contaminants that are in my water. This source flows to my well."

Debating with herself took less energy than she imagined. It was time. Maybe the outcome wouldn't be as bad as she assumed.

"You won't need to have Jake do anything." She kept her words quiet and stayed on the floor, judging that her hair was a convenient curtain blocking his view of her face. The stakes were high, too high for her to want to view what her news would do to his love for her.

"And why is that? We need to trace this chemical. Whoever handled it did so without any precautions, and there are consequences for this." The grate of his boots over rocks and pebbles marked his path to another corner of the cave's large area. She lifted her head to watch him as he stood, hands on hips and kicking at stray papers.

Then he froze, the pause only lasting a couple of seconds, before he burst into motion.

"What the hell! Call 911."

Chapter 40

He might break the steering wheel, he was gripping it so tightly. The smooth road back to Flynn's Crossing and the hospital didn't warrant that kind of control. But the news he struggled to process sure did.

Marguerite huddled in the seat beside him, not saying anything since their heated exchange in the cave.

"I was trying to tell you this morning, but we were interrupted. I had hoped you would have more understanding than this." She was angry, though why she was mad with him, he wasn't sure. Someone else deserved the blame. And she seemed ready to forgive that person in a heartbeat.

When she'd said he didn't need to check the identification on the herbicide container, he didn't realize immediately that she was protecting someone. Fernando. The same man who he'd found lying in the darkest corner of the cave, breathing with difficulty. While she'd called for help, he'd tried to rouse the old man.

"Tell her I'm sorry, would you?" His eyes were swollen and Deke could barely see any color. Coughing hard enough to bring up blood, Fernando had focused first on Deke, then on Marguerite, and looked sorrier than before.

"Fernando, don't talk. Help is coming."

But the old man struggled to sit up and stared at the large container in the opposite corner with remorse on his face.

"I was going to tell you, Margie, really I was. Thing is, I was only going to use a little to kill the weeds growing around my claim. Then I was going to bring the container back and tell you how much I used and have you bill me for it. And report the use and everything."

He gave up when another fit of heavy coughing overtook him. Deke met Marguerite's eyes over the old man's head as he supported him. Hers carried an apology he didn't understand how to read.

When the coughing quieted, the confession continued. "Didn't mean to hurt things at your place, Deke, but things got out of hand. Clumsy old fart, I spilled the container, the whole damn thing, and before I could stop it, it ran into the stream feeding your well. I hoped that the rains would dilute it enough so that it wouldn't be any trouble." He coughed again, but put up a wavering hand when Marguerite tried to push him back to a reclining position. "I should have told you right away. Or I should have told you when you found that container missing in the inventory. I'm really sorry."

The air in the cave constricted, and the fact that Marguerite had known the herbicide was missing burned through him. The pain would be worse when he could examine it closely. She hadn't said anything to him since they'd climbed into his truck to drive to the hospital.

They pulled up to the hospital, the ambulance already in its emergency room bay and the back doors open. One of the EMTs walked out of the hospital and slammed them shut. Deke pulled into a visitor slot and shut off the engine, waiting for her to speak. There was so much unsaid between them that the air seemed to be full of dense storm clouds.

Would she apologize? She had to know that was what he expected. For she'd known the herbicide was missing, had known since he'd presented her with the test results and the nature of the chemical was evident. But she'd kept it a secret for long weeks, time that could have been used to find the source of the contaminate.

When neither of them moved, he turned to face her. She kept her face in profile as she released her seat belt, her expression at once haughty and heartbreakingly sad. She must have sensed his eyes on her, because she turned, and whatever emotion she felt was hidden in a blank stare.

He had to say something. Even if she didn't respond, he had to let her know how he felt about this deception.

"You could have told me right away, as soon as you learned that the container was missing."

Nothing.

"We agreed to find a solution together. Wouldn't it have been easier to be honest with me and get to work than wait until it was too late?"

He saw the flash of anger before she could hide it, and it ignited the same feeling in him.

"Damn it, Marguerite, you knew you could trust me. I've told you I love you. I don't say those words lightly. They mean something to me, and I thought they meant something to you too."

She opened her mouth, then closed it again with a snap that left him in no doubt of her feelings. She was as mad as he was and itching for a fight.

He reached across the center console and grasped her upper arm when she began to turn away from him. Her eyes snapped back to his and then looked pointedly at his hand.

"Let go of me."

"Make me."

He wasn't exactly sure why he wanted to taunt her, other than he was so damned mad that he couldn't think straight. Why hadn't she trusted him with the truth?

She regarded him steadily, her expression slowly melting from its heat to fade into that regal distance. Ah yes, there it was. She raised her chin ever so slightly, and her lips were narrowly shy of a sneer.

Her dismissal of him hurt more than he could process. If he had the time, he might have thought things through. But for once, processing wasn't something he wanted to spend time doing.

He yanked her out of her seat and halfway across the console before realizing what he was doing. They were nose to nose, and her violet eyes were wide with shock. Waiting three breaths, he noticed their color change as shock changed to arousal. And he closed his lips over hers in kiss meant to punish them both.

*****

When she marched through the emergency room doors, she expected to see some of the crew who had searched for Fernando. She anticipated that the Dawsons would be somewhere in the crowd. But what she hadn't considered is that all of the girl tribe and their men would be ranged around the large waiting room as well.

She stopped, wondering what the women would see in her face. Because she knew she didn't have the strength at the moment to hide it. When Deke reached for her and locked on for a kiss that made her head spin, she could only return it. After minutes that she wished were hours, he put her back in her seat, turned away from her, and got out of the truck without another word.

It took her longer to move. By the time she'd slammed the door, he was halfway to the hospital. He beeped it locked without checking to see if she followed.

And now he'd disappeared into the male crowd at one end of the long room. The girl tribe clustered around her, and each one regarded her with a different level of concern.

"We heard what happened. Carl told us before his father got here and he went back when the ambulance arrived. He's with him now. Are you okay?"

She shook her head yes to answer DK's question, then slowed her movement and changed direction. *Dieu*, at this rate, she would be in tears in seconds.

"Oh, give her some space. Come on, sweetie, you come sit down and tell us all about it." Serena wrapped a comforting arm around her shoulders, and that was all it took.

By the time she was seated in the circle of her friends, she was bawling like a baby.

"God, does anyone have any ice cream? Or some wine?" Roxy's questions almost made her laugh through her tears.

Tess pushed tissues into her hands, and Gabby took the chair next to her, rubbing her back and cooing to her. God, she was completely out of control, she, who was always in control.

"You get it all out, honey. Whatever the problem is, it will feel better after you get it out. And then we'll talk about it."

That just made her cry harder.

"Excuse me. Ms. Devereux?"

Her friends turned as one and looked at the tall form of the sheriff's deputy standing just outside their circle.

"Not now, Jake. Can't you see that she's upset?"

"Whatever it is can wait, can't it Jake?"

Roxy sounded like she would punch the man, and Tess had reared up like a lioness guarding a cub. Through her tears, she felt hysterical giggles at the idea that her friends would get into a fight with the deputy, and they would all end up in jail.

"I'm sorry, but I want to make sure Marguerite knows that I need to take her statement." His tone had softened, but his voice was no less firm.

She breathed deeply and nodded, then added words to emphasize that she understood.

"I know, Jake. I will be happy to speak to you whenever you wish." She hesitated, then asked, "How is Fernando?"

He seemed to soften further, giving her a sympathetic nod. "He's holding his own. Between the chemicals he was exposed to, the time over which he was exposed to them, and being out in the elements since he passed out yesterday, he's weak. The doctors haven't told me when I can interview him, but I'll need to take his statement at some point as well."

"I want to be there when you talk with him." She found herself standing in front of him, restraining hands on her arms and back as the women around her reacted to her sudden energy.

"Now you know that's not going to happen. That's not the way an investigation is conducted. From what I understand, he took the container without your prior consent or knowledge, and he never informed you of the spill." He paused as if considered whether to share more before continuing. "The fact that you didn't tell Deke about things as soon as you knew isn't good, but it's not illegal. What Deke decides to do about the situation with Fernando is up to him. First, the man has to recover enough to be able to talk."

Jake turned and squared his shoulders, a movement that she'd seen Deke do so many times when he was about to face something unpleasant. When he joined his brother across the room, the two exchanged words before the both turned to stare at her.

She sank back in to the chair, grateful for the band of friends around her blocking any further view of the room.

DK glanced at the others before dropping down to eye level.

"Do you want to talk about it?"

The words burst out before she could control them.

"I love him."

Gabby stopped rubbing her back and said in confusion, "Who? Fernando?"

"God, no. You really need to stick around more. She's in love with Deke." Roxy's face appeared in her view. "And it's a bitch, isn't it, honey?"

"So catch me up. How long have you been in love with Deke? What did Jake mean when he said you should have told Deke something sooner? And why was Fernando in that cave?"

Chapter 41

"Well, this is one hell of a bachelor party." Vince's voice held no malice, but he waved a hand in Deke's direction just the same, the middle finger appearing right before he smiled.

Deke closed his eyes and leaned his head back, taking a sip of tequila and hoping that the smooth drag of liquor would ease his tension.

"Give the guy a break. He's had a rough couple of months. And it's worse since he and Marguerite haven't kissed and made up yet."

He didn't bother to open his eyes as he gave his brother the finger. The chuckle next to him told him the message was received, loud and clear.

"So what happened with Fernando? Did you ever get the whole story?" Rick's question seemed to be directed at Jake, so Deke kept his eyes closed.

"Fernando got this idea that he'd find gold in the old mine. He's been fooling around in there for years. When we had that last rainy winter a few years back, the ceiling collapsed, and the mine was then open to the elements. Rain washed away some of the sediment, and that's when he found what he thought was gold. Thing is, it was fool's gold, pyrite, but he didn't know that. And by then, he had a new problem. Sunlight came into the opening in the cave ceiling and plants grew in the area he wanted to mine. He brought in the herbicide to spray the plants and kill them off, and the rest you know."

"Will he face charges?"

Jake was silent, and Deke assumed he was shaking his head. The next words he'd hoped to keep out of the story, but before he could stop him, his brother continued.

"Deke refused to press charges, even though he's within his right to do so. The Dawsons have agreed to modify their practices in the vineyards to ensure sustainability and eliminate the use of toxic chemicals. Fernando's retiring from the winery, effective immediately, and since he knows his stake isn't gold, Vegas is off the table. Instead, he's going to work beside Carl at Three Rivers, restoring the area that was poisoned so that in a few years, it can be recertified as organic."

Around him, the men clapped, with a few comments that ranged from how noble his gesture was to what a wuss he was. Mostly, they congratulated him before moving back to a round of toasts for the man of the hour, Vince.

"Yeah, some bachelor party. The food's great – thank Roxy for me, will you Mac? As to my best man, I'm not so sure. Still, this is some kick-ass tequila."

Vince was right. He was the wet blanket at this party, and his friend deserved better. He roused himself and made a production of checking his watch.

"So I guess I should cancel the strippers who are on their way over now?"

Vince and the others laughed, and Vince got up out of his chair and came over to clank glasses with him as the others settled into various conversations.

"No, man, it's all fine. This is what I wanted anyway. I kind of lost my edge for the crazy swinging lifestyle when I met DK."

Deke eyed his friend, taking in his contented expression as the man dropped into the chair next to his.

"And without a single regret?" He couldn't help but ask. Satisfaction was written all over his friend's face. With the wedding less than a week away, he seemed calmer with each passing day.

"No. It was the damnedest thing. One minute I was a one night stand specialist, and the next thing, I'm an engaged man. With a big fuck-up in between, but what the hell can you do?"

"How did you get past that?" He was honestly curious. And a part of him, the part he'd locked away because it hurt too much to examine, wanted to know if there was any hope that he and Marguerite could work things out someday too.

Vince guffawed and took the final sip of his tequila before reaching for the bottle on the table. When he offered it to Deke first, he thought to decline. But what the hell. He wasn't going anywhere else tonight since this party was at his house. And maybe it would take the edge off.

"I didn't get past it, at least not right away. No, I went back to New York, convinced I could drink her off my mind. Instead, I set up a shrine to her. And our mutual friend was smart enough to see that I was pissing myself down the drain. DK was stronger than me, always has been and probably always will be."

Marguerite was strong too, and more stubborn.

"Did she make you beg?" He interjected a harassing note into his words, but Vince gave a reminiscent smile.

"Nah, she's smarter than that. She made me see what I was missing. A couple of weeks away from her and I was putty. One look at her, up close and in person, was enough. Fact is, I would have groveled, but her heart's bigger than that. We both apologized, because there's always fault on both sides. And we figured out how to move on."

He doubted it would be as easy for Marguerite and him. They'd both said some nasty things to one another.

"She hasn't apologized to me."

"So?" Vince looked at him like he missed the point completely. Maybe he did.

"She didn't tell me when she could have. She didn't confess her unwitting role in this. And now that the truth is out, she still hasn't said she's sorry things got so out of control."

Vince shook his head before the words had faded into the afternoon air. "Not the way it happens, bud. Now as I understand it, you blamed her from the get-go, were slow to realize that she wasn't at fault, and then assumed she knew what Fernando had been up to. I think there's culpability on both sides, my friend."

He opened his mouth to protest, and snapped it shut again just as fast. Vince was right.

"So I should say I'm sorry for my part in it and hope that she responds with the same? Because I'm telling you, the Ice Princess won't go for that. The Princess might, but she's feeling kind of cold towards me at the moment."

Vince watched him, tilting his head as if was examining a strange insect.

"No, you just say you're sorry, and you accept the fact that she might never say the same back to you. And you have to decide if you love her enough for that to be okay. Think had about that, my friend. Because you could lose her forever over this, and maintaining a distance from her doesn't give either one of you a chance to work things out."

Vince leaned back and looked around the room, and Deke followed his gaze as it settled for a moment or two on their hooked-up friends. Every one of them looked happy, he realized. Not just satisfied-with-the-moment happy, but deeply content.

"Every one of them will tell you the same thing. A relationship isn't a fifty-fifty thing. It's a hundred fifty-hundred fifty thing. And if you're not man enough to be willing to deal with life's imperfections, your woman will find someone else who can."

*****

"Il ne croit pas dans le pardon."

"What did she just say?" Tess looked to Serena, who looked at DK. They each shook their heads, uncomprehending.

"I said, he does not believe in forgiveness."

Now they all shook their heads again, much more vehemently this time.

They did not know him, not like she did. He might come across as a man who takes life as it comes, but when his protective instincts engaged, he was a man on a mission.

"Marguerite, I don't think you're giving Deke enough credit. Meet him halfway. Tell him you're sorry that you didn't say something to him sooner. He knows you didn't have anything to do with Fernando's escapades." Serena looked to Tess to continue.

"You both had a part in this. He's not without reasons of his own to apologize. But you can be the bigger person and say it first."

She shook her head because they didn't understand, not really. The risk she took if she said the words first were ridicule and scorn.

"You must not love him enough, that's all I can say. Because if you did, it wouldn't matter who said it first. It would just matter that you'd find a way to be together." Roxy flipped a hand in the air to punctuate her words.

She joined the other women in staring at Roxy in disbelief.

"What? I know, men are scum and all that, but I may have overstated things a little in the past." And she blushed.

"Well, well, well. Mac has certainly changed your tune." DK gave Roxy an elbow in the ribs and got a pinch back for her trouble. But instead of continuing the battle, DK turned back to Marguerite. "If the resolute Roxy can find a way to kiss and make up, the diplomatic Marguerite definitely can."

Again, she shook her head.

When her friends would have continued, she waved a hand that silenced them all and got up from the couch in her living room. The place was decorated with paper wedding bells and streamers, the stack of opened presents on the table and spent wrapping paper covering the floor. This was not how she'd planned to conduct her friend's bridal shower slash bachelorette party, but the woman of the hour seemed to be hooked on the idea that everyone needed to be in a couple. Once only the girl tribe remained, DK had pounced like a jungle cat on the continuing chasm between Marguerite and Deke.

"Deke will not see me. He hasn't called. He was so cold the last time we were in the same room that I was going to start calling him the Ice Prince."

"Ah, yes, Vince's nicknaming strikes again. But that doesn't change things. You still need to be strong enough to fight for this, if you truly do love him."

"I do love him. Have no doubts about that. But perhaps it is better if I wait to see if he wants to have any sort of friendship with me. Maybe then we will be able to talk about things. But now? I doubt it."

Chapter 42

He tried to settle, impatience with the traditional ceremony making him jittery. Next to him, Vince was as cool as a mountain spring in winter.

"Man, you have got to chill. You look like the one getting married."

Vince's words hissed in his ear, and he caught the ribbing and tried harder to relax.

"Here they come." Whispers of words through the audience focused his attention on doors from the tasting room to the patio. One of DK's siblings came out first. Another woman of the wedding party appeared, and he planted his feet more firmly on the floor. If Marguerite didn't come through those doors soon, he would lose it.

Then she was there. The bridesmaid's dress was a deep tone that complimented her eyes. Her dark hair hung lose down her back, the curls glowing richly in the candles and torches set around the patio to push back the dusk. She walked the measured wedding march pace looking straight ahead. When she reached the circle of the raised dais, their eyes met, and he saw her step falter before she pulled herself together and took her place opposite him.

That was his girl, always able to pull it together and prove to be a match for any situation. And she was his girl, pure and simple.

He'd intended a frank and open discussion today, once they'd safely married off their friends and done their duties as best man and maid of honor. But seeing her like this, her eyes locked on his, made waiting seem kind of pointless.

Because he loved her no matter what.

She stared at him, and at this distance, he wasn't sure if the shimmer in her eyes was tears or a trick of the light. When she licked her lips, his suit became tighter by degrees.

He didn't see DK come down the aisle, didn't pay any attention to the priest's words, or to DK and Vince as they responded.

He could only stare at the woman he loved to distraction and wonder if there was any hope for them.

"Dude? The ring?" Vince knocked an elbow into him and he fumbled the ring from his pocket, giving his friend a sheepish grin. But he only got a big smile in response.

He lifted his eyes to see Marguerite fumbling DK's bouquet with a startled expression. When she raised her gaze to his again, he smiled.

His heart beat faster when she smiled back.

"I promise to love you, honor you, trust you and cherish you, not matter what challenges life brings our way." Vince's words rang out without any hesitation as he slipped the ring on DK's finger.

"I promise to love you, honor you, trust you and cherish you, oh, and forgive you too." The crowd laughed and a couple of people applauded at DK's cheeky response.

Their undertone conversation nearly did him in.

"I promise to get you for that."

"Promises, promises."

They both looked stunningly happy.

He suddenly knew without any doubt that the love they shared, deep and committed despite their rocky beginning, was exactly the kind of love he had for Marguerite. But did she feel anything close to it?

Vince's wise words a week ago echoed in his head. *'You just say you're sorry, and you accept the fact that she might never say the same back to you. And then you have to decide it you love her enough for that to be okay.'*

*****

She didn't know where to look. It didn't seem to matter. Her eyes were filled with Deke.

She'd never seen him in a suit, the cut of it so compelling on his remarkable figure that she knew there were stars in her eyes. The intensity of his gaze on her made her knees shake, and she forgot where they were for a moment, until DK whispered, "Can you wait for a few minutes until I tie up mine?" The knowing smile on her friend's face as she shoved the bouquet at her and grabbed Vince's ring made her anxious.

Was this enough, this feeling of forever in a simple locking of eyes? She had no experience of this. All she knew was that she wanted more than anything to forget the room full of people and the ceremony between them, step into his arms, and tell him she was sorry she never valued them enough to be completely honest.

Her eyes traced his features, wishing she could brush back the wave of hair that fell across his forehead. Cheekbones chiseled of stone met at lips she knew could be soft or demanding, depending on his mood. His active mind and the intelligence she found to be so attractive brought a race of expressions to his face as he continued to watch her.

Suddenly who was right and who was wrong wasn't important. If she wanted to move forward with Deke at her side, there was only one thing to do. She had to tell him the only thing that mattered. She mouthed the words and hoped that he could read them.

'I am sorry.'

She smiled tentatively, waiting. Her fingers gripped the small bouquet tightly until the tape wrapping the stems cut into her skin. His face filled with such turbulence, she began to doubt the wisdom of her words.

Then those lips moved.

'I'm sorry too.'

"I now pronounce you husband and wife. You two know what to do." The priest's words barely even registered, and if it wasn't for DK claiming her flowers once more she would have continued staring at Deke staring back at her.

The bride and groom began the processional between the chairs, the breeze blowing DK's veil back in a stream that seemed to wrap around the happy couple. Then Deke was coming towards her, and the only thing she could hear was a buzzing in her ears.

Breathe. Three times. It would be very embarrassing if she were the one who fainted at her friend's wedding.

His warm hand wrapped around hers and he pulled it into the crook of his arm. His face was so close, she could see the bright blue of his eyes, and wondered at the depth of emotion she saw there. It was deeper than any ocean. She gulped and prepared herself for the words.

"Deke, I am sorry."

"Marguerite, I apologize."

Their words ran over each other and they stopped a few feet into the procession. Behind them, someone cleared their throat with deliberation.

"Way to go, you two. See you inside at the reception, if you ever make it." Jake's words weren't even whispered, and around them, she was dimly aware of indulgent chuckles.

"I love you." Their identical words tripped over one another as they pulled closer.

She could spend the rest of her life looking into those turbulent ever-shifting eyes.

"Marguerite, *je t'aime de toute ma vie.*"

"Deke, *je t'aime de tout mon cœur et de l'âme.*"

In the end, it didn't matter who said what, because they seemed to be saying things just as they were destined to be, together.

Epilogue

"I really thought that we were going to have to turn a hose on the two of you. I'm not sure DK's mom was crying because her daughter was getting married or because the two of you were stealing her show."

Marguerite blushed, not because they'd gotten caught in their intense attraction, but because the same man was now staring at her across his living room with such intensity, it curled her toes. The fact that he'd curled those same toes so many times last night, and she his, only added to her color.

"Now leave the girl alone. It's obvious that they're lusting after each other so much that we could have cooked the turkeys by setting the birds in the same room with them." Roxy made a show of fanning herself as Mac came up behind her and wrapped his arms around her middle.

"Give the man a break, he's had company here for what, two hours now, and he hasn't had a chance to get her alone in all that time."

The general laughter around her barely distracted her. Yes, it had been two long hours, and she decided she needed to do something about it.

The Thanksgiving parade blared on the big screen and around the room, their friends were in a celebratory mood.

And she and Deke had been celebrating every chance they got since the wedding last weekend.

"Hello Princess. I thought I was going to have to yell fire and clear the room to get a moment with you."

She grinned at him, content to let him wrap her in his arms and kiss her. When whistles and jeers erupted around them, he lifted his head and she could look around at their friends and families, led by Jake, applauding.

Back to the business at hand. The sooner she moved on to a mundane topic, the better. Otherwise, they would be leaving the festivities and locking themselves in Deke's bedroom for the rest of the afternoon.

"Did you check the turkeys?"

"Yes, ma'am, I did."

"Did you baste them?"

He rolled his eyes and said, "Yes, Princess, I did."

"Because if you do not, they will be dry, and Roxy will be *pissé*. And are you taking their temperature, because we want to time the rest of the meal with – "

He grabbed her and kissed her, and she fought him just a little for show.

"Oh, isn't that cute? You two are just like your father and I when we were first together, you know that, Deke?"

Emie came up next to them, her son towering over her small frame. Beside her, Jake chuckled.

"Don't you laugh, young man. It will be your turn next."

Jake denied it, but he winked at Marguerite and gave her a thumbs-up before he slapped Deke on the back.

"Good work, you guys, good work."

"Royan Kermarrec, don't you touch that coffee cake. You know it's bad for you in so many ways that I can't even begin to name them."

Marguerite grinned as Deke's uncle winked at her and hid something behind his back.

Emie was already in motion. "You see? These Kermarrec men need a lot of control and a lot of love to be kept in line. You remember that, dear. And you know you can always come to me for advice if this one gets to be too much for you. Royan? I see you."

Marguerite looked at Deke, his face sentimental as he watched his mother charge across the room and wrestle the cake away from his uncle. When the old man wrapped his big arms around her for a hug instead, his mother only protested a little before smiling up at him.

It seemed that everyone was getting bit by the love bug, and she was glad she had her man in her arms.

"Come on, let's go outside for a while and enjoy. It's supposed to rain again tomorrow, and the clouds are something to see."

They slipped out the doors to the porch and she wrapped her arms around him when he stopped at the railing. Pressing against his back, she felt his deep inhale and contented sigh. His hands covered hers and squeezed.

In the distance, fog shrouded the Witch Hill peak, and she could barely see the Sierras with their new covering of snow at the highest elevations. It was a peaceful place, a wonderful home in which they argue and make-up and love. Maybe there would be children someday. She thought the witch might like that.

"Look."

She followed his pointing finger to the end of the porch and smiled. Deke shifted her around and tucked her against his side as they continued to watch.

"She is a little girl."

The man she loved with her heart and soul nodded and smiled as well.

"She must be happy. She only appears as a child when she's happy."

The young witch apparition smiled and danced a few steps, then glanced over her shoulder, waving as if she wanted someone to hurry.

"Deke, you finally have your wish."

Standing next to the little girl was a young man, his large frame dwarfing the child. He put out his hand, and the little girl put hers into it without any hesitation.

"She found a friend. I hope it's Great-Grandpa, finally able to take care of her the way he wanted."

Marguerite felt the tears in her eyes as she looked away from the two ghosts and up into ocean blue eyes.

"De famille."

The words seemed to echo on the wind. When she glanced back, the big man and the little girl were walking away, fading into the afternoon light. The child glanced back once, waved, then skipped once more before the vision of them melted away.

"You have your happy ending."

He turned to look at her, his eyes blazing with so much passion that she forgot to breathe.

"Yes ma'am, Ms. Devereaux, I do. And our little witch does too."

And he kissed her.

The End

Excerpt from
LOVE'S TOUCH OF JUSTICE

If you enjoyed *Wine Into Water*, stay tuned for the next book in the Flynn's Crossing series, **Love's Touch of Justice**.

Will the girl tribe and the wolf pack ever be the same?

The two men exchanged words that looked harsh and contentious. As they scanned the crowd, she caught sight of their faces. She couldn't avoid recalling the last time she'd seen them. They were older, but no less intense. She'd wanted to escape those memories, but dark thoughts were impossible to avoid. Ducking deeper into the doorway of the shop behind her, she couldn't pull her gaze away.

She wasn't stalking them, not exactly. Besides, it wasn't as if they would recognize her anymore. He'd taken care of that years ago.

"You stupid bitch, how could you get caught? All you had to do was drive down the road, stop where I told you to stop, and hand packages to people. How could you fuck this up?"

The sharp cracks of his fists to her face had not been as painful as the fear that clutched her gut. Curling into a ball and wrapping her arms around her knees so tight she heard tendons pop, she'd given up pleading with him. When he knocked out some of her teeth and blood ran into one eye, he'd finally seemed to be satisfied.

"Just remember we're married, you and me, and you can't implicate your husband." He'd sneered the words in

her ear before throwing her to the floor of their squalid apartment. Through swollen eyes, she'd watched his huge silhouette stomp to the door, slamming it open. It bounced against the wall before snagging on the dingy shag rug. He'd left it hanging there, wide open for anyone to peer in and see her. Not that anyone would care. Even after she'd heard the rattle of his car's holey muffler driving off, she'd stayed in her tight little knot.

Her hands went to her face now, tracing its rebuilt bones. Her tongue ran over straight front teeth. She pressed a steadying hand to her belly. Everything had come at a price, but one she'd paid gladly. A single tear escaped, and she swiped it away. She could do nothing about her past stupidity. She only had the future, however hopeless and empty. Shaking off the self-pity, she resolved once more that things would be different.

She pulled her cap lower and adjusted her large sunglasses, wishing they could conceal the evidence of her fear and mistakes as easily as her make-up and long sleeves. People would judge her and find her guilty. Distancing herself was for the best. Even in a crowd, she stood alone.

From the number of people milling around, it seemed that everyone in the surrounding countryside had come into Flynn's Crossing for the Labor Day parade. Parents hoisted children on to their shoulders to see decorated vehicles and marching bands. Dancers tapped up the street. The lawn mower brigade followed the tractor team. High school teens cheered from home-designed floats. Horses pulled coaches and wagons with waving people on top. For most, it would have been an enjoyable and captivating scene of small town USA. But not for her.

The two men she'd been watching stood back to back now, turning in a tight circle and scanning the late summer crowd. Both equally tall, they looked to be the same age, though she knew years separated them. The older one carried his beefier body with an aggressive fluidness, fitting for someone who'd spent his career in construction. Leaner with the grace of a jungle cat, the younger man barely showed the extent of injuries that almost killed him, the only scars visible to the public carved into his face. The structure of their faces marked them as brothers. She knew they shared bold determination and stubborn independence as well.

When their gazes passed over her without stopping, she let out the breath she'd been holding. It was the closest she'd come to them in years, and she couldn't tear her eyes away. Their watchfulness didn't end, and they continued to turn in a tight circle. Covering each other's backs. That's what they did.

Their watchfulness didn't change when a sheriff's deputy strode over in long steps and questioned them. Their negative head shakes and the older one's gestures indicated frustration. She thought about melting into the crowd, but the exchange made her linger.

The deputy was almost as tall, appearing leaner but just as strong, even under the cover of body armor. His wide-brimmed hat hid most of his expression, but she sensed his alertness as his hands stayed at his waist, close to the belt weighed down with equipment and a big ass gun. He wore it as easily as the authority in his stance. She should be afraid of the danger he represented. She'd already spent too much of her life inviting trouble. Staying on the right side of the law was critical to her success. She doubted he'd understand.

When he added his scrutiny of the crowds clustered on the sidewalk, she froze, willing them all to glance over her in their search. The two civilians did. She was not surprised. Her disguise blurred their perception of her. The deputy's concentrated gaze paused as if searching her area. Through his mirrored sunglasses, she swore he looked right at her, but it was probably a trick of the light. Her heart beat a little faster and she wanted to run. Willing herself not to move, she waited. His gaze lasted five seconds longer before his face turned away.

She was again invisible.

About the Author

I love to hear from readers, so feel free to contact me through my website, www.yvonnekohano.com, or directly on Facebook as Yvonne Kohano, on Twitter @yvonnekohano, and at yvonne@yvonnekohano.com. Please leave an honest review of this novel at Amazon, Goodreads, or your favorite book discovery site of choice.

Yvonne enjoys channeling her characters' voices and passions as they overcome real world problems and discover love. Her Flynn's Crossing contemporary romantic suspense series is set in a fictional northern California foothills town not unlike the one where she used to live. Of course, the beauty and wonders of the Sierra Nevada Mountains and the surrounding counties play costarring roles in her work.

The first six books in the Flynn's Crossing series follow the developing love interests of the girl tribe, a group of successful women who work through real world conflicts and challenges to find acceptance and love - with some suspenseful happenings thrown in! In the next six books, single guys in the wolf pack find their true loves, but not without their own issues to conquer. Periodically, Yvonne will be adding seasonal novellas to the series, featuring the first person voice of a character from one of her previous books experiencing an event that we can all relate to.

www.ingramcontent.com/pod-product-compliance
Lightning Source LLC
Chambersburg PA
CBHW051333250626
47155CB00007B/2580